On Tidal Sand

P. G. Devereux

On Tidal Sand
Published by TISPMG Press in the United Kingdom 2023
www.tispmgpress.com
tispmgpress@gmail.com
ISBN 9798870010007
Copyright ©P. G. Devereux 2023
All rights reserved.
Typesetting and Cover Design by: TISPMG Press
The TISPMG logo was designed by: LittleMouse.
Printed and bound in Great Britain by: AMAZON

Books by P.G. Devereux

The Tidal Sand trilogy

On Tidal Sand

Turning Tides *(forthcoming...)*

Bid Tide Return *(forthcoming...)*

The Larkin Lens trilogy

Under a Larkin Lens (*writing as Phoenix Revanche*)

Spawn of a Larkin Lens (*writing as Phoenix Revanche*)

A Hagridden Larkin Lens (*writing as Phoenix Revanche*)

The Larkin Lens anthology

A Long and Loathsome Murder (*writing as Phoenix Revanche*)

The Third-Buddy Conundrum trilogy

The Third-Buddy Conundrum – A Parody

The Black Woods – A Parody *(forthcoming...)*

Dead End – A Parody *(forthcoming...)*

For two great men:

George Edwin Devereux,
inspiration for the tale.

Derek John Gill (4183871),
inspiration for the teller.

Contents

	Introduction	1
	Prologue	2
1	The man from the Blackburn Iris	9
2	The deal with wasps	30
3	Tram. Bam. Thank you, ma'am!	52
4	*Intervention:* Required	68
5	Millbay Station	72
6	The gargoyle of Gisors	81
7	The hollow smile	101
8	*Intervention:* Paving the way	113
9	The power of parabellum persuasion	119
10	The fall of Argent	130
11	Showdown at Sandplace	138
12	*Intervention:* Kit and caboodle	150
13	Catching the westerlies	155

14	The tale of the Golden Hand	177
15	The captain's connivance	192
16	*Intervention:* The Protracted Stand	202
17	The Isambard	209
18	The man who saw five centuries	227
19	Barty the bull	234
20	*Intervention:* The Campbells are Coming	251
21	Snookered	265
	Epilogue	275
	About the author	281

Introduction

This is a tale of a nobody, a man forgotten but a giant in my world because he was my grandfather, George Edwin Devereux. But this is also a tale of a somebody, a man remembered and a giant in the real world because he was arguably the most famous ordinary person in the early twentieth century and almost certainly the first true social-media star: Tommy Shaw!

My grandfather's tales were extraordinary, and I cannot help but smile at the recollection. The stranger introduced himself as Tommy Shaw and my grandfather had no notion of his real name on their first meeting. A shared journey and a wager would begin their friendship and change everything.

The pair, it seemed, had two things in common: a love of stories and a passion for the green baize. I loved my grandfather's recounting of the day he played snooker against a forgotten hero! Of course, I didn't believe him. How could I? I feel sad to admit I dismissed the tales as pure fantasy conjured up by the imaginings of my wonderful yet doddering grandfather. More than anything I regret that I did not ask more questions.

Only later would I discover it was all true! This, belatedly, is my grandfather's story. A tale of a true hero living a second life under another name. And perhaps a tale of two great men.

Prologue

0017 hrs on 26 June 1930. A near deserted Union Street in Plymouth's City Centre.

No-one involved would ever remember how the fight started. It was simply another late-night brawl that kicked off in the quiet darkness on the pavements outside the Posada Wine Store and Bar on Union Street. A lone and belligerent Scotsman, way beyond merry and looking for trouble, found it easily in the shape of six young sailors making their way back late to HMS Devonshire, at berth in the Prince of Wales Basin in His Majesty's Dockyard Devonport, North Yard.

Egged on by a heady mix of alcohol, arrogance and a mob mentality, the Scot's beating was severe. Even in his drunken stupor, the older man might have managed a fair fight with some dignity. A fair fight was not forthcoming. Laughing and joking as they kicked and punched together, the six left him lying face down in a darkly shadowed gutter, covered in blood, before striding away singing at the top of their lungs, "Blow the man down. Oh, blow the man down, bullies, blow the man down. Way aye, blow the man down. Oh, blow the man down, bullies, blow him away. Give me some time to blow the man down!"

Coincidentally, it was the belligerent singing that brought aid swiftly to the badly injured man. A chambermaid, Annie Farmbrooke, was leaving Farley's Hotel and headed home to her room on Adelaide Street. Running late as usual, she wouldn't normally look the way the sailors were going, but the rowdy singing at the end of the street drew her attention, and a vague bundle of shadows at the edge of the road a few doors down from the hotel entrance caught her eye.

As Annie watched, the shadows seemed to quiver and let out a low melancholic cry, so she ran to see if perhaps someone had fallen. She found the beaten man, moaning in pain and shivering violently despite the relatively warm summer evening.

Not knowing what she might do on her own, Annie ran back to the hotel. Karl Cooperman, the manager, was finalising the day's takings at the front desk and went with her to see what they might do together. A man of strict moral principles, he was more than keen to assist, especially when he recognised the injured man was a regular drinker at the hotel bar.

"Go inside and get some towels, Annie," he ordered, grimacing at the sight of the man's swollen and bloodied face. "Come back and make him as comfortable as you can, and see if you can find Margaret, she'll help." Margaret, his wife, would be prepping the kitchen to make things easier for the following morning.

Karl looked around but apart from the two of them the street was now dark, empty, and silent. He stayed with the shivering man, talking to reassure him until Annie and Margaret returned. The three of them were able to lift him gently onto the pavement, propping him against the thick base of a sturdy gas lamp so they could see him better under its faint light. Annie and Margaret set to cleaning him up the best they could, using towels and a bucket of warm soapy water brought from the kitchens.

"Karl, I think he's in a bad way, and I mean really bad," Margaret noted, her expression mirroring her concerned tone as she turned to her husband who was pacing while she and Annie did their best to clean the man's bloodied face.

"I'll get the saloon," Karl declared without hesitation. "We'll take him to the infirmary and see he's taken care of." He left the two briefly, running off through the shadowed street towards the Octagon. His car was parked less than two minutes away on Bath Street, next to Millbay Railway Station. Karl had a long-standing relationship with the station master that involved free drinks in exchange for secure parking. Both men felt they had the better of the arrangement.

Karl's Sunbeam Saloon was all grey and black and shining chrome, glinting even under the dim glow of the gas street lamps as it pulled up against the kerb, carefully avoiding the tramlines. The car was five years old, looked like a big Ford Model-T and always turned over first time. He left the engine running and climbed out to help get the man into the back seats.

"Annie, help me lift him," Karl ordered, though not sternly. "And Maggie, go and lock up the Hotel, I'll need you to come with me. Let Sidney know we'll be back as soon as we can be. Tell him to take care of things until we return."

"Yes, dear," Margaret agreed before trotting back to the hotel with the bucket and towels to find Sidney, the night porter.

"Come on, sir, let's get you to the infirmary so someone can fix you up," Karl said before turning to Annie. "Take his right arm and I'll take his left."

They lifted him gingerly, and the man moaned continually, his breathing now sounding ragged and burbling. Karl knew there was something very wrong but didn't want to overly worry young Annie right now.

Maggie returned to find the man slumped on the back seat where her husband and Annie had managed to position him. He looked more comfortable than he had on the pavement but was still quietly moaning and otherwise unresponsive. Maggie found herself silently praying that the man would be all right.

"Thank you, Annie. We'll see you in the morning," Maggie said as she climbed in, sitting beside the injured man so she could keep him steady once the car was moving.

"Thank you, miss," Annie responded with a half curtsey before closing the car door and backing away. She had seen the Cooperman's car before, but never been in it, or indeed any other, until tonight. The back of the car smelled of old leather, beeswax polish and wood shavings, and she was disappointed but unsurprised that she was not to be going with them.

Karl jumped into the driver's seat, slamming his door shut behind him before throwing the car into gear. Annie watched as the large saloon sped away. When the car was out of sight she walked home, ate a late supper consisting of a slice of crusty brown bread with margarine, and a bruised apple the cook had let her keep when she cleared away the tables after the evening meals, then slept soundly through the night.

When Annie arrived at work the next day, Margaret

was waiting at reception and greeted her warmly. "You did the right thing last night, Annie," she said to the young girl through a broad smile. "That man is probably only alive because of you."

Annie blushed as Karl came out from the kitchens to stand beside his wife. "It's true," he added. "Three broken ribs and a punctured lung. Right eye socket so badly swollen they're not sure he'll keep his sight. A gash on his forehead that needed more than twenty stitches, a broken wrist, and bruises all over. If you hadn't found him when you did...." He broke off, shrugged, and smiled at Annie.

"I hope he has someone to take care of him," Annie said, thinking about how bad the injuries sounded.

"Well, he's a long way from home, but the nurses are taking good care of him, and his regiment is up at Crownhill Barracks." Karl turned to his wife adding, "He's a sergeant in a platoon from the highlands, so I guess they'll make sure he's ok."

"Well, I hope they catch the men responsible!" Annie said, sounding uncharacteristically angry. She found it hard to believe that people could do something like that to a man, and almost right outside the hotel. The thought of it made her shiver. She curtsied and smiled, happy to have done some good in the world and to be thanked for it. The Cooperman's were like that, quick to praise, quicker to recognise and reward good work when they saw it. She went about her day of cleaning chores with a sense of relief and pride, tempered slightly by a niggling anger she couldn't shake off. Several times through that day she found herself thinking, I hope they catch them, I really do.

No-one involved would ever remember how the

fight started.

No-one involved would ever forget what happened next.

ON TIDAL SAND

1 The man from the Blackburn Iris

0543 hrs on 27th June 1930. The North beach on Drake's Island.

There were two Georges on the beach before the island's caretaker arrived to join them. The first was honest, reliable, hardworking to the point of harshly calloused hands, and looking forward to meeting his friends at the pannier market to tout for work later that morning. The second had been swiftly carved in the sand with a sharp piece of driftwood by the first. George Edwin Devereux was not good at reading by his own admission, and writing was something he did only when he had to. Writing his name was the only thing that had become a habit, and he liked to do so high on every beach he visited. It made him smile to think he would still be there for perhaps several hours after he left, in name at least.

Less than an hour before, George had loaded a small rowing boat with six sacks of coal, lifting each one easily from a sack truck he had used to wheel them from the military store shed at the top of the slipway. Diligent as ever, he had carefully spread the weight between the bow and the stern, placing each load precisely to ensure he maintained an even keel before pushing the boat out into the quiet waters of Plymouth Sound.

Almost silently, George had rowed the cargo across the narrow channel in the stillness of an early dawn that had made most things he could see appear featureless and flat. Buildings, trees, even the normally dominant lighthouse up by the promenade, had been visible only as darkened silhouettes against a slowly brightening haze. To the west the sky had still been a deep blue whilst on the eastern horizon, a pale rusty pink dusted a wide bank of clouds that looked like distant snow topped mountains.

At that hour it had still been relatively cool, especially out on the water and he had been glad to be wearing a warm coat. The extra layer had given him a welcome reminder that the weather could turn on a sixpence. His old da' had always said, "If you can see the Sound it's going to rain. If you can't, it's raining!"

In little more than forty minutes, George had crossed the quiet channel to the island, happy to have watched the clouds sink slowly over the horizon. He had jumped out effortlessly, laying the boat up on the small beach where Stanley Marchant, the island caretaker, would shortly join him. It had taken him only a few moments to find a good stick on the shoreline, then, moving as far up the beach as he could he had carved his name in capital letters about four foot high, using the stick like a giant pencil to dig deep groves into the dry sand. Then he had waited patiently by the rowboat, occasionally skimming stones out across the gently lapping rising tide.

"You gonna do that every time, b'y?" Stanley said as he trudged down from the sloping lane and onto the beach. The wheel of the barrow he was pushing squeaked annoyingly and left a dull grove through the middle of the second G. The caretaker's boots rubbed out the rest of that letter as he followed on behind.

"Of course," George said, not sounding the least bit put out by the challenge or the caretaker's indifference to his efforts.

"Why not carve it on they rocks?" the caretaker asked, pointing to the base of the island's steeply rising rock face. From the beach, one section of the various barracks buildings were just visible at the top of the rocky promontory.

George thought for a moment and said, "I'd have nothing to do next time, I guess."

Together they offloaded the delivery and barrowed the sacks to a red-brick coal bunker built onto the sheltered side of the old, mothballed barracks buildings at the top of a narrow track that spiralled the single hill that made up the main section of the small island.

Stanley was a short and stocky man, clean shaven with thinning dark hair slicked back and tidied using that new Brylcreem that was all the rage. Always dressed in well-worn dark green coveralls and matching gumboots ready for the daily toil, Stanley lived on the island with his wife and four sons sharing three rooms of the barracks set aside as living quarters, including full access to the original and formidable kitchens.

A gentle plume of smoke billowed from the barracks' chimney, confirming that the oven was already stoked with a grand fire and no doubt in use. Around the coal bunker, George always caught the smell of freshly baking bread, cooking fish, sometimes eggs or bacon frying and occasionally a meat or apple pie.

"Stoppin' for a brew, b'y?" Stanley asked, always sounding somewhat stern with his broad Plymothian accent. "I c'n give 'e list for Monday, mind."

George hadn't eaten breakfast yet, and brew always came with a bite to eat. "If you don't mind, sir," he replied, eagerly.

"Not at all, b'y," Stanley assured. "You'm always welcome. I'd rather you 'ear early and carvin' in the sand, I c'n tell 'e. You'm not like that last lad, never on time, messin' me days up. He frightened Mary too, knockin' on her window near 'lem in the mornin'. 'E was so late I'd giv'd up on the bugger. I boxed 'is ears all right."

George smiled nervously and made a mental note never to be late.

Stanley led the way through an oversized door into the pleasantly steamy kitchen, already warmed so much by its large red oven that the room's two windows had been pushed wide open. Taking his place on a padded balloon back chair set at the head of a large rustic table already laid out for breakfast, Stanley nodded towards a stool for George to join him.

George doffed his dark blue waxed fisherman's cap as he entered the kitchen, holding it in front of him and twiddling it before placing it briefly on the edge of the table in front of the stool offered to him. He pulled off his black heavy topcoat, draping it over the seat before sitting and moving his cap to rest in his lap. With his short blonde hair cut with a side parting and taper fade, he looked younger than his twenty-one years. He was clean shaven and smartly dressed, wearing a spotlessly white t-shirt, fishtail pinstripe trousers in blue denim and shining black leather boots. The older caretaker often teased George for his youthful looks, but it was always in good humour.

In the centre of the table on a square cork pot-stand was a large bone china teapot covered with a green and white striped cosy that had been knitted to fit the body and leave the handle and spout ready for pouring. There were enough cups and saucers set on a large kitchen dresser against the back wall to cater for a whole platoon if needed.

"B'ys is still abed, lazy buggers," Stanley half laughed. "Mornin' love," he added as his wife Mary returned to the kitchen from the cold store carrying a small block of lard wrapped in greaseproof and a neatly folded brown paper bag.

Shorter than her husband and plump rather than stocky, Mary Marchant kept her curly brown hair up in a net. She wore a pale blue, spotted dress that came to her elbows and passed her knees, mostly covered over by a full home-made tabard pinafore that looked like it had seen better days, most likely as a fine curtain. The apron was a mustard colour and dotted randomly with what looked like a pattern of daisy chains. Her shoes were plain black and sturdy but had also seen better days and were scuffed with well-worn heals. Like her husband she was ready for whatever work the day might bring.

"Morning, George," she smiled before turning to her husband. "This is the last of the cooked bacon," she said, unfolding the paper bag. "It's cold, but I'll fry some bread to go with it. We're out of eggs, so make sure they'm on the list for Monday." She placed a cup and saucer on the table for George, then poured in a splash of milk from a china jug.

"Tea's still standin', so wait till I pass the bread and bacon," she added, wandering across the kitchen toward the stovetop. She took a large black pan from a hook set into the wall just above the oven and placed it on the hottest plate, then she cut three slices from a crusty loaf before placing a knob of lard into the heating pan.

"'Tis already on me list, darlin'." Stanley rolled his eyes before adding, "Fried bread ok, b'y?"

"Yes please, sir," George replied eagerly. "And thank you," he added, genuinely pleased to be able to enjoy a warm and hearty breakfast. Jobs like this made the extra work worthwhile.

The three of them shared thick-cut slices of fresh bread lightly crisped on both sides in scorching lard, together with a generous slice of cold bacon and a cup of tea that had to be strong enough to dye a handkerchief black, or so Stanley said.

George made a note of the supplies Stanley wanted, adding each item requested to a list in a small notebook he retrieved from the breast pocket of the topcoat he was sitting on. He would deliver the notebook to the duty guards at the Royal Citadel for the attention of the Quartermaster when he got back to the mainland. The notebook and the items requested would then be ready for collection and onward delivery out to the caretaker next Monday morning. That would be another early start and another breakfast to look forward to.

When they had eaten, George thanked his generous hosts and offered to clear and wash the dishes in the trough, but Mary would have none of it, as usual.

"Stop off'rin' to do a woman's work, b'y," she scoffed, shamelessly teasing him.

"'E's just mannerly, that's all," Stanley defended the

younger man before slapping him across his broad back with a clout that would have knocked most men from their perch.

George smiled and stood, replacing his cap, and pulling his topcoat back on. "Would there be anything to take back, sir?" he asked the caretaker.

"Just me rubbish, b'y. 'Tis already down on't beach so I c'n nip down wi' 'e and get 'em loaded."

They walked slowly back to the boat, and as they stowed it with last week's coal sacks now stuffed with rubbish cleared from the old barracks, George couldn't help but notice that at this hour, the waters between the Hoe and the small island remained as quiet as they were likely to be for the rest of the day.

"See thee Monday, mind," Stanley said, pushing the small boat back onto the water. He waved once before turning and walking back towards the barracks and another day of clearing, cleaning, painting and the like.

Delivery completed, it was still early morning and the waters had brightened under the now cloudless sky to a pale blue and green, partly reflecting the few stunted trees, gorse and other plants that grew in stubby thickets on the island around the mothballed military buildings. As George rowed back towards the mainland, he wondered, not for the first time, why the island still had a caretaker family at all. The barracks no longer seemed as relevant as might have once been the case.

George looked over his shoulder briefly, to make sure he was keeping a steady course. He had to squint at the sun that had only now managed to crest the thick towered walls of Plymouth's working sea defences. He would be first to admit to knowing nothing about the run-down buildings on the island, but he was well aware of the history of the city's largest stronghold.

The Royal Citadel was an impenetrable and imposing artillery fort built of wide interlocking granite blocks in the late sixteenth century. It dominated the waterfront, overlooking both the city and confluence of the River Plym and River Tamar, the latter flowing its final stretch as the Hamoaze estuary. For all its age, the Citadel was still in active service, currently a training establishment used by The Gunners, who also kept a watchful eye over Drake's Island's dilapidated barracks buildings, being responsible for supporting the caretaker and his family.

George glanced back towards the island and even in the brightening morning, he spotted a single lantern reflected in the waters from the window of one of the rooms in the old barracks block at its highest point, suggesting that either Stanley was already hard at work, or his boys were finally up and about.

George watched the light casting a gentle rippling line of reflections across the water as he rowed effortlessly back towards the Hoe foreshore. The clinker-built rowing boat would normally be manned by two. Being alone he had chosen to sit in the stern so had loaded the sacks of rubbish he had collected in the bow section. He would offload them at the Barbican Wharf slipway, then lay up the boat before taking them to the rubbish store behind the shed he had visited earlier that morning to collect the delivery.

Coal delivered and rubbish collected, the day was yet to begin for some folks. George was pleasantly content, having eaten well and earned an extra three shillings from some pleasant morning exercise. He had a slow easy rowing style particularly suited to the wide bottomed boats favoured locally for all manner of activities both within the Sound and past the breakwater. He had no problems keeping the craft moving steadily towards the slipway behind him.

Being so familiar with the estuary waterway, its buoy markers and the surrounding landmarks, George only glanced occasionally over his shoulder to confirm he was on course and not headed toward another vessel, perhaps moving more swiftly under power or full sail. A two-man team in this boat might make it back, even against a heavy tide, in less than thirty minutes. On today's calm waters George was confident he could do the same on his own if he wanted to. Having the boat to himself on such a wonderful summer morning, and with a couple of hours to go before catching up with his friends at the market, a leisurely pace seemed to be in order.

The catch and drive of his rowing action was smooth and practiced with the blade of the oar cutting silently into the gently rippling waters before a firm power stroke driven mostly by upper body strength. Only a slight bracing of legs against the footboard in the aft of the boat was needed to generate and maintain a good turn of speed. He had a strength and stamina not immediately evident from his youthful looks.

The usual sounds of delivery trucks, occasional motor car and numerous horse-drawn carts were picking up on Hoe Road. Seabirds cried out, dogs were barking and children already playing along the rocky shoreline and mixed sand and pebbled beaches. As the day wore on, the background noises would increase, early morning sounds merging with the louder clamour of workers and tourists, especially once the pier opened.

George was only fifteen minutes out from the island

when a night trawler he recognised as the Gypsy Reel, originally out of Brixham, passed around fifty yards off his port side, most likely headed for fishing grounds off Southern Ireland. George could see four of the crew checking and stitching nets in the fantail stern, deftly weaving bulky wooden shuttles to close off even the smallest of tears with repair cord. Two others were checking the beam and coiled ropes running through the winch that would be crucial to hauling in a successful catch. The wake of the swiftly passing trawler hit his small boat side on but George was used to riding out a much higher pitch than this presented and didn't miss an oar stroke.

"Ahoy!" The distant cry was a familiar one and George glanced across to see two of the crew at the stern of the trawler waving and pointing at him.

George effortlessly pulled both oars inwards across his body, resting them in his lap and leaving only a short length and the blades resting through the rowlocks over the water, still choppy from the trawler's expanding wake. Cupping both hands around his mouth he shouted back, "Ahoy," and waved casually as the trawler pulled further away, heading on a course that would take it safely between the island and breakwater then out into the main shipping channel.

One of the crew continued to wave and point at George frantically, making him feel a little uneasy. A glance around reassured him that there was nothing on the water he need worry about. The second crewman began shouting again but the trawler was now further away and only some of the words reached him clearly. "Look *something something* boat on the *something* landing *something something!*"

George watched as two others stopped fixing their nets and joined the first pair in pointing frantically at him. He wondered briefly if he might be the butt of some joke and then realised that they were pointing over him, not at him. He turned to look away from the four fishermen but there was still nothing of concern on the waters. When he turned back, three were still pointing but one of them had his arms outstretched on either side. Were they worried about a bird?

And then George heard a low hum and turned away from them again, this time looking up slightly towards the hills on the Cornish side of the river. Finally, he caught a glimpse of what they had seen and were trying to warn him about. No more than a quarter mile upriver but travelling swiftly and heading straight for him was a three-prop fixed wing seaplane, clearly intending to land. He had seen such planes from up on the Hoe but right now he was slap bang in the middle of the channel they used as a landing strip, though not normally at this hour. He briefly considered trying to catch the attention of the approaching pilots, but the seaplane was so low over the water this was almost certainly pointless.

George threw both oars back out through the rowlocks and set to rowing at such a pace that he could feel his face reddening and sweat on his brow within a few powerful strokes. The small rowboat sped away from the central channel and towards the Hoe foreshore. He watched the approaching seaplane as it continued bearing down on him, now dropping to just a few feet above the water and only a few hundred yards off his starboard side.

With two dozen swift strokes, George drove the rowing boat clear of mid channel and then watched as the biplane's centre hull touched down on the waters, creating a huge plume of spray, pummelled backwards by its three large propellers, each secured in nacelles between the upper and lower wings.

The seaplane sped briefly across the water creating a wake that was swift and choppy, and George braced both oars securely, taking no chances as it slowed then stopped no more than twenty yards from where he sat in the now heavily rocking rowing boat. The plane settled evenly, held steady by the underwing floats fixed toward the tips of its lower wings. Once both floats were on the water, the plane sat on an even keel, ready to skim away towards its station on the Devon side of the estuary.

The gently bobbing biplane looked very much at home on the waters of the channel between the island and the foreshore. Being so close, George was stunned by the bi-plane's size and intricate structure, especially between the upper and lower wings that were separated by a tangle of struts, stays and bracing wires. He judged the seaplane's hull to be half as long again as the Gipsy Reel's that was now out of sight beyond the island.

The aircraft was mostly off-white, probably making it harder to spot, which had certainly been the case for George. A blue, white, and red RAF roundel was only now visible on the side fuselage below the rear spotter's cockpit, and three similarly striped struts joined the aircraft's twin rear wings. Two reddish bands circled the upper fuselage immediately behind the front spotter cockpit, empty today, as was the gunners pit immediately behind the aircraft's nose.

George glanced briefly at the foreshore and could see groups of children waving and no doubt hollering excitedly. One of the two pilots in the main open cockpit stood and gave George a thumbs up signal, most likely acknowledging his swift exit from the waters of the seaplane's runway. The three Rolls-Royce Condor engines had been throttled back so that two were now stopped completely, leaving only the central propeller running at idling speed, thumping noisily but not producing enough thrust to propel the plane's heavy hull through the water.

The rear spotter's cockpit immediately behind the main wings and in the centre of the tail section of the plane was the only other manned section, as far as George could see. George watched as its sole occupant also stood before throwing a rope ladder over the side of the plane's hull where it unrolled so that the bottom rungs flopped into the water with a gentle splash. The man who had thrown out the ladder now scrambled out and climbed down, stopping only when his boots reached the rung just above the waterline. Holding onto the rope ladder with one hand, the man leaned out over the water, beckoning with his other hand for George to row towards him! Well, this was a turn up for the books!

The man's face was mostly covered by a brown leather pilot helmet and matching aircrew goggles, but it looked to George as if he might also have been calling to him. Whatever he might have been saying was lost under the rumbling thump of the idling mid-propellor that was also causing the man's long grey coat to flap in its gentle backdraft, revealing flashes of grey jacket and trousers which George presumed to be the man's RAF uniform.

Without hesitation, George pulled heavily on the right oar to turn his boat until the prow faced the stranger dangling from the side of the floating aircraft. Eight strong strokes with both oars brought his rowboat to within a few feet of the serviceman.

"Thank you, young man!" the airman shouted, half appearing to salute as he stretched towards the small boat as it floated towards the bottom of the ladder. "I wonder if you would be so kind as to ferry me ashore! My comrades in the pilot bay were somewhat reluctant to make the landing quite so close to you! If you will assist me, my persistence will be justified!"

George pulled both oars back across his lap then set them carefully to rest in the bottom of the boat so that he could stand and reach across to the ladder. "I'm happy to help anyone on the water, sir," George admitted, also having to shout whilst throwing some of the sacks of rubbish into the stern to make room for his unexpected passenger.

George held one side of the ladder with both hands and braced his feet wide to stop the small boat rocking as the airman disembarked, stepping lightly from the rope ladder into the bow section of the boat before flapping and smoothing his grey long-coat and taking the forward seat with his back to the prow. George returned to the aft seat and switched the oars to a new position so that he could sit facing his passenger. Using the forward rowing system would only be a little slower this calm windless morning and it would be quite impolite to remain seated with his back to the stranger.

"I would not normally summon so urgent a taxi," the airman explained through a broad smile, leaning towards George, and still raising his voice to be certain of being heard. He removed the goggles and head gear before stuffing both into a side pocket of his coat and smoothing back his short white hair. "Today, however, I find myself in need of both immediate assistance and continued abetment. As you have already shown courtesy and courage through your inclination to proffer aid no questions asked, I am already indebted to you for the former and openly offer you first refusal in facilitating the latter. My name is Tommy Shaw, by the way." He reached forward, offering to shake hands formally, either as part of his introduction or his proposal.

"Pleased to meet you, sir." George took and shook the older man's hand. George estimated from the lines of the other's face, the set of his jaw and the narrowed but open smile, that Shaw was at least twice his age, perhaps the same age his father would have been had he been alive today.

"And you are?" Shaw enquired.

"Begging your pardon, sir. George, sir." George took up the oars again and with a reverse rowing action requiring him to push the oars through the water rather than pull, he began to row the boat towards the wharf.

"Thank you, George. I will pay you for your time and troubles today." Shaw waved at the pilots as the small boat moved safely away from the aircraft. Neither of the two in the pilot section showed any indication of having seen the signal that the rowboat was safely clear, but the speed of the single engine still under power increased, and the aircraft was propelled through the water towards its hanger at RAF Mount Batten.

"Beautiful aircraft, is it not?" Shaw asked, finally able to talk normally as the small boat rocked in the gently lapping wake of the plane that was skimming away across the water. "Master of the air and mistress of the sea in one magnificent amalgamation of flight and float. Could you dare to imagine how the design might improve over time?"

"I don't know much about them, sir. Never seen one up close till today, and truth be told I'd like to think as I won't see another one in quite the same way." George continued with powerful forward strokes to row the boat towards the slipway that was still out of sight beyond the outcrop of Fishers Nose.

Other smaller boats, mostly local crabbers, were on the move now. George had to make several adjustments to the path of his rowboat, moving steadily nearer to shore away from the busier channel of working boats departing from their moorings on Coxside and Sutton Pool.

Shaw laughed. "That is a Blackburn Iris, which I have reported to war ministry colleagues to be the greatest reconnaissance aircraft in the RAF today, due in no short part to its versatility. Two-oh-nine Squadron is lucky to have an initial allocation of three such aircraft, and this, I have been told, is only the beginning."

"If you don't mind my asking, sir, is your urgency related to the aircraft?" George was curious to discover the reason for such an unusual encounter on the water.

Shaw thought for a moment before answering. "I suppose in a manner of speaking it is," he confirmed. "We are a day late returning from a convention in Iceland. The waters around Reykjavik were unseasonably tempestuous and so our departure was delayed. I have an urgent meeting I intend to keep this day, with a friend. A payment is due, and I mean to collect. If I return to base, I will be expected to continue my clerking duties and report to my superiors on the events of our visit. Ergo, I determined that the only course of action available to me was to mark myself an absentee without leave. And so here I am."

George frowned but continued rowing. After a moment he felt compelled to ask, with more than a little worry creeping into his tone, "Won't you lose your command, sir?"

"My command?"

"Yes, sir. If you've run away, and all," George paused from rowing for a moment, wondering if he might have made a mistake in offering to assist this strange confusing serviceman, before adding, "I shouldn't like to find my assistance rewarded with a spell in Princetown jail!"

"My dear boy, appearances can often be deceptive. I guarantee beyond all shades of doubt that your wariness is entirely unwarranted. You have nothing to worry about since you will be returning me to my base at the end of today, if you agree to provide me with the assistance that I require to complete my errand, of course. My comrades from the plane have also agreed to cover for me," Shaw admitted with a smile before adding, "And besides, I have no command to lose. I am, in my most recent posting and under my current name, the lowest of the low, a mere Erk." He reached into another pocket of his long-coat and pulled out his RAF service peaked dress cap made of coarse grey wool which he carefully positioned smartly on his head before leaning back to make himself more comfortable.

"Begging your pardon, sir, but I don't know what an Erk is," George admitted.

"It is currently a joy of distraction and solitude for I

can be a nothing and a nobody. I have embraced my title as one which provides a freedom I have not known for a long time. It is short for aircraftman and as such my rank can be no lower." Shaw threw his arms wide and looked first towards the shoreline of the Hoe and then towards the small island some way off on the starboard side. "I am between places, much as now, and I can lose myself in equal measure on the daily toil of my service duties and a thoroughly blinkered immersion in my obsession."

George smiled and frowned at the same time then sighed before saying, "If you don't mind my speaking as I find, sir, but much of what you say sounds interesting and in parts reassuring." George paused taking three more effortless strokes on the oars before adding, "I can't say as I fully understand the actual meaning, mind you. You have the manner of my old school master, sir?"

Shaw looked blankly at the younger man for a few moments then threw back his head and laughed so loudly a small flock of oystercatchers took flight on the inland foreshore, peeping loudly at the unexpected disturbance. "Well and plainly said, my kind and worthy friend on the sea." Shaw nodded to acknowledge the point made by the younger man. "Being an eternal scholar prevents me from ever progressing to the point at which I might consider myself to be a master, young George."

Shaw looked at the shoreline and the citadel, looming over the small boat from the brow of the hillside before adding, "Truth be told, my way is as set as the foundations of that stalwart fort." He pointed briefly at the immensity of the old grey structure before adding, "I am driven to flit between the repetition of my daily duties and the grip of what I recognise to be relentless real work. I have been a storyteller all my life and whilst I have few new stories of my own, I work on translating the works of others from the archaic to the modern, extracting meaning through a shared empathy and inability to accept anything but perfection."

"Ah, stories I understand, sir," George admitted. "Mother always said I could tell a tall tale or two." He smiled but found himself blushing slightly, suddenly feeling that any story he might tell would likely pale against the experiences of his confident and charismatic passenger.

"Wonderful!" Shaw exclaimed, a wide genuine smile setting wider crow's feet at both eyes. "We will exchange experiences to speed the day through its course and ensure that I am not distracted from keeping my appointment."

"Oh! No, sir!" George disagreed, somewhat flummoxed at the prospect. "I'm sure I couldn't begin to..."

"Nonsense," Shaw interrupted before adding by way of reassurance, "I will wager that you know nothing of me, my endeavours, or my provenance just as I know nothing of you, your work, or your aspirations. We are met as equals and to that end you must call me Shaw, not sir. I do not wish you to see me as anything other than your equal."

George shook his head slightly. "Your uniform sets you above me, sir, I mean, Shaw."

"See. My name is not so hard to speak, is it? If you truly do not wish to share histories with me, I will be disappointed but not pressing. I am now quite solitary by choice and rarely engage with others beyond my obsessions with the written word. I would welcome your assistance in securing effective transfer to a location I have visited only once since my posting almost eighteen months ago. Our exchange will be a bonus for me and a chance for you to uncover the hidden truth of the reputation I choose to hide, though I will not make it easy."

"Ah! Current name," George said, remembering Shaw's earlier peculiar statement.

"See? You pay attention to details others might miss. Should you agree to assist me, I will pay you the full sum of one pound on my safe return to barracks at the end of this evening. If you also agree to swap stories with me, I will present you with a singular challenge. If you can uncover the prestige of my true name before I am returned to Mount Batten, I will see the payment doubled." Shaw smiled and extended his hand again, clearly hoping for George to shake on the agreement.

George placed the starboard oar across his lap and shook Shaw's hand again enthusiastically. A full pound for a day's work was already too good to be true, and double could be life changing. Molly, the girl he felt compelled to pursue as his sweetheart, might finally agree to step out with him. She always came up with some excuse or another, but a payment such as this would enable him to offer her a day out to remember so she would have to say yes. Exchanging a few tall tales by way of working to find out who this man might be suddenly seemed wholly worthwhile.

"I look forward to hearing any anecdote of fable or fancy you choose to share," Shaw admitted, pleased that George had agreed to his wager. "And to set you in good stead I will share first, with a tale from my youth, long ago but never forgotten."

George continued to row towards the slipway, wondering what he had done to deserve such a switch from danger to good fortune. A rich and evidently eccentric man had almost got him killed and was now effectively paying him just to listen to some stories! He pinched himself before taking up the loose oar again. The man was still there and still talking.

"Let me tell you about a deal with wasps!" Shaw declared, and George listened intently, all thoughts of spending the day with James and Donald forgotten, as he rowed quietly towards the shore.

2 The deal with wasps

It is early summer on an ordinary day in the June or July of 1897 at Oxford High for boys. Such a school is educational in all ways except those that really matter, or so it may seem to those unfortunate enough to have lived in times of peace, war, and providence.

Some strong recollections from childhood are called to mind as a frozen moment in time. Others convey memories as a sequence of events leading to a singular revelation, recalled not just for reasons of sentiment, emotion, or pain but for the unearthing of fact or fallacy. A moment of instantaneous learning may be remembered intensely, and by its scarring recalled frequently in all its fullness, guarding and guiding thoughts and decisions that might eventually lead to purpose or destiny.

Ned, a gentle but fearless boy, walked boldly through the school courtyard on his way excitedly to his favourite class. New this very year to the school and already recognised as one of the new bastards by at least one family of social climbers who should know better than to judge but believed it to be their right and duty to keep one such as him in his place.

Ned's uniform was carefully pressed, his blond hair neatly combed. His features were not particularly memorable, but his pale complexion was highlighted by a few freckles that made him instantly recognisable.

Languages were fascinating to this hardy boy with keen mind, strong memory, and regard for rules. The structure and repetition of each Latin class slotted understanding neatly into place, soaked into a mind hungry for order, purpose and paradigm, building a fascination with words that would eventually surpass the lure of archaic battles of the dark ages.

His interests were of the time: Teutonic knights, castles and keeps, longbows, crossbows, swords and lances, battles, and defences; these were a sweet escapism, a chance to dream of being more in a world that had moved on long ago from ages of chivalry to more modern societies driven by the mechanics of capitalism, communism, and conflict. The childish charm of sword and sorcery would remain engaging and enchanting for a lifetime, but words would grow to dominate and direct, lifting each day to new heights of achievement and notoriety.

Striding purposefully a few steps behind our eager, sandy-haired hero, was Arthur Newcombe, taller, stockier and three years older than the new boy. Also living on Polstead Road, Arthur was singularly familiar with the rumours which named young Ned and his bothers to be discreetly but entirely illegitimate.

Arthur's oldest sister, Elizabeth, had been married in March and the wedding had brought family from Ireland. Against all odds, Cousin Owen had been quick to recognise Ned's family and to reveal their secret. The boys' father was rich, a 7th Baronet, Sir Thomas Chapman, no less. And this was a very different name to the one young Ned and the rest of his family used now. Ned's mother, almost twenty years younger than the baronet, was Sarah Junner, former governess of the then Mr and Mrs Chapman and their daughters. The pair had run away together and this knowledge, gossip though it may be, gave Arthur the kind of power he relished.

Arthur's accidental stumble and purposeful shove sent the younger boy skidding to his knees, hands reaching out to save his face were scraped painfully across the dusty gravel yard, small shards of stone embedding into soft palms. The young boy's hands were stinging and dotted with spots of blood, trousers now scuffed over already grazed knees, but he stood as silently as he fell. Picking up the small satchel of books he had fumbled beside him, he threw its leather strap across his shoulder so that he would not drop it again, then he turned to face his nemesis.

Arthur smiled and feigned surprise at the sight of the young lad. "Sor...ry, Ned...dy," he smirked, extending, and distorting the younger boy's name, declaring with absolute clarity that he was anything but sorry.

"That's quite all right, my dear fellow," the younger boy smiled up at Arthur. "No harm done." He tried to dust himself off but only succeeded in marking his blazer with faint red lines from his bleeding palms. In part knowing that his response would be received unfavourably, the young boy braced himself, prepared to stand his ground and ride out the merciless bullying until the tyrant grew tired and moved on to other distractions.

Arthur took one step forward and slapped the younger boy so hard across the face that he hurt his own hand, causing him to wince noticeably. "How dare you call my dog a bitch, you bumptious little snot!" he declared loudly, falsely justifying his actions to any in earshot. Then he laughed and walked away, flicking his pained fingers to relieve the sting he had inflicted on himself and leaving the younger boy startled and with his left cheek glowing red.

At a window overlooking the courtyard, Mr Westman, or Old Windy as the boys were apt to call him, the schoolmaster with responsibility for Political Studies, was watching. He was a stern man with wide bushy eyebrows that managed to convey a permanent look of disdain and detachment from beneath his jet-black mortarboard hat. The young boy noticed the onlooker and in particular his odious smile. He watched as the man turned away, his billowing cloak almost as dark as his expression, apparently uninterested now that the fun was over.

Ned sighed and noticing he was now alone in the courtyard set off at a run towards the languages block.

Ned was not late, but he was the last to enter the classroom and take the one remaining seat in the centre of the front row of desks that were spaced out regularly to face the wide blackboard behind the master's desk. Crumpy Smithers, or Mr Smith since none would dare use his nickname to his face, was a stern but fair man with an eye for genius and an expectation for perfection. He was fair in the sense that you behaved as he expected or would be extremely sorry for it, since he was, after all, the master.

Of all his teachers, Crumpy was the one that most reminded Ned of his mother since she exhibited the same fastidious attention to detail and also anticipated excellence.

Mr Smith waited for silence before standing from behind his desk, unfolding his skinny body in a series of jerky movements that made him look quite ungainly. He never had to wait long since he maintained control with an iron will, asserted with a willow cane. He glanced down through his reading spectacles at a notebook on his desk then turned in one fluid motion to the blackboard, grabbed a stick of chalk and scribbled furiously and seamlessly in perfect copperplate, reading as wrote.

"Scrībō......Scrībēbam......Scrībam......Scrīpsī......Scrīp seram......Scrīpserō! We shall proceed," he said, turning to face the boys as he finished crafting the last word in his carefully structured series. "With tenses of continued and completed action."

It was at this point that young Ned thought to ask something he would never forget. A question that would define his own obsessive attention to detail. The room was stuffy, and he was uncomfortably hot to the point of sweat dripping from his brow, in part because his face was still stinging from the slap across the cheek, but mostly due to the fast pace he had set to ensure he was not late for class. He raised his hand and waited patiently.

Mr Smith tilted his gaunt pale face forward to look over the rim of his half-moon glasses and glared at the young boy who had dared to halt his flowing introduction. "I have offered no questions to warrant an interruption," he noted, folding his bony arms across his chest so that his creased and crumpled cloak fell forward to cocoon him. "Make yours a memorable one, boy, for if you do not I most certainly will."

Ned paused and felt his sweat change from hot to

cold. He was no longer sure he wanted to ask but there was no way back, now. "Please, sir," Ned began, a little nervousness creeping into his voice. "Can I remove my blazer?"

Without hesitation Mr Smith replied gently, "Yes, you can," before unfolding himself and turning back to the board and picking up his cane to continue the lesson.

Ned gave a gentle sigh of relief. Perhaps things were looking up.

"Here," Mr Smith continued, slapping the first word in his list with the tip of the cane. "We see the present I write, which can also be..." He turned back to the class just as Ned began to slip one arm from his blazer. It seemed deliberately timed, which in all probability it was.

"What are you doing, boy!" he screamed, scuttling like a four-legged spider around his desk to stand directly in front of Ned, whose eyes were now wide like a cornered animal. Ned froze, one arm in and one arm out of his blazer.

"Well?" Mr Smith loomed over Ned and the room suddenly seemed to grow cold and shrink around him.

What had he done to anger the man so? He'd asked politely, hadn't he?

"Sir, I....I....I," Ned sputtered, nerves getting the better of him.

"Spit it out, boy," Mr Smith sneered as Ned glanced up, noticing the master's grin which looked very much like Mr Westman's, earlier. The man was clearly enjoying making a spectacle of him.

"Sir, you said.... you said....," Ned continued, struggling to find a response.

Mr Smith grabbed the scruff of the neck of Ned's half-on half-off blazer and lifted the boy from his seat, pulling him round to stand in front of his desk and letting him dangle there awkwardly. "What, boy?" he snapped, shaking the collar. "What did I say?"

Ned fought to hold back tears of embarrassment and frustration that suddenly began brimming in his eyes. He could feel the rest of the class with their eyes fixed on him, wondering no doubt if they might be allowed to find Ned's predicament amusing. And, no doubt, holding themselves back until the master himself provided clarity. This day had gone from bad to worse. He had no idea what he had done wrong or what he was supposed to do to put it right.

"Sir, I asked, and you said I could," Ned tried, hopeful that this might at least be a step in the right direction.

"No, boy," Mr Smith shouted directly into his face, letting go of his collar before turning to the rest of the class. "Would one of you please tell me what this fool said to annoy me! This will allow me to cane him and move on with the lesson!" He clicked his fingers in the air several times in an effort to prompt a response.

"No-one?" he continued, somewhat exasperated by the sea of faces all trying not to catch his eye. The master sighed. "Today is your lucky day, boy. Sit."

Ned scrambled back to his seat, slipping his free arm back into his blazer, no longer feeling the slightest bit warm, only grateful that none of his classmates knew what his error might have been. Or, more likely, were at least uncertain enough not to offer a response.

Mr Smith pointed at Ned with the tip of his cane. "This boy did not ask for permission to remove his blazer and neither did I give it. Originating from Germanic kunnan, with a k, through Old English cunnan, with a c, we get the auxiliary verb can which is used to express or query ability only! If you wish to seek permission," he said, leaning toward Ned again, "the word to use is may."

For the remainder of the class Ned sat quietly, listening intently, and soaking up patterns of Latin tenses while he recovered some measure of composure: present, imperfect, future, perfect, pluperfect, and future perfect — a wonderful salve washing over the earlier more stressful elements of the day's lesson.

It dawned on him, not for the first time but certainly with the greatest of clarity, that the rules of English were every bit as important and complex as those of Latin. Mr Smith had been more than truthful in stating his question would be a memorable one.

The study of Latin had provided the first taste of stability and order in a hitherto chaotic life, but Ned decided it would no longer be his favoured subject because there was another which needed mastery not because it was new and difficult, but because it was all too easy to become complacent about it. English would be his new priority. More than anything he would be forever grateful for Mr Smith's startlingly uncomfortable and unexpected revelation from one simple word.

One word can change a life.

Back at home in the evening, Ned met with his older brother Bob in their secret den at the end of their long back garden. Bob was in the same year as Arthur, and by all accounts was equally tyrannised. Though matched in age he was neither equal in stature nor intellect to the relentless bully. It had become the brothers' habit to share tales of the taunts, jibes and drubbings endured each day after school, though only with one another, since neither wished to share the details behind the bullying, especially not within the family. What better way to keep a family secret than to hide it even from those who share it!

In truth, the two brothers were now in open competition regarding the scale of injury or insult endured at the hand, foot or mouth of the bully and his buddies. They came to call their exchanges The Tournament of Torment, a phrase coined by young Ned to bolster defiance and suggest a possible balance of power whilst acknowledging the misery and injustice of a situation not of their making. This first year in their new school had so far been memorable for reasons they would happily choose to forget.

Both boys shared the details of their daily challenges with each other keenly, especially those involving the Newcombe boy. As had become usual, they took their dinner to the den, which was a small, fenced area separated from the main garden by an old outhouse now used as a garden store. It was well hidden and covered by an old beech tree which, together with a tall, slatted fence at the end of the garden, provided shelter from wind and rain.

On a warm evening like this it was particularly comfortable and a place to escape the nuisance of their younger brothers. Though Georgie was only a year younger than Ned he was not yet at school and was often required to care for their baby brother, Frank. Dinner this evening was a simple affair of honeyed bread, something which both boys delighted in.

"Your cheek still looks a little red," Bob noted once Ned had finished the tale of his encounter with the older bully and the equally bullying master. "I will have to sort him out, one day," he promised. "Arthur, I mean. Not Mr Smith."

Ned wasn't worried and took another bite of his sweet treat before adding, "I think after Arthur hit me, he was more worried about his own hand than anything else."

Bob nodded and was about to say something when he noticed something rather urgent. He slowly raised one hand and pointed a finger at Ned's face before whispering, "Ned, don't move. There's a wasp on your cheek. It wants your honey."

"Does it now?" Ned noted, unconcerned. He wiped gently across his face and the honey drips at the corner of his mouth transferred to the back of his hand, as did the wasp. Both boys watched as it remained singularly focussed on the blobs of sweet liquid, mandibles opening and closing as it gorged on as much of the honey as it could. "I can hardly feel it at all."

"You'll feel it if it stings you, you great fool," Bob chided. "Get rid of it."

Ned smiled at his older brother. It was the kind of smile Bob had seen before. A mischievous, cunning smile. "What?" Bob asked.

"Bob, I have an idea," Ned beamed, looking from the wasp to his older brother. "What if I could smother Arthur in honey, right next to a wasps' nest?"

"What?" Bob asked again, the pitch of his voice

higher this time, as if he wasn't quite sure he had heard correctly or couldn't believe it.

"I've seen a spectacular nest, bigger than a football," Ned continued, eyes now alive with ideas. "It's in the hedgerow between the Trap and the canal. He didn't see me, but Arthur was scrumping last Sunday, so I know he goes there."

"I think that slap has addled your brain," Bob offered, still thoroughly shocked by Ned's suggestion.

"No, think about it," Ned continued, flicking the wasp gently from his hand so that it flew off into the tree canopy. "It's just a three-step plan. I lure Arthur to just the right spot, throw a jar of honey over him, then push him into the hedgerow. The wasps will do the rest."

Bob scratched his head. His hair was darker than his younger brother and he was somewhat taller, but apart from that you could see they were brothers. "You make it sound easy but he's bigger than both of us so how exactly are you going to push him anywhere?"

"I'm not sure yet," Ned admitted. "I may have to find a way of tripping him somehow. I'll find a way, though. It's just a matter of strategy. Will you help me?"

"Hmm." Bob wasn't convinced but knew how stubborn his brother could be so thought it best to show willing. "I suppose so. Help with what?"

"That's easy," Ned declared. "When Mother sends you for groceries, buy one extra thing. A jar of the cheapest honey. I'll do the rest."

Bob sighed. "Fine, little brother. But you have to let me help with the plan."

Ned stood and shook his head. "Sorry, Bob. It has to be just me because then Arthur won't be able to resist."

The weekend came quickly, and Bob had delivered on his contribution to the plan, as promised. Ned had a jar of the thinnest, runniest honey he had ever seen. It was probably watered down but that didn't matter, it would be the better for it.

It was a fine warm Saturday, just right for scrumping. Of course, Ned couldn't know for sure that his bully would go to the Trap today, but he had contrived a way to trigger Arthur's interest.

Ned and Bob left home early together, straight after breakfast to set things in motion. They walked down Polstead Road towards Aristotle Lane and stopped just short of the corner of Kingston Road, right outside Arthur's house. Ned ran to the other side of the road as if going on ahead then yelled across to his brother, "See you when you get back with Dad's ales, Bob."

"Ned," Bob shouted in reply. "Don't forger mother would like blackberries as well as apples."

"Thanks," Ned yelled back, noticing a curtain twitching at a second-floor window of the Newcombe house. "I'll see what I can find on the Trap Grounds. I tried Port Meadow last week, but pickings were lousy." Could it be Arthur, listening to them?

"Ok," Bob called back, just as loudly. "Be seeing you."

"No need to rush," Ned replied, then added with a final holler, "I'm not at school so no fat dolts to worry about." The curtain twitched again, more vigorously this time. It had to be Arthur!

Bob turned left onto Kingston Road in the direction of the Old White Horse. He wasn't really buying beer for his dad, but Ned had convinced him it all had to look and sound right. Bob was just going to walk home via St Margaret's Road, doubling back past their school, then down Polstead Road again to wait at home. After all, he'd promised Ned he would.

Ned crossed the Hayfield Road to Aristotle Lane directly opposite the Anchor Inn to the old red-brick bridge across the Oxford Canal. He walked slowly, optimistically carrying a tuneless whistle first across the bridge then down the narrow steps to the trampled towpath, so dry and dusty Ned might as well have been walking a path through the dunes of a desert.

The canal was quiet, its waters still and blue under the cloudless summer sky but it would get busier as the day went on. Ned could see one canal barge at a gentle bend a few hundred yards ahead just short of Medley Wier, a large black and tan Shire horse with brilliant white foot feathering pulling obediently.

The barge was most likely filled with feed for livestock or potatoes, beets, or other root vegetables on the way back to midland markets or to Warwickshire to load with coal for a return trip back to London. Several coal loads would pass through on the way to Britain's industrial heartland every day, and Ned would sometimes watch from the bridge over the canal, but never for long as the slow pace made him restless.

It could have been any usual Saturday except today he was here with a plan bigger than just collecting fruit from hedgerows, or scrumping for bitter wild apples. A short way down the towpath he was able to look back along the canal and just see the rooftop of Arthur's house above the market stalls setting up on the other side of the canal, across the Hayfield Road from the Anchor.

Ned had no way of knowing if the bully had taken the bait, but he intended to proceed as if he had. Even if Arthur never came after him, it would be good to double check the location was still good for his plan. Ned thought of it as more than revenge, he wanted to strike at the bully in a way that would make him think twice in future before doing anything to him or his brothers. That seemed fair after the catalogue of attacks recounted in their Tournament of Torment exchanges.

Ned continued along the canal, reaching inside his Norfolk jacket every so often to check that the hidden jar of honey was still safe. It was wrapped in an old wool sock tied at one end, partly to protect the jar but mostly to make it more comfortable, stuffed as it was in the side of his jacket, a little way below his armpit. He had thought to hide the jar in his knickerbockers, but it was too big to fit comfortably in either a pocket or even down the leg. He had a small hessian sack bag crumpled into one of his jacket pockets so that he could look the part of collecting blackberries when he reached the hedgerow.

"Hey, Neddy," a familiarly unfriendly voice called from somewhere behind him. "Fancy a swim?"

Ned turned to see Arthur leaning over the short brick wall of the bridge crossing the canal. Two boys with unknown round faces flanked him, like Tweedledum and Tweedledee. So much for a practice trip, Ned thought, as he set off at a sprint down the towpath towards a narrow gap in the hedgerow a little further ahead. His heart was beating fast, and he couldn't help but smile at the thought that Arthur had not only heard him but felt the need to come after him immediately. This was more of a rush than he would have liked, but boy did he have a surprise in store for Arthur and his buddies. Dealing with three larger boys presented an unexpected degree of difficulty so he would have to think fast.

Ned risked a glance and saw Arthur and his friends strolling casually down the steps to the canal path. The three were dressed in matching fawn britches and tops and the two Ned didn't recognise had Eton collars, brutally starched over the lapel of their tweed jackets. Arthur was wearing a plain grey flat cap whilst his companions sported matching brown summer Gatsby's. From this distance the two looked like they could be twins. Arthur's cousins perhaps?

Ned immediately thought of a plan to deal with three bullies. First, he would need to throw the honey onto them, and then he would hurl the ball of wasps at whichever of the three was standing in the middle. The thought of destroying the nest made his stomach turn, but with so little time it was the only option he had.

"Oh, Neddy, boy," one of Arthur's friends called out with an accent Ned thought might be Irish. "We know who you are."

So, Ned thought, the two new boys were almost definitely Arthur's cousins.

Ned ducked through the gap in the hedgerow to enter the wooded scrubland of the Trap Grounds, and wondered with a brief smile if he had enough honey for the tea party. Ideally Ned would have liked a little more time, but he was certain his idea was a sound one, that it would work, even against three bigger bullies. He knew he had the advantage to counter his enemy's superior numbers, he was drawing them to exactly where he wanted them, he had a plan, and they had no notion of it. This was going to be perfect!

There was a narrow well-worn path along the inside edge of the hedgerow, which was thick with brambles in places this time of year, making it a hotspot for gathering blackberries. Ned was quick to notice that he wasn't the first to arrive this fine morning. There was a young girl wearing a yellow smocked dress and pinafore, much farther down the path and she had already collected a fine harvest of fruit in an old wicker basket.

Ned sprinted to the part of the hedge he had previously found the wasps, dust from the dry path billowing up behind him. He needed to know that the nest was still there. He knew roughly and slowed when he was alongside the bushes in which he thought to find them.

Ned scanned the lower part of the hedgerow hoping to catch sight of one or two workers buzzing around so that he could see where they were headed. He was beginning to worry that perhaps the wasps had moved on, died, or had their nest destroyed by someone else. If the wasps were gone his plan would be gone with them and he would have to make a hasty retreat with his tail between his legs.

With a sigh of relief, Ned spotted what he was looking for, wasps scuttling around a small hole at the base of their football shaped nest that was well hidden in the undergrowth that covered the lower part of the hedge. Ned was near enough to hear the buzz of the swarming insects, and he was confident he would be able to pull the whole ball from its attachment in the hedgerow. The bullies were on their way, so it was time for him to get things ready.

Ned reached into his jacket and pulled out his secret weapon. He smiled and in that instant a large stick caught him a glancing blow across the back of his head so that he dropped the sock and its contents onto the baked earth path. Even though it was partially cushioned by the woolly sock, Ned heard the glass jar shatter as a loud guffaw confirmed that Arthur or one of his cronies had thrown the stick from somewhere on the path behind him.

Ned stooped to pick up the now sticky mess, dripping with thin honey, shards of broken jar protruding awkwardly through the darned thing. Glancing across at the three boys running towards him, Ned did the only thing he could think of. Carefully gripping the sticky sock filled with broken glass and dripping honey, he backed himself into the thick greenery with his hands behind his back, holding onto a sliver of a plan, one final desperate hope; the memory of a single wasp trying to steal a spot of honey from his cheek!

"What are you doing, Neddy, boy?" Arthur sneered, pushing the younger boy further into the thick hedge so that he would be out of sight of the girl who was already moving away from the rowdy gang.

"Where's his manners?" one of the boys with Arthur barked. "Where's his tongue?" said the other, as he poked Ned's shoulder with a stick at least three times the size of the one that had made him drop the honey jar. They were indeed twins, and so like Arthur, except for the accent, it almost made Ned laugh: Tweedledum, Tweedledee and Tweedledolt.

"Hello, Arthur," Ned beamed. "And who might these friendly chaps be?" Time. He needed time.

The three bullies looked at each other and laughed so loudly into Ned's face it almost hurt his ears.

"Ned, what kind of a fool are you?" Arthur said slowly, poking a bony finger into Ned's chest with every word, so that he was rocked backwards, rebounding each time due to the spring of the thick greenery he was pressed against. Ned could feel some sharper branches and thorns digging into his back, but his hands were free, and his hands were busy.

"I was really hoping to see you here today, you know," Ned smiled at Arthur. "I thought perhaps we might discuss the possibility of a truce. Before things... get out of hand."

"A truce?" Arthur mocked. "My dear boy, things haven't even started yet."

"That's very true," Ned admitted, still smiling. "Things haven't started yet, and I believe you might like to keep it that way."

Arthur took a long look around, wondering if perhaps Ned was not alone. "Billy, go back to the cut-through and see if the path is clear. I don't want anyone around when I throw this wretch in the canal. If we're lucky he might drown," he sneered, sounding as if he really meant it.

"Arthur," Ned smiled, feeling things coming together. "Is this really necessary?"

With no warning, a large stick smacked him so hard in the shins Ned almost stumbled, only managing to keep his balance at the last moment using the hedge for support. His smile changed to a grimace, and he was forced to inhale sharply at the sudden jagged pain radiating up through his leg.

"So, you're the misbegotten little shite-brain?" the cousin who had struck him shouted into his face. Ned could smell the older lad's foul breath which, together with the pain, helped him keep from smiling as the older boy swiped mindlessly at something buzzing near his ear.

"Excuse me? Billy's brother? Sorry, I don't know your name," Ned began, still stalling for as much time as possible. "You wouldn't happen to have a lozenge of some kind, would you?"

Billy's brother spat at the floor, probably aiming for Ned's shoe but missing. "If I did, I wouldn't give one to you, you gobshite."

"Ah. I know that. I'm smaller than you but that doesn't automatically make me the most stupid," Ned pointed out. "If you had one, and please forgive my crude analogy, I was going to suggest you suck on it yourself because your breath is like a bag of month-old turnips dipped in cow dung." Ned smiled and braced himself for more pain.

Billy's brother turned red and pulled back one enormous fist only to be stopped by Arthur grabbing his arm. "Wait, someone's coming." Arthur pointed to the cut through which Ned couldn't quite see from his position sunk back in the hedgerow.

"Ah, you'll like this, Ned," Arthur scoffed as soon as he could see who was headed down the path towards them. He also flicked thoughtlessly at something buzzing near his face.

Billy pushed a boy slightly shorter than him into view and Ned only just managed not to roll his eyes. "Hello, Bob," Ned greeted chirpily, at the unexpected sight of his brother. "I thought you were shopping," he added pointedly, realising that he would not be able to wait much longer before going ahead with his new and unexpectedly desperate plan.

"Billy, do you have a lozenge? Or a mint, perhaps? If you do your brother is in dire need of a breath freshener." Ned leaned his head towards Billy and sniffed loudly before adding, "You might want to have one yourself."

"Enough!" Arthur shouted stepping forward so that he towered over young Ned. "You!" he shouted, pointing at Bob. "Get lost or get ready to join your brother in the drink! Billy? Danny? Let's teach this rancid little oik some manners."

Billy and his brother pressed in on either side of Arthur, exactly as Ned hoped they might. Ned could see Bob behind them, rooted to the spot by tendrils of indecision.

"Arthur, I'm wondering. Can I teach you a lesson?" Ned asked, looking up and staring defiantly into the eyes of the older boy.

"Really?" Arthur scoffed, glancing left and right at his cousins who were clearly just waiting on his word, "You are such a ridiculous little bastard. Only you would ask for permission."

Ned smiled. "Arthur, you really need to listen more carefully. Can is never used to ask permission; can is a question of ability. And besides, I already know the answer. Let me show you what I can do."

Ned leaned forward slightly and in one swift and sweeping movement brought his hands from behind his back and placed one on either side of Arthur's chubby cheeks. Only his hands didn't look like hands at all.

They looked more like boxing gloves that had somehow come to life to writhe and scuttle and buzz. Both were a seething mass of angry yellow and black.

The hair on Arthur's head appeared to stand on end, as if the buzz were one of static. His eyes widened, then he screamed, first in shock then increasing in pitch as it changed to one of pain. In panic, Arthur punched upwards then outwards, pushing the demon hands away from his face in one swift desperate motion, smacking one hand into Billy's nose, and the other into Danny's left eye. The cousins joined in Arthur's chorus of screams as the fists of fuzzy anger connected with their faces, evaporating the swarm around them.

Bob laughed as the bullies backed away in great bounds, screaming and flapping wildly at the wasps that had so happily collected themselves over Ned's honey drenched hands. In picking on Ned, the three older boys had disturbed the insects satisfied feeding frenzy. Now they were paying the price, all three enveloped in a haze of humming vengeance and stings.

Ned's desperate last-minute plan was turning out way better than he might ever have imagined. Sometimes the natural world was also a wonderful one.

Ned turned and knelt on the floor, leaning in against the hedge. The jagged glass of the broken jar had made things difficult, and he had barely managed to smother his hands and wrists in the thin honey before dropping the sock and awkward shards behind him. Quite a few from the nest were already feasting there, and Ned gently coaxed the last reluctant wasps from his hands onto the sweet sock, before rising swiftly to find his brother.

"Ned, that was unbelievable!" Bob declared as they

both ran, leaving the three older boys swarmed by the cloud of anger they had stirred up, their attention solely focussed on the predicament they found themselves in.

"It didn't go to plan at all," Ned admitted. "But on reflection that was probably for the best."

The pair ducked back under the cut-through as soon as they reached it. Ned lay immediately on the towpath, leaning his head and arms over the canal edge and dipping his sticky fingers into the cooling water, rinsing away the last traces of honey.

When Ned stood, Bob pointed and with a voice laced with concern said, "Ned! Your hands!"

Ned looked down. Both were dotted with red blotches on his palms and fingers. He was in part responsible for the ending of the insects' spectacular feast, so a few stings were only to be expected. Spots on the backs of his hands were already beginning to swell.

"Doesn't that hurt?" Bob asked, amazed that his younger brother had endured so many stings.

"Oh, it hurts! It hurts rather a lot, so I say we go and raid mother's lotions cabinet," Ned suggested, quite matter-of-factly.

Bob shook his head and admitted, "You know, I'd probably be screaming right now. What's the deal with that, then?" Bob demanded, amazed at his brother's stillness, especially in comparison to the whoops and hollers of the three bullies and the fight they were clearly losing against the army of wasps.

Ned looked up and smiled. "The deal, dearest brother, is not minding that it hurts."

Bob laughed, threw one arm over his younger brother's shoulder and together they marched home.

3 Tram. Bam. Thank you, ma'am!

0833 hrs on 27 June 1930. On a rowboat now less than 100 yards from the Barbican Wharf slipway, Plymouth.

George couldn't help laughing through the latter part of the tale. It had the kind of ending that gave you a buzz, lifting your spirits. A day with his odd new companion would certainly pass swiftly.

"Don't go expecting me to be as grand as that, mind," George declared, still smiling as he continued to row gently towards the slipway which was now just a short stretch ahead.

Shaw looked back at the nearby shoreline and could see their destination was almost upon them. The slipway was always busiest between eight and nine each morning regardless of the tides. At the top of the slope at least a dozen older fishermen were gathered around lobster pots, crab creels and nets, some smoking a pipe and chatting away, but all of them taking care in checking and fixing anything untoward.

"I'm glad you appreciated the deliberate levity which, in truth, I may have slightly embellished purely for the purposes of achieving an aesthetically appropriate ending," Shaw admitted. "Mostly the truth is enough, but there can be occasions where the story demands a little more."

"I wish I had your way with words," George declared. "I'm grand at listening, not bad at doing, but not so good at talking and never had much luck with reading or writing. Any story I share is apt to be a little short."

"My dear boy, a story is a story, no matter the length or detail included," Shaw reassured. "Take it from me that all tales are worth telling, and all tales worth telling are worth telling well."

"I take it you are Ned?" George asked directly.

"I am," Shaw admitted.

"But I also take it that Ned is not your name," George stated, pushing hard with just the right oar to steer the rowboat to the side of the slipway.

"It was the name my brothers and closest friends called me, before the war." Shaw leaned forward and added, "It wouldn't be much of a challenge if I told you who I was from the beginning, would it? I am definitely Ned, though."

George laughed again, then pulled all but the blades of both oars into the boat, laying them up beside and behind him making a giant V. He stood confidently and grabbed one of the thick posts that lined the side of the slipway about a yard apart, bracing the boat to hold it steady.

"You'll be jumping off here, mind," George pointed out politely. "I'll get these out," he added, with a nod towards the sacks of rubbish. "Before I tie up." He pointed to a space between two similar boats moored about 30 yards further down the walled quayside beside the slipway.

Shaw could make out a rusty looking ring for the

boat to be tethered, beside that a sturdy wooden ladder which George would likely use to climb ashore rose to the quayside.

Shaw stepped lightly from the boat onto the lower slope of the slipway, carefully avoiding patches of green and black seaweed that would no doubt be hazardous under foot. He was relatively sturdy and stocky at only five foot five but might still take a fall if he didn't watch his step, so he moved up the slope with great care.

George waited until his passenger was safely away from the edge, then neatly lifted the sacks of rubbish to make one stack on the slipway before rowing the boat to its mooring.

Shaw watched as the younger man deftly knotted a line to the crusted ring, carefully checking the length of rope was sufficient to ensure the boat could rise or fall in the changing tide unencumbered. From higher up the slope, Shaw could see that what he had first mistaken for rust, was in fact a myriad of sea life. Barnacles, limpets, and other small, shelled animals he couldn't name made the mooring ring appear older and more rust laden than it truly was.

After climbing ashore, George was swift to join Shaw again, wheeling a sack truck he had collected from a rickety looking shed built against the steep cliff that rose to the main Hoe Road above the quayside path. George steered the truck around the sacks and pushed the blade of its carrying scoop under the bottom one until it wedged and would move no further. With a practiced kick on the fulcrum bar at the base of the truck, the blade of the carry scoop scraped noisily up and across the slipway, sliding niftily under the bottom sack before George tipped it back so that all six were deftly balanced and ready to wheel away.

"I'll offload these," George said, nodding towards an area beside the shed which was already piled with similar rubbish. "And then we can be on our way."

"Wonderful, my dear boy," Shaw boomed, slapping George between his shoulders, before following him towards the rubbish store.

"I have to ask. Did the bullying stop?" George queried as he returned the sack truck to the shed after offloading it. It was a question he'd been poised to ask since Shaw first mentioned it.

Shaw thought for a moment before replying. "My dear George, the bullying never stops, as I am sure you already know. You either learn to live with it, avoid it, or harden up so much that you embrace the act of bullying, yourself."

"I've known more than a few bullies in my time, I must admit," George conceded.

"I should be dumbstruck if you had not," Shaw declared. "We are a people whose historic empire was built by blinkered bullies commanding bullied belligerents. In truth I have found it to be so ingrained in some institutions that were it to be rooted out there would be nothing left but empty buildings."

George shrugged. "I don't find bullies stick around too much," he admitted, closing the door to the shed, and slapping his jacket to remove dust fibres from the old sacks. "I've a bit of a temper and that seems to put 'em off." He slipped his jacket back on and straightened his cap. "Right. Where do you need to go first?"

"The Banjo Pier is where we will find my friend," Shaw confirmed. "I should like to be there before mid-day, if that is achievable."

"I hope you mean the Promenade Pier just down the hill there." George pointed. Scratching his chin thoughtfully he added, "The only Banjo Pier I know is miles away in Looe!"

Shaw frowned. "That is the one," he confirmed merrily. "I knew you would know of it! My friend stays in that quaint village several times each year. I had forgotten the name! And it really should be quite memorable. I have been told it is possible to travel there in under two hours by train."

George removed his cap and scratched his head. "I've only been to Looe by train once," he admitted. "And it can take more time than you think if there's problems. We need to be making our way to Millbay Station now if you mean to be there before noon."

"You will accompany me, remember," Shaw added. "I will pay the fare."

George smacked his hand to his forehead. "Pay! Oh, cripes!" he exclaimed. "I have to get the Marchant's supplies list to the quartermaster. Come on," he added frantically. "You can wait for the tram while I run to the main gate and back."

George set a brisk pace leading Shaw along the quayside then up a steeply sloped path set with thick granite steps to the main Hoe Road. The road itself was getting busier with people walking to and from places of work. There were also quite a few cyclists and any number of horse-drawn carts transporting all manner of goods from the barbican wharfs to just about everywhere in the city.

"Just wait here," George said, pointing at a small bench that was positioned to mark the last stop of the tramway. "We'll need tickets to Millbay Station. The walk would take us the better part of a half hour, but the tram will get us there in minutes. Make sure you get on even if I'm not back. I'll catch up." And with that he sprinted away towards the towering walls of the Citadel.

"Think on the story you wish to deliver on your return," Shaw called across the road as he watched the young man run up a narrow path past Smeaton's Tower, the bright red and white striped commemorative lighthouse that had been moved from the Eddystone for some obscure reason. Shaw new only snippets of the tale and to him it seemed odd that anyone should want to move a broken lighthouse to the shore, especially since it was no longer ever used as a lighthouse.

Shaw turned away as George disappeared over the brow of the steep grassed slope, headed on his way to the Citadel's main gate which was out of sight.

Alone for a while, Shaw took some time to take in a view he had never seen from this vantage point. From the West Hoe tram stop, he could see back across Plymouth Sound to Drake's Island with its small landing stage, walled cliffs, and old dilapidated buildings above. The water between the foreshore and island looked cool and blue, dotted with boats of all shapes and sizes all moving easily and lazily about their tasks.

Beyond the island, to the right of the wide Hamoaze Estuary, was the Cornish side of the river. The Mount Edgcumbe estate could just be seen on the Cornish slopes, whilst to his left on the other side of the confluence of water courses, three miles from the Cornish side, he could see the landing stage and barracks buildings of Mount Batten, and the coastline round to Jennycliff and Staddon Battery above Wembury Point. Both sides skirted the water with rocky outcrops rising to lavish fields and woodlands.

In the widest section of the channel was the Breakwater, a mile of interconnecting limestone blocks, some weighing several tonnes, it was two hundred feet wide at its base below the waterline and over forty feet wide at the top, which remained over eighteen feet above the highest tide. Through his reading Shaw new that it had been built almost two centuries ago to break up stormy waters and ensure safe passage around hazardous rocks into the various harbours and ports from the three connecting waterways: the English Channel, and the Rivers Tamar and Plym. Most importantly it also made it possible for the RAF seaplanes to land safely in all but the stormiest of conditions.

From the Hoe, the Breakwater looked vaguely curved inwards towards the Sound, but was actually three sides of an irregular hexagon when seen from above. At the eastern tip was a beacon, built from concentric rings of stone topped with a metal tower and cage provided as a place of refuge for any seaman stranded in bad weather. A stumpy lighthouse, still in operation but unmanned, stood sentry over the western end.

At its midway point and some thirty yards inside the Breakwater, rising from Shovel Rock, was Breakwater Fort. It looked circular from where Shaw was standing but he had seen it from above and knew it to be a perfect oval.

On the near shore, at the bottom of the incline that was followed by the main Hoe Road, Shaw could just see the end of the Promenade Pier with its collection of buildings and clocktower. Its attractions were likely just opening ready for tourists and locals alike. It already looked busy.

A light wind was blowing gently out to sea, but would no doubt turn about-face later in the day if the sky remained as clear as it was, the wonders of predictable land and sea breezes.

Shaw could just make out a faint odour of cut grass, roses and horse manure carried on the air from the manicured gardens that were tended daily along the outside of the west wall of the Citadel.

A sudden screech shook him from his all-too-rare moment of relaxed observation. An electric tram had rounded the corner at the bottom of the hill and was letting people off at the pier stop. It would soon be making its way uphill, to where Shaw was waiting.

Shaw looked up at the wide green slopes of the Hoe, hoping to see George returning. Two women dressed in what appeared to be matching Nannies uniforms were pushing perambulators, one made of wicker the other wood, no doubt out for a morning stroll and exchange of gossip.

A man in a smart tan three-piece suit and a woman in a bright yellow summer dress walked arm-in-arm. She stopped briefly beside Smeaton's Tower, but he pulled her along playfully to continue down the path.

A group of boys had started a game of kickabout on the sloped grass, interrupted occasionally by three dogs that vacillated between play fighting and trying to steal the children's ball.

When Shaw glanced back down the road, the tram was already halfway up, sparks crackling occasionally where its power pole scraped against the overhead catenary. He would do as George said and take the tram on his own if needs be, but he really wouldn't be happy doing so.

With another screech, the tram stopped just short of the end of its track, directly in front of the seat where Shaw was waiting. The tram looked somewhat like a single squat railway carriage, curved around at the front and the back and with an open top surrounded by a meshed railing.

A smell from the power system below the tramcar wafted out, strong, sweet and a little overpowering after working at full throttle to bring the tram up the incline to this last stop. Shaw always imagined the clean smell of electric motors to be somewhat like a coil of copper wire that had been dipped in chlorine: sickly but clean.

The tram displayed the number 124 and between the lower deck windows and the upper deck railings were decorative advertisement boards. 'BOVRIL' was written in large white letters on a bright red background above the destination sign declaring 'WEST HOE.' On the nearside panel, Shaw could see another placard, this one for 'HARDING'S FURNISHING ARCADES OF UNION STREET.'

Three men and two women disembarked from the front of the tram, as did the motorman once he had made sure the slipper brake was wound fully on and the tram's engines disengaged.

"Be a wait of about five minutes afore we set off," the motorman declared as he stepped from the tram, checking his pocket watch. "The Guard'll take your fare, sir," he added as he walked to the other end of the tram and applied the slipper brake there too, before taking a seat for a short break.

"Perfect, thank you," Shaw declared, happy to wait

for as long as possible.

Shaw walked around the tram to see it in full. He had ridden such vehicles many times before, but not in Plymouth, and everywhere you went they were different. This one was shorter, squatter than those he had ridden in London, and apart from the advertisement panels, the main body of the tram was a deep dark green, whilst the window surrounds were a pale cream.

The back of the tram was facing down the slope of Hoe Road and since this stop was the end of the line it would now become the front for the return journey. The tram could be driven from either end making it perfect for this kind of route where the vehicle would spend the day trundling along a single line from end to end.

The motorman would stand all day in the curved section at the front, driving the tram using a swing arm that could only be turned slowly, one notch at a time to ramp up power to the electric motors. A cranked handbrake would slow the vehicle at each stop, and a wheeled slipper brake would be applied to hold the tram on any incline. Finally, a foot pedal could be used to release sand onto the rails to prevent skidding.

Shaw noted that the destination sign at what would now become the front declared 'PRINCE ROCK' to be the final stop on the return journey. An advertisement below the front railing read 'PANIER MARKET FOR FINE WOOL 2d AN OZ,' and on the long offside, a panel read 'BEECHWOOD MILD COOKED HAMS AND BACON.' Upon reading, Shaw realised that he was somewhat hungry.

As he approached the step up to the tram, Shaw

could see a small sign detailing the upper and lower deck fares. There was also a clear instruction in larger letters below the fare prices: 'NO SPITTING!' Since the top deck would almost certainly fill with smokers, Shaw decided to pay the dearer fare.

"May I have two for Millbay Station? Inside, if you please," Shaw asked the guard who was stood at the bottom of the staircase that led to the top deck.

"Two, sir? Are you sure?" the guard asked, looking around and past Shaw.

Shaw turned to look towards the Citadel. "My companion will be here shortly," he assured quietly. "He is returning from the fort as we speak."

"We'll not be able to wait if he's late, sir," the guard advised. "And I can't refund once I've issued a ticket."

"He will be here," Shaw declared certainly.

"Very good, sir," the guard turned the handle on his ticket machine twice and handed both stubs to Shaw. "Sixpence, please?"

Shaw reached into an inner pocket of his long coat and pulled out a brown leather wallet which he opened, extracting the fare from a coin flap, and handing it to the guard before taking a seat facing the windows overlooking the green slope and path that ran up past the lighthouse.

The man and woman that had stopped briefly to look at the tower had now reached the road. Shaw watched as they walked over to the tram, the gentleman politely supporting his lady friend's hand and arm so she could step easily onto the platform. The man then followed her, paid the guard and both climbed the stairs to take seats on the upper deck. Neither of them gave Shaw a second look.

How quickly fame died with time's passing, Shaw thought to himself. A blessing in every respect! The flow within the hourglass relentlessly pursuing its course to a new destination, leaving its old and empty section devoid of all but a vague memory of sand.

Shaw estimated it had taken the couple at least two minutes to stroll from the lighthouse to board the tram. Over his shoulder he could see that the motorman was still looking out to sea, puffing on a cigarette. Shaw was beginning to get a little anxious. He would have no problem making his way alone to his appointment today, but he was already invested in the young man having shared a personal history. On top of which he had set a very real challenge which, if bested, he intended to honour.

A series of clicks from the downhill side of the tramcar caught Shaw's attention and he turned to see the motorman pulling the connecting pole free from the overhead catenary line. A tether rope was used to swing the pole down and around 180 degrees to its new position above what had been the front, but would now be the back, of the tram. Once the pick-up groove at the end of the connecting pole was safely hooked up to the overhead line again, the driver tied off the pole's tether neatly to a cleat just to the right of the rear step platform.

With the power restored, the driver jumped to the rear driving position and switched on a red light to confirm which end was now the back. Then he turned a wheel to fully release the rear slipper brake so that when he released the same at the front, the tram would instantly be under way.

Shaw scanned the brow of the hill, but George was

still nowhere to be seen. He watched the motorman hop off the back then stroll to the front of the tramcar, taking every last puff on his fag before throwing it down, standing on it and twisting it into dust under the sole of his right boot. Finally ready, he boarded the front driver's section and declared loudly, "Next stop. Pier!" before turning the releaser wheel for the second slipper brake just enough to allow the tram to begin running downhill purely under the influence of gravity. The brake would not be fully released until nearer the bottom of the hill to prevent excessive speed and difficulty stopping.

As the tram began to move, Shaw caught sight of a familiar figure cresting the grassed hillside beyond the lighthouse and beginning to descend at breakneck speed. George had clearly spotted that the tram was already headed down Hoe Road, so he had picked a route at a tangent across rather than directly down the green slopes.

Shaw could see George was sprinting so fast he had to remove his cap and was carrying it in his right hand which made the run look slightly awkward but didn't seem to mar the speed. It looked as if he might be headed for the Liner Lookout from which he would be able to follow a path directly to the Pier stop. Shaw was pleased to see that he had not been abandoned by his young companion.

As the tram continued down the slope of Hoe Road, Shaw lost sight of George again, the steep section on which the Liner Lookout was constructed blocking his view. With a fair speed on the incline of Hoe Road, the tram soon reached the Pier stop and three more passengers boarded, all taking to the upper deck. Shaw watched anxiously, wondering if he should ask the driver to wait once it was clear that George hadn't quite made it. Knowing such a request would be rejected, he continued to watch expectantly.

"Next stop. Grand Parade!" the motorman called before turning the brake release. As there was no longer a downward incline, he also engaged the trams electric motors, slowly turning the handle of the Westinghouse control panel clockwise, one notch at a time to build a smooth acceleration.

Shaw thought he caught sight of George briefly at the top section of the tiered Colonnaded Belvedere, which stood like a monumental wedding cake built almost parallel to the Pier itself. The structure had been built in the late nineteenth century to mimic a grand summer house from which visitors could enjoy views of the pier and out over the Sound.

Shaw saw him again, half jumping half running down the structure's wide stairways. The steps between the four tiers would provide George with a quick drop to Hoe Road.

As the tram reached the Belvedere's ornately decorated raised garden level, Shaw's view was blocked again, this time by a horse and cart loaded with barrels of ale, stout, and porter, which passed between the moving tram and the lower concourse of the pillared structure.

Shaw heard one of the cart's drivers suddenly shout, "Oi!" and then there was a thud, a gentle shriek, and a sound of general commotion from the upper deck.

Before the guard could take the stairs to see what the fuss was about, a young man, looking somewhat flushed and flustered came down and took a seat opposite

Shaw. The lad wiped his brow with a clean white handkerchief taken from his coat pocket, then placed his fisherman's cap back on his head and smiled at Shaw. Shaw handed his young companion one of the tickets he had purchased. "I did tell you he would make it," he said to the guard who was looking at them both and scratching his head.

"It was... touch... and go... until that cart... came along," George said breathlessly. "Just at the... right moment, it was. Regent Breweries... make strong casks... so one quick jump... from the wall... to the barrels... then a second... to the upper deck."

"You might have hurt someone you bloody fool," the guard chided.

"I'm really sorry, sir," George admitted, and meant it. "Today might change... my life, is all... I had to risk it."

The guard looked from George to Shaw shaking his head, "Do I know you?" he asked, looking directly at Shaw.

"You've possibly seen me on another route," Shaw lied.

"I suppose," the guard conceded. "I ought to throw you both off and fine you." He pointed at George, adding, "For reckless behaviour."

"I'm truly sorry," George offered again, "I didn't mean to make the young lady scream, so. I should probably apologise again. Her companion stood to clobber me; I think. She made him sit back down."

"You've done enough, just wait here. I'll let her decide what to do with you," the guard said, marching up the stairs and leaving George on tenterhooks.

When the guard returned a few minutes later he

made his way straight to George and said, "Lucky for you no harm done. She doesn't look at all happy, but she wants no trouble for you."

"That seems very kind of her, I'm sure," Shaw interjected.

"Thank you," George said. "I'll not be trying that again."

The guard chortled. "Mind, it'll make a grand tale down The Phoenix tonight, wont it, Harry?" he said, slapping the driver across the shoulders. "Don't see something like that every day!"

George thought for a moment, relieved but also suddenly inspired now that he had his breath back. "Really?" he said, then, folding his arms, he looked at Shaw. "There's my first story. Delivered as requested. Just, not to you."

Shaw, momentarily gobsmacked, was utterly speechless. Then he filled the lower deck with a sudden burst of laughter that was every bit as heartfelt as George's had been at the end of his own tale. He had to admit, George had delivered, and it was almost certainly going to be shared as an entertaining yarn that would bring merriment to the bar and leave everyone in good spirits. George had got the exchange off to a grand start, albeit in a most unexpected fashion, and without speaking a single word. This really was going to be a memorable day.

4 *Intervention:* Required

0900 hrs on 27 June 1930. Brigadier O'Dochartaigh's Office at Crownhill Barracks, Plymouth.

"Tell me Colonel, under what circumstances exactly was Colour-Sergeant Campbell found?" Brigadier O'Dochartaigh barked at his second in command over the busy landscape of his wide oak desk. He liked things to be tidy. He liked them to be orderly. Colour-Sergeant Campbell, he had heard, was neither at the moment and this disturbed him to the core.

"Th' colour-sergeant failed tay return tay barracks oan an forenicht ticket 'n' wis reported missin' yest'day mornin', sur. Private Blackwood suffered a deep gash o'er th' arm whilk wantit mair attention than th' squad medic cuid gay. Th' private wis taken tay a ward at yon infirmary fur his wound tay be cleaned 'n' sutured. 'Twas oan this ward that th' private immediately kent th' colour-sergeant. Th' private refused treatment, returnin' tay barracks 'n' informed me o' his discov'ry, sur."

Colonel Wallace kept an even tone to his report, ensuring it was a direct and accurate response. He was distinctly Scottish in all ways highlighted by his broad accent, but most would spot that immediately from his kilted uniform. He stood at ease but kept his eyes firmly fixed on a watercolour of Stirling Castle, hung deliberately on the wall behind the brigadier: Regimental headquarters of the contingent of highlanders currently based at Crownhill Barracks.

"Damn it, why didn't Blackwood just return the colour-sergeant to camp, colonel?" the brigadier demanded.

"Private Blackwood requested tay da exactly that, sur. Th' ward matron intervened 'n' wid nay allow Colour-Sergeant Campbell tay be moved, sur."

"Wouldn't allow?" the brigadier snorted, incredulously.

"Nay, sur."

"Blackwood? We are talking about our Blackwood, aren't we, colonel? Six-four, eighteen stone, burly, sour disposition, short tempered Blackwood?" the brigadier asked, still struggling to accept what he was hearing.

"Aye, sur. Blackwood initially dingyed her refusal 'n' tried tay hulp th' colour-sergeant oot o' kip, sur."

"And...," the brigadier prompted.

"Th' matron dragged Private Blackwood oot o' her ward by his lug, sur," Colonel Wallace had to admit.

The brigadier just stared at the colonel. Eventually he had to ask, "Well, didn't Blackwood struggle, man?"

"He did, sur," the colonel cringed visibly.

"Heaven's, man!" Brigadier O'Dochartaigh yelled, slapping his desk, "I'm almost afraid to ask!"

"Gey sensible, sur," Colonel Wallace agreed. "Let's juist be sayin' that whin Private Blackwood's een stopped waterin', he hud some difficulty traivelin, sur."

"A nurse? Incapacitated Blackwood?"

"Matron, sur," the Colonel corrected, then added, "She wis an' aye th' foremaist tay bring him a pack of ice, sur."

The brigadier shook his head in disbelief.

"Private Blackwood is a grand fighter bit wid ne'er skelp a wifie, sur," the Colonel offered by way of explanation.

"I should think not, Colonel," the Brigadier agreed.

"Th' matron, however, hud nay qualms hittin' yon man, sur. Wi' her knee, sur."

The brigadier shook his head again, "It comes to something when a nurse is capable of lashing out like that at one of our private's, colonel."

Wallace coughed uncomfortably.

"Move on, colonel. What do we know about the colour-sergeant's accident?" the brigadier demanded.

"Colour-Sergeant Campbell wis nay in an mishanter, sur!" the colonel responded. "He wis heavy goin in a drunken brawl 'n' badly gubbed, sur! A maid ferr fun him, sur! Ah been tay her works 'n' hud wurds wi' th' landlaird, sur."

"I don't believe it, colonel," the brigadier snapped. "Blackwood is formidable, but Campbell could kick him round the yard with both hands tied behind his back."

The colonel hesitated, took a deep breath, and said, "Th' colour-sergeant wis ferr mingin, sur."

"He usually is colonel!" the brigadier snapped. "That doesn't generally impede his fighting prowess."

"A gentleman guest tell t' th' landlaird that th' noise o' th' barnie woke him, 'n' he saw th' end o' th' rammy fay his winday, sur!" The Colonel swallowed and finished, "'Twas mirk, bit th' guest said thare wur a lot o' thaim, sur. A' kickin', punchin', shoutin', 'n' spittin', sur. He said thare kin hay bin aboot a dozen, sur."

Brigadier O'Dochartaigh rose so quickly his chair toppled over behind him, crashing into the wall. He stood stock still and Colonel Wallace watched as his brigadier's face changed from pink to red to dark purple.

The brigadier stood silently until he had regained a little natural colour then stared at the colonel and said coldly, "Who did this to us!"

"Navy lads, sur! Th' chambermaid heard thaim, sur! Th' guest saw thaim, sur!"

The Brigadier grabbed his swagger stick, tucked it under one arm and said, "All men to muster parade, Colonel. But first, Chief Constable Daniels at Charles Church. Get him on the telephone for me. Get him on the telephone for me, now!"

5 Millbay Station

0903 hrs on 27 June 1930. On board Plymouth Corporation tram number 124 currently passing the Grand Parade stop.

"You certainly have a way of thinking on your feet," Shaw noted of George, as the tram made its way around the streets of Millbay.

"I do what I do always looking ahead, is all," George replied, after a few moments.

"What was the urgency at the Citadel?" Shaw enquired, curious to know the reason for his sudden abandonment, which had been the cause of George's mad dash to re-join him.

George explained how the caretaker and his family on Drake's Island relied on deliveries of supplies arranged by the Gunners in the Citadel. "I'm currently the favoured errand boy. Food on a Monday and coal, oil, candles, and the like on Fridays," George finished.

"But if not you, then someone else would step in, I presume?" Shaw surmised.

"They would," George admitted. "And I'd be three shillings short on the week and two mornings down on a good breakfast."

The tram pulled silently away from a stop that had been earlier declared as Millbay Park and the motorman called, "Next stop! Station Causeway!"

"Speaking of breakfast," Shaw replied. "I have eaten nothing since the very early hours of this morning."

"There's a place at the station serves food," George suggested. "Depending on when the train leaves, that may be your best option."

"And yours, George. Do not forget you are my guide but also my guest," Shaw offered.

"Why?" George asked, looking directly at the older man.

"Why, what?" Shaw replied, a look of genuine surprise on his face.

"Why me?"

"So far I would call it serendipity, dear boy," Shaw smiled.

"And speaking plainly?" George asked, one eyebrow raised at Shaw's continued use of words that meant nothing to him.

Shaw sighed and thought for a moment before adding, "Put simply, you were in the right place at the right time. Or, perhaps, I was."

"But you must know people around here who might have helped you?" George pressed, determined to understand a little more about this strange man's motives.

"Nancy is the only close friend I have here. She would do anything for me," Shaw admitted. "But alas, I understand from our most recent correspondence that she is currently engaged in affairs of government in London."

The tram began to slow, and George stood, nodding at Shaw to indicate that this was where they should get off.

The woman in the yellow dress had descended from the upper deck and was already waiting on the platform to dismount with her friend. She glanced at George, and Shaw noticed that her face, framed as it was by her well styled shoulder-length auburn hair, still appeared fearful and deeply unhappy. If George's unexpected jump onto the upper deck had left her in such an obvious state of discomfort, why had she not pressed the guard to take some action?

Before Shaw could give it any further thought, the lady and her companion had alighted, just as the tram came to a halt, and were headed across the wide station loading area reserved for carts, lorries, vans, and taxis. They appeared to be in even more of a hurry to catch a train than he and George.

George and Shaw made their way in the same direction as the couple, entered the main station entrance, and headed straight to the ticket office. It was a little after nine in the morning and travellers from liner arrivals late the previous evening could be seen everywhere, easy to spot from their fine clothes, finer luggage, and more obviously from the personal staff attending to them. Most were clearly headed for London, but a handful could be seen waiting on platforms that would take them either to quaint villages in Cornwall, or further north to bustling cities like Edinburgh, Birmingham, Liverpool, Bristol, and the likes.

George enquired about the next available train that would get them to their destination and was told that the 09:38 to Penzance from platform three was on time, with a single change at Liskeard to pick up the 10:21 to Looe, arriving by 10:59. Return journeys were every eighty minutes or so and a day-return ticket would be one shilling in third class, or one-and-six for first. Shaw paid for two first class tickets, and they made their way to the station tearoom, which Shaw was pleased to discover served a range of breakfast options all day to accommodate late travellers.

Shaw ordered toast with condiments of marmalade and jam but made a point of stressing he did not like honey. He also wanted strong black coffee, which unfortunately the waitress said they were unable to serve due to a late delivery. Having already eaten, George politely refused to take up Shaw's offer of more food but agreed to share a large pot of tea which came with a selection of biscuits.

They took a window seat, partly because it was in a small section near the door set aside for non-smokers, but also to watch the hustle and bustle of the early morning rail services. The tearoom was not particularly crowded, but neither was it quiet, and the smell of food was interlaced with the more pungent smell of tobacco smoke from patrons sitting at tables in smoking, nearer the counter. George placed his cap on his lap and enjoyed the view.

Looking through the window they could see the platform was typically packed with carts of luggage, parents with children, people with dogs, wheeled crates loaded with sacks of mail and other goods, servicemen of all kinds, tourists mostly from the United States and any number of train guards and personal staff assisting with fetching and carrying.

"We'll be lucky to get a seat if this lot is anything to go by." George nodded toward the window and the crowds beyond.

"I should be most happy to stand," Shaw replied. "Thank you, my dear," he said, smiling at a young waitress who had just brought a tray loaded with their breakfast order and placed it on the table. He tipped her threepence and she curtsied and trotted away contentedly.

"If you're the lowest of the low, in the RAF, I mean; how come you're so rich?" George blurted before he could stop himself, half regretting it the moment it was said. It almost certainly made him sound a little envious, which, if truth be told, he probably was. He'd never spent time with anyone with cash enough to be so generous in giving gratuities or proposing such an extravagant rate of pay for a single day's work. He wouldn't be one to complain at the end of the day but couldn't hold back his natural curiosity.

Shaw did not bat an eyelid. He took a plate loaded with four slices of well-done toast from the tray and buttered a slice before slathering it with thick cut marmalade. He took a large bite and made a great show of savouring the experience, clearly happy to be eating some much-needed sustenance.

Shaw finished the whole slice then poured two cups of tea, passing one to George and inviting him to add milk and sugar if he wished. Then he replied, "I would never consider myself to be rich, although I have worked to secure a modest income, most of which I have already bequeathed to others." He took another slice of toast.

"Sorry, Shaw. I don't mean for you to explain your good fortune and I'm glad you took no insult. None was intended," George apologised, taking a sip of tea from the china cup Shaw had passed to him. "It's just I rarely rub shoulders with the likes of you. This strange day is both a first and likely only in my lifetime, of that I'm certain."

This time Shaw took more immediate notice, pausing mid-slice and putting his half-eaten toast back on his plate. "The likes of me?" he sputtered, folding his arms across his chest.

George reddened noticeably and explained, "Educated, sir. I mean, Shaw."

Shaw resumed his breakfast, apparently satisfied with that short response.

"That's all right then, George," Shaw continued as he buttered a third slice. "I was concerned for one moment you might have thought me a snob," he observed.

"Not likely, sir. Sorry! Shaw." George was still finding it hard to call the man by his name. "Snobs don't speak to the likes of me." He took a homemade oat biscuit and promptly dunked it in his tea before eating it.

Shaw gave a short laugh and replied, "In my experience, George, snobs rarely speak at all except to other snobs. They have a kind of club, you see. A way of recognising one another."

George thought for a moment while he took a second biscuit, this time dotted with dried fruit, then said, "I should guess there's a few out there," he said, nodding towards the bustling platform.

Shaw glanced through the window as a grand looking lady in a billowing full-length dress of pale green finished with fine white lace and a matching leaf shaped hat walked past carrying a dainty parasol and fine silk purse. A servant, evident from his demeaner and deference to her leading manner, followed behind in a smart but plain grey uniform and cap, carrying four cases with some difficulty.

"Perhaps," Shaw admitted.

"If I ever make something more of my life, I'll never look down on no-one," George said. "Don't need no-one waiting on me."

"Quite right," Shaw agreed, then added, "What do you mean, if?" He took a sip of tea having finished the last of the toast then leaned back in his chair, comfortably satiated.

George thought for a moment before replying. "Well, I've always thought it all depends on hard work, luck, and circumstance. I live as I find, and I find as I live."

"Hard work, I agree whole-heartedly. Luck, I concur but with reservations," Shaw accepted, "But circumstance? There we must disagree. A friend whose name I... currently share, once told me that life isn't about finding yourself, but about creating yourself."

George took a good swig of tea before he replied. "I believe I can meet your friend half-way. I live as I find, and I create as I live." He looked across at a large wall clock and added, "Right now I find it's time to go. Three minutes until our train leaves." He grabbed a napkin and pointed at the few remaining biscuits. "I find these to be surplus to our immediate needs," he noted wrapping them up before shoving them into his pocket. "I'm creating an opportunity for a snack later."

Shaw shook his head, laughed, and followed George out onto the busy platform.

With Millbay being an end of the line station, it was a relatively short walk to platform 3, and since they were in first class, shorter still to their carriage. Many passengers had already boarded and each of the compartments in the first carriage had at least a couple of seats already taken. Shaw couldn't help but notice, as they passed the windows of one occupied compartment, the woman in the yellow dress and her gentleman friend.

The next carriage was still first class and they found that most of the separate compartments in this were vacant. They settled on the very last in the carriage as it was a no-smoking compartment near to the exit, which would be ideal for the relatively short trip to the station at Liskeard. George removed and folded his coat, placing it neatly on the netted overhead shelving above his seat together with his cap. Shaw did not appear inclined to remove his service long-coat or cap and sat quite comfortably as he was.

They heard a final call for all-aboard from the main guard on the platform, and a few moments later there was a loud tooting from the large steam engine several carriages away. The train pulled away under a great cloud of stream from the main engine's smokestack and a lesser amount from the steam chests in front of the locomotive's front driving wheels. Being under a covered platform meant the carriages appeared to momentarily disappear, engulfed in a billowing cloud as the train left the station. This cleared quickly once they were out in the open where the stream could dissipate easily.

"I have a second story for you, George, if you wish," Shaw offered, "Which should pass the time nicely on this part of the journey. It may also offer you some further clues towards our wager. I do not need to suggest you listen carefully since you seem to be a natural."

"Listening has never been a problem," George admitted. "Fully understanding is what catches me out. If you gave any clues in your first tale I know I missed them."

"This is a simple tale of childhood obsessions. Castles, keeps and insufferable rain," Shaw began.

George listened intently, only slightly distracted by the many views he had so rarely seen as the train began to wind its way through Plymouth towards their connection stop at Liskeard.

"There is a castle at Gisors in France which, I was told as a young boy, holds the treasure of the Knights Templar. In my youth I thought myself bold enough to find it, or at the very least, to look for it." Shaw began. "I found no treasure. Only the gargoyle of Gisors."

6 The gargoyle of Gisors

It is mid-morning on 11 August 1907, and I am sitting beside a muddy country track three miles east of Villers-en-Vexin, a small town in the county of Eure in Normandy.

My father and I have spent most of the summer here travelling on our trusty bicycles, I with my father's Beck camera in a leather case I wear across my back, whilst its sturdy wooden tripod is strapped across the handlebars. The device can be somewhat cumbersome but has proven to be worth its weight in gold. I am confident that the images I have captured, should the plates all develop as I expect, will convey an astounding account of our most grand adventure, capturing the spirit and feel and history of glorious times past, set within the memory of magnificent stonework. My father challenges my suggestions for photographic positioning at times, but when I am most adamant, I tend to get my way.

My eighteenth birthday is in one week but whatever that day may bring, I know in my heart it could never surpass my time already spent with my father. We have been fortunate to be able to visit every castle and abbey on my extensive list, and yesterday, at Chateau Gaillard in the idyllic Petit Andelys overlooking the River Seine,

I found a piece of heaven itself. The magnificent castle harks back to none other than Richard the Lionheart and his disputed simultaneous reign as Duke of Normandy. A truly majestic medieval stronghold, it was far better than I had dared to dream with the highlight being the earliest machicolations I have had the good fortune to observe. Its concentric construction, dry moats and formidable keep made it stand out as the most auspicious monument to the perfections of fortified defence. A bombastic bastion shamelessly showing the true strength of stone that can only be achieved when combined with the most perfect positioning afforded by high ground.

Father said I may, if I chose, travel on alone to the Chateau de Gisors today, and I fear I may regret my decision not to wait for him to complete his business with Monsieur Bartenique, who joined us in our guest house when we arrived two days ago. Barty, as my father fondly calls him, is a jovial, fat dandy and has been pressing father to invest in wine through a partnership arrangement that will see a grand old coach house in Rouen converted into a base for exports to London and Edinburgh. They have agreed to travel to Rouen together today, and my father will return to Petit Andelys tomorrow, as will I, giving me ample time to prove I am more than capable of taking care of myself on my own round trip.

It had rained through the night, but as I set out keenly to cover the twenty odd miles of roads and tracks, the sky appeared to be lightening from the west which seemed at odds with an unseasonably cool easterly breeze prickling its way through the narrow country lanes, driving bulbous clouds that painted the sky with every monochromatic shade you might imagine. I wondered then if there might perhaps be a shower or two in the offing. Had I paused to ask the locals I might have learned what was ahead.

I struck out as fearlessly as ever with nothing but an old wine bottle I have filled with water, some local cheese from the fromagerie which I find both agreeable and moreish, and a slab of crusty bread I kept from our last evening meal specifically to sustain me through my independent adventure. I have the camera and tripod, of course. Father insisted I take it so that he could be sure of at least one surprise when all our Agfa plates are developed on our return home. The camera takes whole plates ensuring the best quality, the only downside being the weight since we brought six boxes with 12 plates in each. I used ten plates from one box at Gaillard yesterday so have brought the remaining two protected safely in their thick card box, wrapped with the camera in a waterproof sack as well as the usual leather box-case. This is both easier to carry and assures greater protection from the elements.

Never has a waterproof been so tested. I am currently resting against the trunk of a large sweet chestnut tree watching rain the likes of which I have never seen in my lifetime. I'm sure that on the other side of the muddy track that has finally defeated me there is a field of cabbages and views beyond across this flush fertile farmland towards Sainte-Marie-de-Vatimesnil or such, but I cannot see it. My jacket and trousers are soaked through despite the sou'wester I was quick to bring fearing the possibility of further inclement weather. The French would say, "Il pleut des hallebardes," which is fitting given my destination. For myself, stair rods do not do this rain justice; it is coming down in newels, the kind you might find at the bottom of the most palatial escalier.

I tried to cycle through this onslaught when it started just before I reached Villers-en-Vexin. The roads, if I can call them such, are nothing more than earthen tracks used primarily by locals who bumble along contentedly on horse and cart betwixt farmstead and homestead. Monsieur Bartenique brought his Darracq, which he assured us he travelled to Italy to collect personally in May. He is immensely proud of it, and it is the first such vehicle that has made me want to get behind the wheel of a charabanc. I was impressed by the sturdiness of its ten spoked wheels, and its black leather seats were most comfortable. It was painted a hideous green but that did not detract from the visual beauty of its shape, with its sleek rounded mudguards and wide running boards. Should Barty and my father have the misfortune of encountering this freakish weather, I fear they will be far wetter than I in its open topped cabin.

My staunchest efforts secured me an additional three miles or so and I think I might have continued longer were it not for the interminable mud. The cooling breeze dropped when the downpour began, and the air became stiflingly warm and humid. When this deluge is passed, I wonder just how warm the journey may become. For now, I am pleased to wait below this sheltering canopy, uncomfortably wet, uncomfortably warm, and wondering if there is any danger of lightning. I have laid my bicycle flat against the floor on the other side of the tree trunk just in case. I could easily succumb to an urge to eat or drink, but I decided when I set off that I would take no sustenance until I arrive at Gisors.

It is too early in the season for my shelter to provide me with any bounty, but there will be wild berries, plums, and cucumbers aplenty within easy reach of the track when I continue my journey.

The sound of the downpour is all encompassing, like a constant nagging hiss, drowning out the possibility of hearing anything else. It is not so much a gentle patter, more a raucous natter, and to ensure there is not the slightest possibility of you giving it anything other than your fullest attention, its volume is such that it might as well be using a loudhailer. I am certain this extreme weather event is one I shall not forget. *La pluie en France ne connait pas de limites*! Of that I am most certain.

When the rain begins to ease, I decide to set off again. Sticking to the verge where there is enough short vegetation to give the wheels of my bicycle some traction away from the mire of the sodden track and I am soon able to pick up a reasonable pace. The rain is just rain again and I can see ahead and across the wide flat fields dotted with occasional rows of tall conifer trees that appear so out of place and have most likely been grown as windbreaks for crops or cottages.

The track I have chosen to take me to Gisors is so straight it has the feel of a Roman road. I believe I am past the halfway point of the journey and my idea of using the verges to make the ride easier and avoid the cloying mud is paying off. The closeness in the air has passed, and now that I am a few miles further on from that brief pause at the sweet chestnut tree, I can feel the rain easing further to nothing more than a light drizzle. The cooling breeze has returned, the dark clouds are behind me, and the sky is clearing towards the east. To my left I am delighted to catch a first glimpse of Voile de la Bienheureuse Marie, hanging in the sky, a shock of blue breaking through the interminable overcast, a promise of the brightness to follow. There will doubtless be rainbows behind me if the sun breaks through. With that in mind I peddle ever faster, thinking about how surprised father would be if I manage to frame the castle beneath such a wondrous phenomenon.

Passing through Neaufles-Saint-Martin, a quaint and quiet village dotted with characterful cottages, the rain clears completely, and I am happy in the knowledge that I am no more than ten minutes hard peddling from my destination.

At the Rue Saint-Martin I make a brief stop at the church, strolling between the gravestones of its cimetiere and soaking up its history. I say bonjour to a cowled figure placing flowers on a grave and they stiffen briefly as if momentarily frozen by my unexpected interruption before continuing their act of sorrowful remembrance, placing seven blood-red roses on a grave the headstone of which is unreadable. Their cloak, which might have once been a glorious scarlet, is now dramatically faded, perhaps through an age of repeated washing and the bleaching effect of the sun. It is so creased it has the appearance of a patchwork stitched together from shards of cloth in every shade you might find between the palest of pinks and the deepest granite grey. What might have once been a fancy fringe in white lace at the hem, is now yellow, tattered, and threadbare, torn and hanging in strips that rest on the drying mud.

I decide to continue with my journey, warming now that the weather has cleared, and the clouds and rain are behind me. Before mounting my bicycle, I cram my sou'wester into the leather satchel that already holds my food and water. I realise that I have missed the possibility of any rainbow but will at least be assured of good light should I choose to use the camera at Gisors when I arrive. I take one last look across the monumental headstones and notice that the cloaked figure is gone, or more likely out of sight behind one of the larger mausoleums dotted around. No doubt the crows I notice perched high on the church tower can see us both.

As I continue towards Gisors, I am fortunate to see le Croix Percée at the edge of the road and stop to see if there are any surviving inscriptions on this ancient monument. My research prior to this visit confirmed it to be one of the few remaining Romanesque crosses in Normandy. I have read that most French historians believe it to be a Christianised menhir, somewhat akin to le Croix Roger at Heudebouville.

I recalled that Leon Coutil suggested in his *Inventory of the megalithic monuments of the Norman Departments*, that the stone was likely Christianised in the 9th Century, commemorating an agreement between Charles II le Chauve, the then King of Aquitaine, and the region's Lords. The king would fund the construction of what would be named Neaufles Castle, and in return the Lords would occupy it in his service. This would simultaneously pave the way for a future in which the River Epte would become an agreed border between France and Normandy, but more immediately it would serve to bolster defences against Viking raiders.

The Cross of the Templars, as it is also called, is very old, very weatherworn, and very short, being under five feet. The knotted ropes and crossed swords of the rounded head that I have read about in some books, are completely indistinguishable. Being so close to the roadside as it is, the stone reminds me of a similar ancient cross I encountered on a trip a few summers ago. We were staying with some of father's friends in the quaint village of Gweek in the far Southwest of England and had heard tales of a dilapidated chapel and old fallen cross. We found the cross very much standing and it was much like this one, except the cross in Cornwall had been carved to show four dimples within the wheel shaped head, whilst this one at the roadside at Neaufles has four holes carved straight through, giving its name.

I had thought that I might also try to find the Tour de la Reine Blanche given the fanciful stories that the old and crumbling tower is still connected to the Chateau de Gisors through a series of secret underground tunnels. Since Gisors is still almost three miles away, I have my doubts about such a legend. If I find any hint of hidden subterranean shafts at Gisors, I will make every effort to find a route back to Neaufles Tower through such a lair. Should I find nought but a crawlway I will endure its hardships for the chance of achieving the kind of notoriety that a discovery of such magnitude would bring. Now that I have seen the Pierced Cross of the Templars, I am keen to complete the final stretch to Gisors.

Considering the vast area of flat and cultivated farmland in this region, I remain quietly impressed by how scarcely populated it seems to be. I can only imagine that the few locals I meet work incredibly hard at certain times, perhaps affording them the opportunity to remain more relaxed throughout the rest of the year, living off the rewards of the many substantial crops I have passed this day. The pace of life is slow, measured, almost savoured.

For the last part of my journey, I feel I could just as easily be in Worcestershire as Northern France. Approaching Gisors, I leave behind the tracks of mud and dust and wind my way through cobbled streets dotted with a mixture of homes and businesses constructed with external beams, reminding me of old Elizabethan cottages. A sign identifies this as Rue du Faubourg de Neaufles and there are more modern homes built of limestone interspersed with the older properties, some under construction, but they are relatively few and the town of Gisors appears to consist of one long road dotted with a mixture of establishments constructed in diverse architectures. I turn onto the Rue de Penthievre at the junction with Rue de Vienne, and finally see the immensity of the outer walls surrounding the Chateau de Gisors. To capture the best picture of this wonderous castle I decide to continue around to the west side which will present the best light at this time of the afternoon.

The Rue de Penthievre is quite steep but not so steep that I am unable to cycle it and as I approach what looks to be the castle's prisoner tower, I switch to an old track to the right that flattens off and then gives me a speedy downhill section around the castle walls, eventually leading to a wonderful lawned area dotted with occasional spruce and alder. With the sun behind me, I stop below an ancient horse chestnut and the view across to the castle is magnificent. From here I can see four distinct fortification sections, making this the perfect spot to capture a record of the splendour of this final bastion of the Knights Templar.

I lean my bicycle against the trunk of the tree, then untie the straps holding the tripod to my handlebars and carry it clear of the canopy to a spot with an uninterrupted view across to the castle. The camera is in one section of my large leather satchel, carefully wrapped in an oilskin, and once removed I mount it to the tripod by means of a double clasp that rigidly supports the flatbed that folds out from the neat leather-lined wooden box. I unclip two retaining lugs and the camera bellows is revealed, concertinaing out like a tapering squeezebox until fully extended. I carry the main lens in my jacket pocket with a focusing glass, carefully wrapped in a handkerchief, and once the lens is screwed in place on the front standard, the whole thing is ready to focus.

I check the ground glass set in the rear standard to see that the image includes all that I want captured. The image is inverted and so faint that most would want to cover the back of the camera with a black hood and tuck themselves under to secure a better view in the darkness beneath. I content myself with pulling my jacket-back up and over my head, shielding the camera from as much of the sunlight behind me as possible.

The initial view, I find, is a little too dominated by sky so I tilt the camera forward gently until the top of the castle's keep is at the lowermost of the inverted image on the glass. Then I release a holding catch and slide the bellows towards me until I am happy that the image is in focus. To be certain of the best possible picture, I use the focusing glass, which father calls a loupe, placing it upon the ground glass and making final slow adjustments until I am certain that the now magnified image achieves perfect sharpness. Then I cover the lens with its cap, release a mechanical catch to set the shutter mechanism ready and in place, and collect one of the two plates I have brought, loading it into the plate holder which I slide into place so that it sits exactly where the ground glass was focussed.

The protective cover of the Agfa plate has a tab which is gripped in a cover slide and with one swift pull I remove the cover from the glass now safely inside the camera housing, stopping once I see a red line protruding from the side of the camera to ensure that I can slide the cover back in place across the glass plate once the photo has been taken. The shutter is set for around half a second, which in this light should capture a perfect image with very little blur given the gentle breeze in this late afternoon. I remove the lens cap, hold my breath as I always do for some strange reason, and gently press the shutter clip on the side of the lens. There is an audible click confirming that the shutter has opened and an instant later a second click to confirm that the shutter is closed. I can breathe again and immediately replace the lens cap and push the cover slide back into the camera which presses the plate cover firmly onto the photographic glass again.

My first image of the Chateau de Gisors will be amazing, I am sure, and I decide that given the wonderful light and clear sky, I will take my second picture this late afternoon, as well. Should I wish, I might then return to the guest house at Petit Andelys this evening, rather than find a local hostellerie. I feel confident that I can make it back before dark.

I remove the exposed plate from the camera and slip it into a small black silk bag, which serves to confirm that it has been used, before placing it back into its box, protected by the stiff card and the other unused plate. Then I pack everything away again and refasten the tripod onto the handlebars before setting off for the castle's main entry which I had seen at the top of the Rue de Penthievre.

At the opening into the castle, I dismount and push my bicycle over the final stretch of cobbled road and pathways to enter the castle's outer bailey, passing between two buildings that, like the rest of the fortification, make a show of confirming that defence is everything. The tour du prisonnier to my right has three openings facing out toward the town, arrow loops, each around three feet high but no more than two inches wide on the outside. What appears to be a roofed gatehouse to my left makes up for a slightly reduced height by having five such defensive openings. The high stone curtain that circles the remainder of the fortification has similar defence slits at regular intervals, all difficult to reach from the outside since the walls themselves are built upon naturally raised rocky slopes, affording no opportunity of a breech by tunnelling. Whatever gates might have been constructed to form the barbican have long since rotted and fallen away. Similarly, there is no evidence of a portcullis at the end of the wide entryway. Two cast iron gates are all that control access to the outer courtyard now.

Glancing around the inner bailey, I close my eyes. In my mind, I construct the kind of image the Knights Templar might have seen upon arrival, perhaps returning to homes across Europe from conflicts or defensive duties in the Holy Lands, and I am more than impressed with the obvious impregnability of this castle's outer structure. For those brave selfless souls this haven must have seemed a tranquil, cool, and fertile refuge in comparison to Jerusalem, Aqaba, Tripoli, Damascus, or the harsher challenges of other Arab states.

I wonder how I might have fared in their sabaton? Charging across the majestic dunes of Saudi Arabia, encased in armour, and fighting to be a hero under the scorching heat of the relentless sun. In my heart, I understand that I will never know. There can be no quarter for such chivalrous adventures in this era of modernity, so I will content myself with my explorations and work to be the best archaeologist I can be, uncovering lost wonders and striving to unlock their secrets.

My imaginings have fired up my inquisitiveness, and after a quick bite to eat and swig from my bottle, I make my way across to what was almost certainly the castle's stable block, overlooked by the upper bailey constructed on top of a large man-made conical mound. A narrow doorway, most likely the entrance to a feed store, is open, and though the whole building is dilapidated by time and neglect, the interior is still protected by the stone roof and so presents a haven for my bicycle. I decide to take the camera and tripod with me. I am not overly concerned about theft, since the whole place seems deserted, but it is better to be safe than sorry where father's camera is concerned. It is so quiet I am feeling bold enough to consider a little unconventional exploration. The camera is not the only thing I thought to bring in the leather case. *Ad malleum praemium venit*, as my friends and I would declare behind the master's back in archaeological studies.

When I walk across to the base of the giant mound and look up towards the substantial chemise that encircles the upper bailey, I am overjoyed to also catch a closer glimpse of the upper section of the magnificent, octagonal keep and tower within. This is undoubtedly the most exceptional example of a motte and bailey castle I have ever observed. A wooden bridge section almost certainly joined the open gate I can see at the top of the steep slope to the stables block behind me when the Knights Templar were in occupancy, though there is no evidence of such now.

I scramble my way up the steep incline, which is at least forty-five degrees, using the thick stems of stubby couch grass and ivy as makeshift ropes which I hold onto with my left hand occasionally to stop from sliding to the bottom again. I carry the camera and my stonemasons hammer in the case strung carefully across my back, whilst the tripod is balanced so that the weight is taken by my right shoulder and my right hand holds it steady in front of me. At the top I stand before the magnificent open gateway which is four yards wide and twice that in height. I am even more impressed to find that the wall the entryway passes through is at least two yards thick with wider sections of Romanesque buttress every six paces or so.

Standing in the centre of the wide entry, I turn to look at the view from the top of the mound and am amazed at how far I can see. The wonderous rich farmland beyond the town that has grown around this ancient fortification is even more impressive from this vantage, revealing a patchwork of fields, some recently tilled but most in shades of vibrant green, interspersed with wooded areas, farm buildings and distant hills of wilder moorland.

I can already see beyond the church of Saint-Gervais-et-Saint-Protais, which to me has the look of a cathedral with its enormous flying buttress supports that flank each section of intricate stained-glass windows. To the west, I see a wide bank of rugged looking hills at least 15 miles away, the towns of Clermont, Criel and Chantilly are just beyond. To my south, the limestone dotted hills of the Vexin are thickly forested in places, hiding the distant communes of Saint-Gervais, Nucourt and Bouconvillers.

My attention is drawn back to the castle, and I turn and enter the upper bailey, finally seeing the keep in all its glory, looming over me at least seventy feet to its highest point. A single doorway into the tower section is flanked by even more impressive buttress supports, each protruding almost three yards at the base, progressively narrowing in long upward sloping sections until they are almost flush at the top of the keep. Perhaps because of its magnificence, I have a sense of disquiet in the stillness of this innermost sanctuary. All about me is hushed, almost unnaturally muffled, as if I have clapped my hands over my ears. Apart from the stubby green grass below my feet and blue sky above, all about me is shades of grey and so seems more a prison than a refuge. I cannot help but imagine that this tower has had a great many uses through its history in addition to its main purpose as a lookout.

It is so quiet I decide to seize the moment, removing the hammer from the side section of my case, then leaving the tripod and camera on the floor just inside the entry to the upper bailey. I trot across to the portal opening at the base of the tower and find that the thickly latticed gate, which has the look of a portcullis, is hinged, and locked with a wrought iron clasp and thickly rusted padlock. A furtive glance around confirms that I am still completely alone, so without hesitation I raise the hammer and strike the padlock firmly three times. The sound reverberates up through the tower, as if it holds a tolling bell, sounding mournfully like an ominous summons. I instantly regret my attempt, and though no-one has seen me, I feel my face redden bashfully.

The padlock is clearly far sturdier than it looks and is unmarked by my endeavours to force it, so I decide to make no further attempt to gain entry. A fine archaeologist I am! Though I have seen no sign of security about the place, I scamper back to my case to hide the hammer, defeated, deflated, and feeling more than a little rueful. The loud clanging noise has changed the feel of the place further still, emphasising the intensity of the silence so that the cold grey stones around me become almost sepulchral.

The feeling of foreboding increases with the arrival of a murder of crows, alighting on the upper edge of the tower, as if summoned by my resonant signal. Most pay me no heed, but one, looking down at me, caws raucously and continues to do so until all its companions turn their dark and beady eyes to me. Once all are staring, the leader falls silent. It feels as if they are judging me, and my earlier flush is replaced by a sudden chill. With a shiver I decide to take my picture swiftly so that I can leave what is beginning to feel an unwelcoming place.

I set up my camera at the entryway so that I may be

as far from the tower as possible. As I swing the ground glass into place, I realise that I am faced with a dilemma. Do I take a picture of the lower section of the tower and courtyard, to emphasise the magnificent and frustrating entry into the tower? Or do I angle the camera upwards to capture the feel if its imposing height and the integrated tower section? I decide that the base will be the most rewarding, since the top, though viewed more distantly, will feature in the picture I have taken from the lawns. My decision has nothing to do with the birds, but I notice they are still watching me.

When I have set the camera ready for the final focus, I pull my jacket-back over my head again and hunch myself over the ground glass to get the darkest view I can and make fine adjustments of focus. I bring the bellows towards me again, much further than was needed for the last picture, since the focal length is much shorter for this second photograph.

As the image begins to clarify, my eye is drawn to a taint that spoils the look of the flat wall at the base of the tower. The blocks appear smudged and twisted, as if seen through an old bullseye windowpane. I use my handkerchief to carefully wipe the lens to remove any blemish or dust and then check again. The smudged image remains and is somewhat bigger, so I unhunch my jacket and move to the front of the camera, removing the lens housing and cleaning the glass at both ends this time before screwing it back into place again.

Checking the ground plate under the cover of my jacket once again, I gasp, then jump upright, my jacket still over my head, and look to the wall with my own eyes. The grey blockwork looks just as it did when I arrived. I close and rub both my eyelids then crouch again, allowing my jacket to shield the camara glass from as much light as possible. In the lonely darkness beneath my own jacket, I freeze, holding my breath, afraid to look further but more afraid to look away. A face is visible in the wall where the blurring had been. Its eyes are focussed on me more intently than even the crows. As I watch, the stone face leans forward, emerging out of the wall, gurning as if the struggle is an act of agony. It has the look of a gargoyle, snarling, angry and striving.

I stand to see.... nothing!

I can feel a cold sweat has beaded on my brow, but the wall is just a wall.

I shake my head, straighten down my jacket, and walk a few steps towards the keep, determined to dismiss my confusing fears, but feeling them just the same. The light in the late afternoon must be playing tricks on me, or my camera, at least. The few slow steps through the cloying silence reveal nothing, and I dig into my resolve, taking several more until I am standing directly before the stones that presented the frightful illusion.

One of the crows, the leader, I suspect, croaks loudly, breaking the stifling silence so abruptly that I jump despite my resolution to keep a grip on the dread that clouds my mind. Is it laughing at me?

I glance up and as I do, stone hands grab me, pulling me towards the wall where the face has appeared once more. The icy grip seeps through my jacket at the shoulders, my heart is now the loudest sound I can hear, and I feel frozen to the core. My mind cannot comprehend what is happening and I can feel myself succumb to a panic that scrambles all logical thought.

My mouth is open, my eyes are shut, and I am

screaming. I know I am screaming. I can feel the exertion, my mouth is open so wide my jaw muscles are straining. My lungs are exhaling so violently my ribs are aching. The scream should be echoing around the upper bailey, far louder than my tolling on the lock. And yet I hear nothing in my state of chilled despair.

In the violence of my own silence, I open my eyes and I am nose-to-nose with the stone face, no longer twisted, no longer straining. The monstrous gargoyle holds me easily as if I were constricted in the jaws of a keen vice. Sad grey eyes gaze balefully into mine and a voice like velvet whispers, "*Vous ne pouvez pas tomber. Il n'y a rien pour vous arreter.*"

The piercing cold hands push me roughly to the floor, and I look up at the sad face, now leering over me.

"*Partir! Votre avenir est de sable et non de pierre!*" The face screams at me this time and still in shock and confusion I scrabble away backwards on all fours, unable to take my eyes off the wall until the gargoyle has faded back into its lair.

Still shivering in shock and chagrin, I grab at all my things and bolt through the opening before sliding roughly down the side of the mound to the outer courtyard. I run to my bicycle and in a matter of moments I am off, peddling away from this terrifying place as swiftly as I am able.

The streets are either deserted or my brain too addled to register anyone. This is a place of nightmare, for me at least. I do not know how to process the terror I feel. When I write to mother, I shall simply confirm what I will swear to all who ask me; that this place was locked and thoroughly disappointing.

My journey back to Petit Andelys is a blur, as forgettable as my journey to Gisors was memorable. I am back before dark. I am back in what seems the blink of an eye.

Ordinarily I choose not to drink, but on return to the guest house I ask for wine with a late evening meal, which astounds the propriétaire, since he is aware of my hitherto habitual demands for water.

I do not sleep well, despite swiftly finishing off a bottle of Chateau Margaux whilst barely touching the plate of cold ham and cheeses that were served to me with warm bread.

I wake the following morning to find myself more determined than ever to remain teetotal. I shall remember this headache for a long, long time. The rest I shall endeavour to forget.

7 The hollow smile

0957 hrs on 27 June 1930. A first-class railway carriage on the Plymouth Millbay to Penzance direct service, 10 minutes from Liskeard Station.

"Well, that was a creepy one," George said, shivering slightly despite the warmth of the carriage as Shaw ended the tale.

"It was not my finest hour," Shaw admitted, glancing out to watch the countryside racing past them. Some farmers were already baling hay and pickers hard at work in fields of cucumbers, carrots and other root vegetables were clearly used to the backbreaking toil.

"Did anything like that ever happen again?" George asked.

"Not like that, no," Shaw replied. "And I have since been able to identify a possible explanation for my spectral encounter. A proposition that removes the experience from realms of fantasy and suggests a more down to earth reason for the bizarre exchange that day."

"Which is...?" George pressed, wondering what might cause such a strange and terrifying ordeal.

"Cheese," Shaw said simply.

"Cheese?" George repeated, uncertain he had heard correctly. "I thought you were going to say it was a dream. Or that perhaps you made that part up. You know, an embellishment for the purposes of achieving an appropriate ending."

Shaw smiled. "Sadly not. For this tale I have added nothing. Even the rain was as harsh as I described. I had taken with me a blue veined cheese, not unlike Stilton but somewhat softer. That is what I recall eating when I arrived inside the main castle, before I climbed up to the keep on the motte. It had become quite warm that day and I suspect the spores in the cheese were particularly active on ingestion."

"What did the ghost say?" George asked, adding, "I barely speak your version of English and I don't speak French at all, so the foreign parts meant nothing to me, as grand as they sounded."

"Gargoyle, not ghost," Shaw corrected. "It spoke twice, the first being a literal nonsense which I reflect upon frequently but have yet to comprehend. The second time it told me my future was not written in stone, but in sand." He smiled enigmatically, as if perhaps there was something important about what the gargoyle had said, like it might be a genuine clue to his identity.

"You didn't make that part up either, then?" George asked.

"I did not," Shaw confirmed quietly. "At the time I did not understand why my vision said what it said. I can only surmise that in some way my mind was reaching forward through the hallucination, predicting my own future in some bizarre fashion."

George thought for a moment and then clicked his fingers excitedly, "I've got it! I know who you are!" he exclaimed sounding genuinely pleased with himself.

"You were in the papers several years ago."

Shaw nodded but said nothing. He would not mind being discovered so early in the journey; it would still be fun to share stories of his adventures.

"For discoveries in Samaria or Egypt," George continued. "I don't recall the details, but your achievements were slightly overshadowed by the destruction of an ancient temple."

Shaw raised one eyebrow. "I..."

"No, don't tell me," George interrupted, drumming the fingers of his left hand on the seat beside him. "I know your alias! It's Smith!" He pointed at Shaw excitedly. "No. It's Jones. Yes, that was it! You're that famous archaeologist, aren't you?" He smiled proudly, delighted to have presented a guess which he genuinely believed to be correct.

Shaw laughed. "Henry?" he said seemingly in disbelief. "He is Dr Jones, now, I believe. I knew him. We worked together in Palestine. Briefly."

George was crestfallen. "Ah! I was sure that must be you."

"No," Shaw admonished. "I am not that maverick of misadventures; of that I can assure you. Dr Jones is a good man, but his penchant for the wanton destruction of the ancient, however accidental he may claim it to be, is matched only by my own dogged determination not to damage anything I recognise as sacred."

"Is that why you gave up?" George asked.

Shaw prickled slightly. "Gave up?"

"Wanting to be like Dr Jones, I mean," George explained.

"My dear boy, I never wanted to be like that. Well. Perhaps I did when I was very young indeed," he admitted. "My childhood interests were peeked by tales of heroics, journeys of discovery and acts of chivalry. My true obsession was with the Templar Knights since they seemed to be inherently noble to me. At first, anyway."

"I've only heard mention of their name but don't know much about them," George admitted.

"They were a force for good against legions of evil, until they became rich, at least," Shaw sighed.

"Did getting rich stop them from being good?" George asked.

Shaw nodded. "In a way. Riches made them lazy, then fat and then greedy. Greedy for more riches, anyway. I suspect they still thought themselves good. But their rise and fall can be mapped out by the simplest proverb."

"Money is the root of all evil," George suggested after a moment's thought.

"Almost," Shaw noted. "The love of money is the root of all evil," he corrected.

The door to their compartment from the connecting passageway flew open suddenly, startling both. They turned to watch as an unexpected visitor entered, slamming the door shut behind them, then yanking down all three sets of blinds, masking the three of them from the corridor. Then the stranger sat in one of the chairs, looked at them both and said in a desperate and frenzied whisper, "Please help. He's going to kill me!"

It was the girl in the yellow dress.

"Well that at least expounds your reticence in regard to my compeer," Shaw nodded towards George.

"What?" she asked quietly, sounding slightly annoyed and frowning deeply.

"You'll get used to it," George noted, standing, and ushering her to take his seat before moving to the door and firmly wedging one boot against the base, jamming it shut.

"Now, I surmise that you are being taken to Penzance against your will," Shaw said, before the girl could add anything further.

"Yes," she said, her frown deepening as she glanced from one to the other.

"Then you are in luck since we intend to alight at Liskeard, which will be the next stop. If you accompany us, we will do what we can to secure your safety."

She shook her head, clearly doubting the reassurance. "Thank you, but I fear my brother will find me again," she said, sounding pitiful and defeated.

"Your *brother* wants to kill you?" George asked incredulously.

"May I first ask your name, my dear?" Shaw interrupted before she could reply to George.

"Marjorie, sir. Marjorie Ayres. Miss," she replied.

"Thank you, Marjorie. This is George, my friend," Shaw indicated George who nodded and smiled to try to reassure her. "And you may call me Tommy if you wish."

"You look familiar," she said, looking at George.

"We met on the tram, miss," George offered, and Marjorie nodded.

"I remember. But you look familiar, too, Tommy," she pressed, turning to face Shaw.

"I have a very familiar face," Shaw proposed.

"Are you with him?" Marjorie asked, glancing at them both, nervously. "Is that how I recognise you, Tommy? Have you been following me?"

"Are we with whom, miss?" Shaw asked.

"My brother. He claims to be alone, but I do not believe he could have found me by himself," she observed, seeming a little uncertain now about the choice she had made in seeking help.

"Marjorie, my dear, I have no idea who you are," Shaw admitted. "I promise you upon my life that neither George nor I have any connection with your bother. None that we know, at least."

"So, how did you know where he was taking me?" Marjorie asked, still sounding sceptical. She was determined to challenge them fully before trusting them further.

"We followed you into the station and were next to purchase from the ticket office," Shaw replied. "I noted that the booking clerk had the timetable sheet for trains to Penzance in front of him. He had to swap it for local branch-line listings when George asked about tickets for our journey today."

Marjorie looked at George who shrugged but nodded.

"I have an eidetic memory," Shaw added by way of explanation. "Anything I notice remains with me forever. Sometimes I try to be too clever for my own good," he admitted.

"We'll definitely help you if we can, miss," George said, trying to sound as reassuring as possible.

"I need all the help I can get," Marjorie admitted, allowing herself to relax, but only a little while she remained uncertain. "My brother is the last of my family and alas I have made few friends that I might turn to."

"Why is your brother trying to kill you?" George asked again, clearly angered by the thought.

Shaw watched Marjorie intently as she answered. "It's a long story which begins with my late grandfather and his estate left solely to me." She opened her yellow handbag which matched her dress, taking out a small handkerchief.

"Which your brother stands to gain if you die!" George interrupted, furious at the thought someone might be so callous.

"No, if it were that simple, I should be dead already," Marjorie stated bluntly.

"But you still believe he intends to kill you," Shaw pointed out.

"He does," she insisted. "But first he will force me to marry his business partner, Edward. Edward and I were due to be married tomorrow in Hugh Town, St Mary's on the Isles of Scilly. My brother, Mark, is trying to take me by force to St Mary's from Penzance this afternoon. From my uncovering of their plans, I suspect that shortly after my marriage I will meet with a most unfortunate accident. Either that or be forced to suffer a lifetime with a man I abhor."

"I take it there is a marriage clause in your grandfather's will?" Shaw asked.

Marjorie nodded. "Everything from my Grandfather's estate will transfer to my husband on our wedding day, nullifying any will I might have chosen to make for myself."

"Not an unusual thing," Shaw admitted. "Your grandfather was opposed to the right to vote campaign?"

"Vehemently," Marjorie agreed.

George rolled his eyes and groaned. "Not another one," he whispered under his breath and Shaw and

Marjorie both looked at him.

"Uh. Next one is us," George said, smiling disarmingly.

"If you do not mind my asking, your brother looked older than you when I saw him with you earlier. How is it that your grandfather did not see fit to leave the estate to him? Especially given his obvious aversion to the aptitude of the female mind," Shaw noted.

"My grandfather saw to the heart of Mark," Marjorie replied, looking at the floor in front of her.

"He did not approve of his character, then?" Shaw asked bluntly.

"No! Grandfather even told me to be wary of him," Marjorie replied sharply, looking at Shaw. "I could not believe it when I discovered what my brother was planning! His business partner is near twice my age. They have no doubt come to some financial agreement, which, which..." she sobbed into her handkerchief.

When Marjorie had recovered some composure Shaw said, "I suspect your grandfather knew something of your brother's tendency to greed."

Marjorie scoffed. "My brother is far worse than merely inclined to personal gain. Mark has no heart; grandfather could see that as easily as could I. My brother once admitted that he deliberately started the fire that killed our mother and father. He claimed he did it just to teach them a lesson, but he couldn't help gloating. He was glad they had died."

Shaw looked at George then back to Marjorie. "So, your brother is a murderer already?" Shaw asked.

Marjorie nodded again. "At first grandfather tried to excuse Mark's dark moods, said the fire must have addled his mind, made him lose his way. He said it must have been the shock of our loss that caused Mark to act so heartlessly."

Shaw nodded. "That could have been the case."

"No. I always feared my brother long before our parents were lost. Mark has a black heart and relishes in causing hurt to others. When my brother smiles it is empty, a mask, like he has no notion that a smile ought to be connected to a feeling, an emotion, to happiness." Marjorie sounded defeated. "I think he killed my best friend, too!"

"My dear, I am so sorry," Shaw offered.

"Madeline was the only one I could trust when I found out about my fiancé and my brother. I wept and I retched when I discovered their betrayal and Madeline helped me escape, said she would always be there for me. I tried to telephone her yesterday and her mother is distraught. Madeline hasn't been home in days." Marjorie paused and looked out of the window as the train began to slow.

"This is us," George confirmed, grabbing his coat and hat. He opened the door to check the corridor. "There's no-one out there."

"Come with us," Shaw offered. "I have a friend who is very good at helping people to hide. And believe me, I should know."

Marjorie looked from George to Shaw and nodded. "Thank you," she said, somewhat tearfully.

The three of them left the compartment and walked swiftly to the door section where the bellows joined their carriage to the next.

"Marjorie! Sister. Here you are," Marjorie's brother said as they came upon him. He was leaning against the door, barring their exit, and smiling in a way that made

Shaw's skin crawl. Everything that Marjorie had said made sense. Shaw had encountered men like her brother before. This man's face was so devoid of emotion Shaw felt he might as well be looking at a bleached skull.

"You must be Mark," Shaw said swiftly, offering his hand to shake by way of introduction whilst also stalling for some time to think.

"And you must be mad," Mark said, ignoring Shaw's gesture and folding his arms across his chest, one hand reaching into his jacket. "If you're thinking of leaving the train with my sister, that is."

"No, I must be mad," George said, barging past Shaw and Marjorie, as if impatient to get off the train.

"And why is that...," was all Marjorie's brother managed to say before George's fist connected swiftly and solidly with Mark's lower jaw, knocking the disturbing smile from his face, and rocking his head back so hard it shattered the glass of the carriage door window. All three watched as Mark crumpled into a heap, out cold.

"That's why," George said, before turning to Marjorie and adding, "Sorry. I can be... a little impulsive." He smiled and she smiled back.

George turned to Shaw. "There's another good one," he declared. "Delivered to you, this time."

Shaw looked momentarily perplexed and then he realised what George was saying. "My dear boy, I know you said you may not be good with words, but..."

"I seem to be more creative than I imagined," George interrupted, "And anyway, actions speak louder than words." His wide and genuine grin immediately made up for the disturbing smile that had been worn by

Marjorie's now unconscious brother.

Shaw was momentarily stunned by George's speed of thought before filling the exit cubicle with laughter. This was becoming a habit! Then he shook his head. "I think we should move to the other end of the carriage." Looking down he added, "This end seems a little cluttered. Well-done," he said, clapping George across the shoulders again.

The three of them made their way down the narrow corridor to the next exit, reaching the door just as the slowing train came to a complete stop. They alighted onto platform 1 of Liskeard station directly in front of the ticket office. One stooped and elderly lady, apparently in mourning from the look of her veiled hat and puffed out black dress with crinoline skirt, exited the train from the carriage behind theirs. She hobbled away towards the footbridge that crossed the tracks. Apart from this one passenger no-one else boarded or left any of the carriages. All three watched until the train pulled away a few moments later at which point Marjorie breathed an audible sigh of relief.

"Your brother will certainly have some explaining to do," Shaw said. "When the train guard finds him, in any case." He began to walk towards the footbridge that crossed the track, following the signposts for Looe. "He will, no doubt, be quite creative with his explanation, most likely avoiding any mention of us."

"I hope I never see him again," Marjorie admitted, following close behind Shaw as he marched ahead up a shallow shingle slope to the footbridge over the railway lines. "You should, too, you fool," she said, slapping George, who was walking beside her, across his right arm.

"I think I can handle myself," George said confidently.

"No," Marjorie chided. "You can't. If he ever sees you again...."

"Come, come," Shaw interrupted. "No further moroseness. Your brother is headed for Penzance, and we are not. When we get to Looe, I shall introduce you to Ferdinand Bartenique. Barty to us."

Shaw looked at his pocket watch. "Barty will be most impressed if I am at the pier before mid-day. Come. It's this way," he said, following the signs that pointed down a long sloping path onto platform 2 before levelling out and crossing a wide cobbled road to an additional set of station buildings at platform 3. "A new life awaits."

8 *Intervention:*
Paving the way

1014 hrs on 27 June 1930. Brigadier O'Dochartaigh's Office at Crownhill Barracks, Plymouth.

Colonel Wallace stood at ease having carried out his orders to the best of his ability. It had taken him far longer than his brigadier was happy with, and his brigadier had made that known in no uncertain terms. If Brigadier O'Dochartaigh said jump you just did it and worried about when to stop going up afterwards.

Being a member of the armed forces did not always give you the kind of clout you expected. The chief constable had not been available when the operator secured the colonel's initial call earlier that morning, and a desk sergeant had told him to call back around ten. The chain of command did not hold sway with those outside the military. Civilians did not understand that orders were orders, which all-in-all was extremely frustrating when you could not follow yours if they did not do as they were asked.

The Colonel tried twice before ten, but it was only on this third attempt at almost quarter past the hour, that the operator was able to confirm a direct connection to Chief Constable Daniels. The colonel handed the telephone to his commanding officer and stood listening, only able to hear one half of the conversation.

"Danny?" the brigadier began, "It's Tig."

"... ... ..."

"Yes, well, thank you, and the girls. Mrs Daniels still hitting the gin?" he scoffed haughtily, apparently sharing a personal joke.

"... ... ..."

The brigadier laughed and said, "Well I suggest you find a better place to hide the Gilbey's, old boy."

"... ... ..."

"Now listen, we have a situation which I'm sorry to say requires an Intervention."

"... ... ..."

"Yes, exactly like the one I told you about in the Sudan three years ago." The brigadier rubbed his forehead as if searching for the right words.

"... ... ..."

"Yes, I'm sure this will be the first of its kind on home soil," the brigadier admitted.

"... ... ..."

"As a courtesy, of course. I want you to be prepared. Bring as many men as you feel necessary."

"... ... ..."

"Tonight. It will start early in the evening. Late enough so that business premises other than those serving drinks are shut. Early enough to ensure things are kept sober."

"... ... ..."

"Hold one moment. I'll just confirm with my colonel." The brigadier turned to Colonel Wallace and asked, "Can we be precise about the timing and location of our exercise, Colonel?"

"We kin, sur," Wallace confirmed. "Th' Intervention wull tak' steid at six th' day in Union Wynd fay th' Octagon, tay th' Palace, sur."

"Did you hear that, Danny?" Brigadier O'Dochartaigh asked curtly.

"... ... ..."

"Yes, that is good considering my colonel's accent. It will all be contained between the Octagon and the theatre, beginning at six-o-clock."

"... ... ..."

"Necessary? Necessary? Of course, it's bloody necessary."

Colonel Wallace could see his commander getting a little agitated. Colour was returning to his cheeks and not in a good way.

"... ... ..."

"Look, I don't expect you to understand. You're a civilian, old man."

"... ... ..."

"No, I don't mean to offend but do you work with your family?"

"... ... ..."

"I mean literally and figuratively."

"... ... ..."

"Yes. An Intervention keeps things under my command and ensures minimum fallout."

"... ... ..."

"Yes, you do whatever you feel necessary to be prepared. Just have your men keep things clear and I'll hold my men under full command." The brigadier appeared to be calming again.

"... ... ..."

"This is not just the best option, Danny, this is the only option. This nips it in the bud preventing months of tit-for-tat escalation that could lead who knows where."

"... ... ..."

"Justice? Justice is your jurisdiction. You're talking to the army, old boy."

"... ... ..."

"No, it's not about revenge. It's the opposite in fact. It's about discipline and empathy and obligation."

"... ... ..."

"Our motto demands it." The brigadier paused and added, "No. It damn-well commands it."

"... ... ..."

"*Sans Peur. Ne Obliviscaris.* Understand, old boy?" the brigadier said curtly.

Colonel Wallace saluted as was the tradition on hearing the regimental motto spoken aloud.

"... ... ..."

"That's just a direct translation!" The brigadier was slowly changing colour again. Wallace knew the mistake the Chief Constable was making.

"... ... ..."

"Being well educated is not always a good thing, Danny. That may be what it says but that's not what it means!"

"... ... ..."

"No! It has one clear meaning, not two! *Beyond all doubt, we will never forget!*" the brigadier snapped. Colonel Wallace saluted again.

"... ... ..."

"Yes, it does shine a different light on things, doesn't it, old man." The brigadier was calming again. The chief constable appeared to be reaching some understanding.

"... ... ..."

"Thank you, Danny," the brigadier said calmly. "I think that would be best for everyone."

"... ... ..."

"Of course. And perhaps you could brief the naval and military hospitals in Stonehouse. I really don't mind who knows. A military exercise is a military exercise. There will be casualties."

"... ... ..."

"Yes. Goodbye, Danny. I look forward to seeing you at the Octagon. And better luck hiding the whisky next time."

Brigadier O'Dochartaigh replaced the handset onto the cradle of the telephone and turned to his second in command. "Well, Wallace. That went better than might have been expected."

"Apologies it's tak'n say lang tay connect tay th' chief constable, sur! It wi' nay happ'n agin, sur!" Colonel Wallace half shouted.

"Damn it, Wallace, I know the delay wasn't down to you! Bloody civilians are a law unto themselves. Especially when the civilians you want to speak to are literally the law unto themselves," the brigadier snorted.

"Sur."

"You know who to call next, of course," Brigadier O'Dochartaigh nodded at his colonel, before adding, "Unofficially, of course."

"Commander-in-Chief Hansen, sur," Colonel Wallace confirmed. "'N' howfur detail wid ye like me tay be, sur?"

Brigadier O'Dochartaigh laughed. "Spell it out for him, Wallace. Spell it out in no uncertain terms. Tell him

I will be in personal attendance should he wish to participate."

Colonel Wallace hesitated. "Yi'll waant me tay threaten a commander-in-chief o' th' navy, sur?"

"Threaten? Good heavens, no." The brigadier smiled. "Extend it as a courteous opportunity to, to... engage in rigorous and spontaneous training opportunities with another of His Majesty's Armed Forces."

The brigadier stood, saluted, and marched smartly out of his office. Colonel Wallace saluted as his commanding officer left, then he shook his head, smiled, picked up the telephone, dialled for the operator and said, "Aye, awright, please connect me tay th' commander-in-chief's affice at Adm'ralty Hoose. It's gey urgent 'nd ah mist bade oan haud 'til ah kin be 'n touch. Th' commander-in-chief must hear whit ah haes tay say."

9 The power of parabellum persuasion

1026 hrs on 27 June 1930. A first-class railway carriage on the Liskeard to Looe branch line service departing Liskeard 1021; delayed by approximately ten minutes.

"How about a strong hot cup of tea, Marjorie?" Shaw asked. "You still seem somewhat anxious, and I should like to do all I can to reassure you."

Shaw, Marjorie, and George had taken a vacant compartment in the first-class carriage immediately behind the engine that was busy taking on water from a tower beside the track whilst simultaneously building up steam in preparation for the delayed departure.

Marjorie took a moment to think and breathe. She was still feeling shaken by her abduction, rescue, or both. "Fine!" she snapped, almost as a challenge.

"Excellent. Lead the way, George," Shaw invited. "I believe we can take tea in the next carriage."

George steered the three of them from their compartment, along the narrow corridor to the restaurant car, which was set out with tables, each covered with fine cotton tablecloths, napkins, fancy lamps with tasselled fringes, curtained windows, and softly cushioned seating.

Marjorie sat at the first table of the carriage, taking a window seat that looked out onto a storage area and the Looe Valley Line engine shed. Two tables at the other end of the carriage next to the serving counter were taken by a group of three men and three ladies who were nattering away happily, clearly travelling together. Shaw sat opposite Marjorie and George beside him. After a few moments a waitress came to take their order which Shaw insisted on paying, much to Marjorie's annoyance.

"I hope you don't mind my still having trouble with all this," Marjorie said to Shaw, sadly. "Four days ago, I travelled to Plymouth to avoid my wedding day. Only my best friend knew and yet my brother came for me this morning."

"There is only one logical explanation," Shaw suggested. "And it is one to which you have already alluded."

"Your brother made your friend reveal you," George said angrily.

"That is one possibility," Shaw agreed. "And it would explain her disappearance. I should hope a more likely explanation would be that your brother had some inkling that his duplicity had been discovered. He might then have set an accomplice, perhaps a private detective, to observe you and report to him."

"So, it could be anyone," Marjorie said nervously, glancing at the group of passengers at the far end of the restaurant carriage again.

"Not anymore," Shaw suggested, trying to calm Marjorie as best he could. "I suspect that once your brother found you, his accomplice went their own way."

Marjorie smiled slightly for the first time since they had boarded the train to Looe.

"And now you are under my..." Shaw paused, then added, "...our protection." Acknowledging George, especially in light of his swift action in dealing with Marjorie's brother.

George nodded before taking a small napkin full of biscuits from his pocket and placing them on the table.

"Forgive me if I still have doubts," Marjorie said bluntly glancing from one to the other. "But this just seems too good to be true."

"Shaw would say it's serendippy," George smiled.

"Serendipity," Shaw corrected. "And yes, that is exactly what I would say."

"Chance!" Marjorie sneered. "You want me to believe our meeting is down to blind luck."

George smiled and was about to say something when their waitress returned with a tray loaded with a large teapot covered in a smart blue cosy, three cups and saucers, an ornate milk jug and a cut glass bowl of sugar complete with silver spoon. There was also a wonderfully art deco coffee pot.

"Thank you, my dear," Shaw said, tipping her his customary amount. "I shall be mother," he added reaching for the teapot.

"You were just in the right place at the right time," George offered.

"Or we were," Shaw added, pouring tea into Marjorie's cup first.

"Exactly," George agreed, offering the biscuits around.

"Thank you," Marjorie said, holding out one hand to stop Shaw pouring. She reached for the jug and tipped in a splash of milk before adding four heaped spoons of sugar and stirring vigorously.

"And how is it that you just happen to be going to see a man that can help me hide from my brother?" Marjorie asked pointedly.

Shaw looked at George as if searching for the best way to respond.

"Would you like me to leave for a moment?" George said, looking at Shaw. "I shouldn't want our wager spoiled."

"Wager?" Marjorie said frostily, folding her arms defensively as the train began to pull away from the platform. "I sit in fear for my life, and you worry about a wager?"

"It's nothing to do with you, miss," George reassured her, realising too late that the emphasis in his reply was not quite right.

Marjorie arched one eyebrow and kept her arms tightly folded.

"You need not leave us, George," Shaw said before turning back to Marjorie and adding, "What young George is trying to say is that I laid a wager which he feels may be compromised by my answering your question."

Marjorie waited.

"I have challenged George to call me by my true name," Shaw admitted. "The man I am travelling to see has been instrumental in helping to hide my identity on more than one occasion."

"Well, that makes perfect sense!" Marjorie replied waspishly.

"It would if you knew who I was." Shaw smiled charmingly.

"And who are you?" she asked rhetorically, before continuing with, "Oh, that's right, you can't tell me while George is sitting here because of some childish wager!"

"It really would be easier if I left for a moment," George said again, starting to feel somewhat uncomfortable. "Or we can end the wager, if you wish," he said to Shaw.

"No, no!" Marjorie chided, "You stay here, George. It is George, isn't it?"

"It is, miss," George replied sheepishly.

"And this, this," said Marjorie, unfolding her arms and gesturing at Shaw's RAF long-coat and cap. "What is this ridiculous uniform about?"

Shaw looked perplexed. "Ridiculous? This is me," Shaw said plainly. "Aircraftman 338171, Shaw. Reporting for duty, ma'am." He poured a full cup of black coffee and took a sip carefully since the train was turning a steep slow curve, which was rocking the carriage slightly.

"You don't have the sound of a common aircraftman," Marjorie challenged.

"I shall take that as a compliment," Shaw smiled, relishing another sip of coffee.

"And you, sailor boy?" Marjorie said, looking pointedly at George's cap. "What do you do?"

"Me?" George thought for a moment before replying, "Jack of all trades and a master of none, miss. Right now, I'm in the employ of Mr Shaw."

"And you have a wager with your employer?" Marjorie pressed.

"Yes, miss," George confirmed.

"And what do you stand to lose?" Marjorie asked.

"Nothing, miss. If I can name Mr Shaw before the end of the day I shall have double pay, is all, miss,"

George confirmed chirpily.

"And you, Tommy?" Marjorie asked Shaw. "What do you gain from such a wager?"

Shaw thought for a moment, took another sip from his cup and replied easily, "Company, Marjorie. I have company. It has been an eventful morning and I already think of George as a friend rather than in my employment."

George smiled at the compliment.

"You really have no reason to mistrust us, miss," George tried to reassure her.

Marjorie sighed and took a sip of her hot sweet tea before turning back to Shaw. "Tell me about the friend you are travelling to see. Barty?"

"Ferdinand Bartenique is a second-generation family friend," Shaw replied. "I trust Ferdinand with my life, as my father trusted his father, Francesco, with his reputation and the good name of all our family."

"Your family's reputation?" Marjorie interrupted.

"Indeed," Shaw confirmed. "The details are as captivating as they are calumnious."

"Calumnious, how?" Marjorie said. She looked at George who just shrugged again, clearly uncertain of the meaning of the word.

"Scandal, my dear. But do not fear. I am extremely proud of my history," Shaw continued. "My father met with Francesco Bartenique sometime in the 1880s whilst on a trip to France. I am told they shared stories of loss, longing, and love. My father had left his wife, choosing to run off with the family governess, my mother. Apparently, I have four half-sisters from his marriage. We have never met."

"You mean previous marriage?" Marjorie asked.

"No. Father married once. I and my brothers were born out of wedlock. Barty Senior supported my father with securing documents for the family that would at least hide the indiscretion, though not always effectively," Shaw admitted, looking at George.

"I did not mean for you to share such personal detail, Tommy," Marjorie admitted. "My fear is clouding my mind in ways I have never thought possible. I'm so very sorry."

"I'm not," Shaw said, matter-of-factly. "I should not have lived the life I have if things had been different."

"But how is it that you are visiting with Barty today of all days," Marjorie asked. "It seems too good to be true. I do not mean to continue to doubt you so, but you will understand that recent events leave me wary."

"Barty saved my life, and now he is now my business partner," Shaw admitted. "My agent, in fact. He maintains contracts with a number of publishers I write for, and they pay me through him."

"But you said you're an aircraftman," Marjorie pointed out.

"I am an aircraftman by choice because I am comforted by the habitual military regime. I am a writer by vocation since I am obsessed with the technicalities of effective prose," Shaw confirmed.

"He does tell a good tale, miss" George said cheerfully.

Marjorie shook her head, still uncertain. "And Barty saved your life?" she asked.

Shaw nodded slightly. "I had a price on my head. Literally. Twenty thousand guineas," he confided. "Barty facilitated a new identity in partnership with the War Office which assured my anonymity allowing me to remain hidden in plain sight."

"Twenty thousand guineas?" Marjorie exclaimed. "What did you do? Plan the assassination of the Archduke Ferdinand?"

Shaw sat expressionless for a few moments then said quietly, "In times of war, one side's saint must always be the other's sinner." He thought for a moment before adding, "In my time I was truly worshipped as a saint and knowing the consequence I came to accept that I deserved whatever Fate might bestow upon me. But you need not worry since the bounty lapsed several years ago."

"Why are we stopping?" Marjorie said, immediately distracted and suddenly sounding uneasy again.

George looked out of the window as the train continued to slow. "If I recall there's four stops before Looe. This is the first, Coombe Junction Halt," George advised as he spotted a sign through the carriage window.

Marjorie drained her cup as the train began to move again. "So, why are we now going back the way we came?" she asked, still sounding panicky.

"My dear, I think you might need another," Shaw offered to pour again. "The route is a circuitous one elicited by the intersecting main-line and the topography around this station."

George and Marjorie looked blankly at each other before Shaw added simply, "I have seen it from the air."

"But we're returning to Liskeard," Marjorie complained as the train clearly appeared to be in reverse.

"It only feels that way. Look," said George, pointing through the window at an intersecting track. "There's the line we came into this halt station from, and now we've switched."

Marjorie watched as their carriage passed the track that George insisted was the one that led back to Liskeard station, then she calmed slightly and took a second cup from Shaw.

"If anyone can help you, Marjorie, it is Barty," Shaw advised, pouring a tea for George and a second coffee for himself. "With his assistance you will be well hidden if you wish, and his fees are fair. I do not know of your inheritance but based on your brother's intentions I would deduce that you should easily be able to afford his services."

"I'm so befuddled," Marjorie said, placing her head in her hands.

Shaw paused for a moment, staring blankly at the verdant greens of the countryside passing the train, then he said quietly, "I know from experience that it is a most distressing feeling, my dear. I believe Mark would have used it, you know, if George had not been so... quick to act. He was reaching for it as he fell to the floor."

Marjorie sat up again, looked at him and nodded slightly. "How did you know?"

"You do not strike me as one who would be dragged easily against her will. Let alone go quietly as if out for a morning stroll." Shaw was thinking back to the lighthouse. "Which means you were in fear for your life."

"And for those around me," she confirmed.

"Did he have a knife?" George asked, wondering what they were talking about.

"A parabellum," Marjorie whispered.

George looked blankly but Shaw's eyes widened.

"A luger!" Shaw declared quietly.

George had heard of that one. "A gun!" he exclaimed as some of the colour drained from his face. Shaw and Marjorie glared at him as one or two of the group at the other end of the carriage fell silent and looked their way.

"I think perhaps we should return to our compartment," Shaw suggested as the train began to slow again.

George looked out as they came to a stop at another empty platform. A sign declared it to be St. Keyne Wishing Well.

"Lead the way, George," Shaw invited. George stood and made his way back along the corridors to their compartment in the adjacent carriage, Marjorie followed, then Shaw. Marjorie sat first, choosing to sit in the middle of the wide forward-facing seat and George sat next to her taking a window seat, Shaw sat opposite George, taking the window seat with his back to the front of the train.

In the relative privacy of their compartment, Shaw said to Marjorie, "I can tell you about the merits of my friend before we meet him, if you would like."

Marjorie sighed, "I just need to know I can trust you."

Shaw took that as an affirmation and said, "George?" he nudged his friend's knee with his foot to make sure he had his attention. "I accept your latest non-verbal adventure as a valid contribution to our exchange. It certainly gives me a story I can share at... the Phoenix?" Shaw smiled. "The tale is particularly elevated by the fortuitousness of your actions in preventing what might have escalated to become a wholly unfortunate encounter. Vis-à-vis, Mark's hidden firearm."

"Thank you, Shaw," George smiled. "I think."

"But that must be the last," Shaw stated emphatically. "When I have shared my tale, the next in our exchange must be yours. Wholly verbal. That was our agreement, after all."

"Of course," George confirmed. "You're in for a treat now," he said, turning to Marjorie. "I've heard some fine stories today already."

"You are most kind," Shaw thanked George. "This is perhaps the shortest tale I shall recount today, being mostly poetry. But it is the most unusual and most vividly recalled. It concerns the fall of Argent, a lost god of the city of Carchemish, and a friendship that endures to this day."

Marjorie leaned towards George and whispered, "Is your employer always this melodramatic?"

"I don't know. We only met this morning," George whispered back. "But he has been like this all day, yes."

Marjorie blinked disbelievingly at both and whispered, "Honestly. Men!" under her breath. Then she leaned back into her seat so that she could watch the countryside pass whilst listening to the strangest man she had ever met.

10 The fall of Argent

The Egyptian city of Akhebaton was nothing but a ruin buried and all but forgotten when I encountered it in 1912 under the tutelage of my dear friend, Charles Woolley. The ebb and flow of driven dust storms had scoured it, burying it beneath dunes that had been creeping for centuries across the desert landscape, tidal sand, as unforgiving as the harshest ocean.

Even in its state of desolation and abandonment, it held an allure that seemed to far exceed that of other more intact excavations. Echoes of a very different past seemed to hold council upon a landscape of dust and decay, devoid of any shade for as far as the eye could see. No tree or shrub could tolerate the blistering heat of that barren, arid landscape. The occasional helichrysum petiolare could be seen, though stunted and not thriving, liberating the faint aroma of liquorice on even the faintest breeze.

And yet our preparatory studies had already confirmed that as recently as one hundred years ago, the entire desert upon which we stood had been a forest of olive trees, farmed and traded both as oils and stone fruits across the whole of Northern Syria, possibly feeding into trade routes of the old Silk Road. Stepping back further through thousands of years to the times in which our interests were invested, the Hittites would have no doubt looked upon a very different scene, lush and green and covered in wide swathes of woodland and pasture. Perhaps it is the memory of that vivid living landscape that permeates to this day, creating an aura of potential that belies the desolation laid out before us in sand, shale, and splintered stone.

Under the rule of the Turkish Ottoman Empire, this region had been doomed to devastation, and all due to misguided levies enforced against unfortunate tenant farmers and applying to every single tree that grew upon their land. Much as an Englishman in the 1700s might brick up four windows to darken their homes and halve their taxes, so those farmers, under the dominion of the Ottoman, might burn a forest to secure the same. The few surviving havens of woodland might have reinvigorated the terrain were it not for a new and relentless demand for logs engendered by the arrival of the railway. The insatiable appetite of new and heavy steam engines provided a perfect opportunity for locals to secure a modest income whilst denuding the landscape of its remaining tax burden.

Upon this land was written for me a destiny of archaeology and adventure. The first, unearthing secrets of the dead from many thousands of years before the construction of Akhebaton was a very real objective, but also a cover for the second, our true purpose of spying on the development of the Berlin to Baghdad rail line and in particular its crossing of the Euphrates River. International tensions notwithstanding over the ambitions of Kaiser Wilhelm, we could not have known that we were treading the kerb of a tinder path that would eventually ignite into war.

Those tales, however, are for a different day and this particular adventure is not even mine. It concerns a revelation born of a discovery lost on the same day it was found, and the hallucinations induced by a fever from which I might never have recovered were it not for the determined care and attention of a loyal family friend.

On arrival at the site of our works at Carchemish, we were quick to divide our proposed excavations into clearly demarked sectors so that in our notes we could always be abundantly clear about the exact location of our finds. During this initial apportionment, an area of the north-west sector engaged our immediate interest since it appeared to indicate a strong fortification, though what its purpose might have been and whether it derived from the early Hittites, the Mesopotamians under Sargon, or Tell el-Amarna built under the direction of the Pharaoh Akhnaton, only time and our patient investigations would expose.

It was during our second week of careful digging in this area that I began to feel unwell. Had I known how quickly I would succumb to the parasites that had infected me through one or other of numerous mosquito bites, I should have taken more care, and possibly secured a swifter recovery. Unfortunately, my stubborn nature and determination to prove my resilience alongside our native contingent of Arab workers got the better of me.

I can recall one of our Arab workmen shouting for Orange, a nickname gifted to me by the unbridled sunshine, and one which would stick with me in one form or another throughout my time in the desert. He ran to me excitedly, carrying a small stone tablet, inscribed with Hittite hieroglyphs on both sides. My head was pounding in response to the infection I was not yet aware of, and I thought to blame only the heat, so after thanking him I retreated with the find to a covered tent to note the exact location of his discovery and to begin the immediate task of translation. What I believe I read that day will stay with me forever, though I can never prove the truth of it since, when I recovered six days later from the illness that almost killed me, all trace of the tablet and its remarkable inscriptions were gone.

In what I can only believe now to have been an extreme fever dream, I did not just read the translation, I was possessed by it. Through the power of its ancient carvings, I was spirited away to live as fatherless child, son of a god, demon spirit, and broken outcast. Ichor flowed through my body; wounds of the flesh healed instantly since my blood was not the impotent red liquid of man, but the infinite silver white light of a Hittite God. Filled with limitless puissance, I would eventually grow to fear nothing.

In the days before the mighty Torhunz ascended the throne of my brethren and bound us all to him as servants, the thousand gods dwelt among mankind. Some towered above their mortal company like giants or monsters, whilst others hid their divine powers, living in plain sight, unrecognised among humans whose visage they could easily mimic or wear like a cloak through beguilement. I was one such as this, though not by choice. I was raised and lived as a child of man with no notion of my true heritage. My divinity was hidden as much from me as from those I encountered. This is my song:

ON TIDAL SAND

My name is Ushune. This is my story.
Now living in shame. No longer in glory.
I grew as a child. I played with my friends.
Fighting with bullies. Then making amends.
I struck at a playmate. Lashed out with a stick.
He cried for his mother. And said I was sick.
Why did you hit me? He wailed as he said.
You know you're like me. Your father is dead.
His words cut me deep. I started to cry.
I ran to my mother. I had to know why.
She snatched at my stick. And took it away.
Then promised to tell me. Just not on this day.
Anger flowed through me. I raised up my fist.
Lashed out at my mother. Only just missed.
Her eyes opened wide. She begged me to stop.
My power was unfettered. Now I was on top.
Please do not strike me. I beg you, she said.
Your father is alive. You've a journey ahead.
Give me your mercy. Don't smite me, take pity.
Your father's divine. Urkes is his city.
Your brother is Teshub. The heavens he rules.
Your sister is Sawuska. Queen of the fools.
You are greater than both. You are stronger and free.
Go forth and find him: your father Kumarbi.
The Gods cannot harm you. Make sure you fear none.
I listened and thought. Until mother was done.
Then let light envelope me. Drawn from my power.
Took the name Argent. And set off that hour.
I followed the sun, and the moon, and a star.
My journey was long. I travelled afar.
To the depths of the oceans. The heights of each peak.
Till I came upon Urkes. The city was bleak.

None there could help me. My father had left.
The cold pierced my heart. I felt so bereft.
To the heavens one told me. Your father has gone.
Ascend to his dwelling. If it can be done.
Take your place by his side. Be the one that is true.
Though he may try to stop you, show him what you can do.
A stick is a plaything. I needed a sword.
So, I sought out Lelwani. The queen of the horde.
Her demons all fell. With one smite of my hand.
Lelwani was angered. She took one last stand.
Her sword pierced my side. Which was always my plan.
I just laughed then and turned. And away with it ran.
Lelwani ruled evil. With a sword forged from good.
A haft carved with runes. In pistachio wood.
But now it was mine. And the gods I would goad.
From the safest of towers. To their darkest abode.
None would be safe. From the might of my blade.
I should grow stronger. And watch their powers fade.
I soon found Kumarbi. To his palace I strode.
The birth of my godhead. The end of his road.
To balance my sword. I took father's spear.
He sang out my praises. But trembled in fear.
Arma and Arinna. I dragged from their seat.
Both paid me homage. As they cowered at my feet.
Arinna was Sun God. Arma, God of the Moon.
I might leave the world darkened. From midnight to noon.
Please do not kill us. My fellow Gods pleaded.
You may light up my lands. I warmly conceded.
My own radiance is pure. It also shines bright.
But I can't watch all day. And I won't watch all night.
Thank you, dear Argent. My luminaries said.

Then away to the heavens. The two of them fled.
Love of the moon. Blood of the sun.
Playing at god was such impish good fun.
Teshub was angered and paid me a visit.
His tone was emphatic. His words were explicit.
I said he should kill me. Or at least he could try.
Perhaps I might make the God of Storms cry.
You foolish impetuous dandified oaf.
If I should kill you. I'd be ending us both.
His words were anathema. Nothing to me.
My sword! My spear! My ruling decree!
His scream then was thunder. Unbridled. Unleashed.
Spear shaft turned to dust! Sword buckled and creased!
A lightning bolt struck. My blindness complete.
An assumed victory, swiftly turned to defeat.
So now as a pauper I wonder each city.
Pleading for food, begging for pity.
My potency gone. Succumbed with my vision.
I was blinded by power. Struck down in derision.
If dominion you seek, be righteous, not corrupt.
Or your fall, just like mine, may be justly abrupt.

I awoke with this experience, this lamentation, burned like a literal lightning scar into my consciousness. Standing over me as I opened my eyes was my best friend, Ferdinand Bartenique. He was mopping my brow with a flannel dipped in cool water, and I later learned that he had watched over me for the entirety of my illness. Forcing me to drink a weak vegetable broth and as much cold water as I could swallow in my delusional state, he secured my recovery from the most dreadful malaria.

The ancient carved tablet was gone when I returned

to the excavation site and the tent in which I had sought comfort and shade. I had started to scribble some initial translations of glyph phrases from Hittite into English before darkness claimed me at the start of the illness, but there was no sign of my work. I did not care then, and I do not care now. I was alive.

11 Showdown at Sandplace

1057 hrs on 27 June 1930. A first-class railway carriage on the Liskeard to Looe branch line service departing Liskeard late at 1033; now approximately 15 minutes from Looe station.

"You really should be in the theatre," Marjorie complimented Shaw when he finished. She had been particularly impressed with the cadence and projection of the poetry element of his tale.

Shaw beamed. "Why thank you, Marjorie."

"To recite as you did so flawlessly and without hesitation from memory is uncanny," she said, then added, "Where did you first hear it?"

"Hear it?" Shaw replied. "I read it from the stone tablet, my dear. It felt like I lived it. Just as I have recounted."

"The tablet that just disappeared?" she asked, sounding slightly disbelieving.

"The one that was stolen. Yes," Shaw confirmed.

"How do you know it was stolen?" George asked, trying to seem as interested as Marjorie.

Shaw looked at George. "I know it was stolen because it was never seen again. There is a tremendous black market for such marvels. I have no doubt it will surface again one day."

"And you only looked upon it once to work through its translation from an archaic language...Hittite, wasn't it, into English?" Marjorie probed, sounding somewhere between searching and sceptical.

"Yes," Shaw repeated.

"And from that single viewing of a stone written in ancient hieroglyphics you remembered that whole poem?" Marjorie folded her arms, clearly finding Shaw quite unfathomable.

"Some of it I believe I remembered, but in truth the whole of it might have been an hallucination, nothing more," Shaw admitted.

"Now that seems more plausible." Marjorie smiled. "I can at least understand your loyalty to your friend."

"It was just the first time he saved my life, of course," Shaw conceded.

"Why did they call you Orange?" George asked quizzically, wondering if this might be a clue to the man's real name.

"My fair complexion tended to burn very easily, and my hair was not always like this." Shaw ran his fingers through his shock of white locks.

"Golden, perhaps?" Marjorie pondered, her eyes widening briefly, as recollections of old news stories began to hint at why Shaw looked so familiar to her.

"Indeed," Shaw admitted.

"Did the Arab workers speak English?" Marjorie asked.

"A few," Shaw admitted. "Most spoke Arabic, some old colloquial French. I had swiftly learned to speak and read both."

"I see." Marjorie leaned back into her seat. "I trust you now, Tommy. And you George." She smiled at them both.

"To what do we owe your most welcome and sudden acceptance?" Shaw inquired.

Marjorie leaned towards Shaw conspiratorially and whispered to be out of earshot of George, "I know who you are, Orange."

Shaw replied with a wry smile, "Well that at least makes one of us."

Marjorie giggled, sat back, and declared, "I shall enjoy hearing how your wager plays out. For as long as I am with you, at least."

"I'm afraid that will not be for as long as you might have hoped," a figure said, barging into their compartment from the corridor and slamming the door shut behind them.

George leaned forward, intending to stand and confront the stranger as he had Mark, but Marjorie pressed him back into his seat beside the window. It was the old lady that had alighted from the train at Liskeard, and she was pointing a gun at Shaw. She pulled off the headgear of her widow's weeds and the matching veil came away with it, revealing a far younger woman than the attire and gait observed earlier suggested. She looked to be younger even than Marjorie.

"Madeline!" Marjorie yelled, standing herself. "I thought you were dead!"

"Marjorie! Sister. Here you are," the woman half sneered before throwing her hat and veil onto an overhead shelf and shifting the gun to point at Marjorie. At the same time, she pulled down the shades to shield the compartment from the eyes of any passengers that might be passing through the corridor, just as Marjorie had done on the earlier train. "Just sit down, you silly goose!" she ordered.

Marjorie sat again, visibly seething, and trembling at the same time. George held her hand to provide some comfort, which seemed to help slightly.

Staring intently at the new arrival, Shaw said quietly, "Good morning, Madeline. How good of you to join us. If I know Mark, and believe me when I say I do, he will be so pleased you had the foresight to follow us from the train. He will not, however, be quite so forgiving of the fact that you have left him on it."

"What?" said the new arrival at the exact same time as Marjorie exclaimed, "Pardon?"

Marjorie frowned and found herself wondering all over again if Shaw was the man she now believed him to be.

"My dear, put the gun away before you hurt someone, or worse, yourself." Shaw smiled thinly, staring intently at the weapon.

Madeline returned his smile, narrowed her eyes, and sat with her back towards a now covered window, taking the seat beside the door to the corridor but looking extremely uncomfortable in the puffed-out laced crinolines of her black garb. "Do you take me for a fool, old man?" Madeline said with obvious disdain.

"Time reveals all, my dear," Shaw said calmly, brushing the shoulders and sleeves of his long coat as if to remove some invisible dust or dandruff. "Should you wish to speed along said judgement, I have three simple questions which will confirm the exactitude of your foolishness," he added, looking directly at Madeline.

"Madeline, how could you?" Marjorie interrupted. "I thought you were my friend." She was still shaking, and George was now holding both her hands, trying to find some way to console or calm her whilst wondering what he could or should do in this most distressing of situations.

"And you honestly thought I might help you escape?" Madeline mocked. "Mark is not the sort to let family go so easily. I know I am a despicable person but at least I am not a fool like you, Marjorie."

"Seeing the good in people does not make Marjorie a fool, Madeline," Shaw pointed out. "Just as being despicable does not make one infallible. It only makes one pitiable."

Madeline laughed. "You think you know me, old man?"

"I wasn't talking about you." Shaw looked coldly at her. "I was talking about me. But if you feel the shoe fits...," he added, leaving the statement hanging.

"Why, Madeline?" Marjorie couldn't help but mutter.

Madeline replied stiffly, "We all have to work for a living."

"And most find a way of doing so that does not involve murder," Shaw pointed out simply.

"And many of those die with barely a penny to their name," Madeline derided. "And besides, my part in all this is just delivery. Whatever Mark has planned is between him and Marjorie."

Shaw sighed, looked at Madeline and said, "I have a question ready for you. I just wonder whether you are prepared to face the challenge. And of course, the inevitable consequences."

Madeline turned the gun back to Shaw and laughed, derisively. "Go ahead, you doddering old crackpot. Do your worst," she challenged.

Shaw smiled enigmatically. "Thank you, Madeline. This is a simple one to kick things off, so to speak." He cleared his throat and said, "What exactly is your plan?" He crossed his legs and interlaced his fingers before hooking them around one knee.

Madeline snorted. "Really? That is your burning and insightful first question?"

"If it is too difficult for you or perhaps you feel somewhat compromised, I will understand," Shaw added nonchalantly.

Madeline sighed. "I take Marjorie off the train at the next stop. We meet up with Mark again. The end. It's a simple plan. I won't bore you with details."

"Excellent," Shaw commended. "Simple is best, I always find." He turned to look out through the window and added, "Are we slowing?"

"If we are, it's been great to chat, but this is where we get off, Marjorie." Madeline stood and flicked the barrel of the pistol up to indicate Marjorie should stand, too.

"It's probably for the best that you are going now. You really wouldn't like to hear what I have to ask next. I think it might break you. Though on reflection you have the manner of one already broken." Shaw continued to look out at the passing countryside, seemingly completely uninterested in Madeline.

"Just ask, you old fart!" Madeline snapped.

Shaw turned to face her again and said quietly, "If you insist. You look so young and pretty, my dear. What is it that has made you so twisted, so ugly before your time, so exquisitely vile on the inside?"

Madeline's face contorted into a snarl, and she stomped awkwardly in her puffed-out skirts to stand directly in front of Shaw. George and Marjorie now sat timidly behind her, Marjorie still shaking and George silently fuming. She pressed the muzzle of her gun into Shaw's forehead. "Don't judge me!" she barked into his face.

Shaw sat very still, looked up into Madeline's watery angry eyes and said, "My dear I never judge anyone. I allow their own actions to present judgement for them. And to answer your earlier question, yes, Madeline, I take you for a fool." He smiled passively.

Madeline sneered into Shaw's face, "Ask me the third damn question! I dare you!" she said, through gritted teeth, as she pulled back the hammer of her gun with an audible click.

"I'm sorry. You misunderstood, Madeline. I don't have a third question for you. Which clearly makes you somewhat foolish from the off, wouldn't you agree?" Shaw explained.

"I'm not stupid, you old goat, and I'm not deaf!" Madeline snorted. "You said you wanted to ask me three questions!"

"Oh, I understand that you would think that. It is my way you see. I am indeed an old goat. Think of me as a veritable ancient billy, sharp of tooth, long of horn, and wiry of hair. And I will think of you as the troll under the bridge," Shaw said calmly.

"Shut up!" Madeline shrilled, pulling the gun away and slapping him with her free hand before pressing the muzzle against his forehead again.

"Sadly, for us both, that is unlikely," Shaw smiled despite his reddening cheek. "Words are my obsession, you see. They have been for a very long time, and I am very good with them. I have three questions," Shaw admitted finally looking for and seeing the confusion on Madeline's face. "It's just that the last is not for you."

Madeline just glared at him. "Get up, Marjorie!" she ordered. "We're leaving," she said as the train began to pull into Sandplace station.

Marjorie stood slowly, still trembling.

"My third question might have been for George. But I think given the circumstances it is infinitely more suited to Marjorie," Shaw stated loudly, turning his gaze away from Madeline.

Marjorie locked eyes with Shaw, everything was moving so fast around her but somehow seemed almost not to be moving at all. She was fearful, fretful and... she paused, caught in mid-breath, and thought, *wait, did Shaw just wink at me?*

"I said shut up!" Madeline spat at Shaw one more time. She pulled her hand back ready for another slap across his face. Shaw caught her swinging arm at the wrist, stopping her from hitting him a second time. His other hand quickly snatched at, and fixed around, the barrel of the gun, holding it in place so that it remained aimed at a space between his eyes.

"Marjorie," Shaw said evenly as the train came to a stop at the final station before Looe. "How impulsive do you imagine George might be if he knew Madeline's gun...," he paused and turned to look Madeline in the eyes again. "Was a starting pistol!"

Madeline opened her mouth as if to say something, but no sound came out. Her eyes widened and she looked simultaneously shocked, chagrined, and livid.

Marjorie, on the other hand, was relieved, angry, and decisive all in the same instant. "Open that door, George," she ordered sternly, and George obediently pulled the latch so that the door beside him swung open from their compartment directly out to the side of the train with no platform. Marjorie placed both hands against her would-be kidnapper's shoulders, pushed with all her might and simply said, "Bye, then!"

Shaw released Madeline's wrist and watched as the woman in black literally flew out through the open door, only to succumb instantly to the inevitable force of gravity and fall in a heap of black lace and cushioning crinoline, onto the sloping ballast shale beside the train. The ground beside the track was overgrown and sloped away towards a narrow section of the East Looe River.

"Try not to drown!" Marjorie shouted down as she watched Madeline roll towards the water's edge. Then she slammed the door shut, harrumphed, sat down beside George again, folded her arms and just glared at Shaw. George tried to hug her by way of congratulations, but she swatted him away, still shocked at both herself, the situation she had found herself in, and her own actions in eventually dealing with Madeline.

George turned to look through the window and as the train pulled away, he could see Madeline sitting at the edge of the river, seething. He couldn't help waving but wasn't the least bit surprised she did not wave back. He was half expecting her to shake a fist at him, like the outsmarted villain in one of those Chaplin movies.

"You couldn't have diffused that situation by, oh, I don't know, let me think," Marjorie snapped at Shaw, still in a state of bewilderment. "Telling us that in the beginning?"

"If I had been certain, I would have," Shaw admitted. "But my eyes are not what they once were.

On Madeline's arrival and my first look at the pistol, I had only a suspicion. I do not like to play the odds, which meant I needed to see the weapon up close so that I could undertake a visual assessment. I had to be sure."

"So, you taunted her!" George noted, sounding excited and relieved.

"Indeed, George," Shaw confirmed. "Only when I had seen that the barrel was blocked, was I able to confirm and share my observations with you both."

"And then *I* threw her off a moving train!" Marjorie snapped at the pair of them, sounding outraged at herself. "Who does something like that? Not me!"

"We were at the station, Marjorie," George noted. "We had just stopped."

"Really?" Marjorie said, her voice rising slightly in pitch and volume, clearly a little put out at being corrected. "I'm so sorry! I didn't notice! I was a little busy worrying about the gun that my ex-best friend, who I foolishly thought might have been killed by my brother, kept waving in my face! Here, let me correct my inaccuracies. And then I *threw* her off a stationary train. There. Is that better?"

George turned bright scarlet.

"In my experiences I have found that it is only when you believe yourself to be in mortal danger that you truly discover who you are," Shaw said. He sat quietly for a moment as he watched a field of black-face sheep on the far side of the river. After several moments deep in thought, he turned to look at Marjorie and added, "And what you are capable of."

"You would say that, wouldn't you!" Marjorie snapped back. "George knocked my brother senseless,

I pushed Madeline," she turned from Shaw to George, "off this train. And you!" She faced Shaw again. "You sit and pontificate, sharing your sugar-coated sententia according to Shaw!"

"Oh! I really like that!" Shaw said, smiling at her. "I will remember to use it at some droll and appropriate time, or should it take my fancy some entirely inappropriate time. You have a wonderful wit, my dear. Cutting, critical, merciless, and observationally accurate. Wouldn't you agree, George?"

"I probably would," George replied. "If I had any idea what she just said," he turned to face her and apologised, "Sorry, Marjorie. If I had any idea what Marjorie said," he corrected. "You're not a she. She's the cats mother."

Marjorie sat with her mouth open, unsure which of them to respond to first.

"Marjorie said that I am exhaustively inclined to speak in apothegm," Shaw replied to George.

George looked blank.

"I am overly fond of aphorisms," Shaw tried.

Still George looked at Shaw with no obvious understanding.

"I speak in epigrams?" Shaw offered.

Nothing.

"He likes to talk in riddles and use big, uncommon words to make himself sound clever," Marjorie explained to George with a sigh.

"Ah!" George replied, "Thank you, Marjorie. Yes, definitely. I mean I definitely agree with what you said to Shaw, then."

Shaw smiled, looked out the window again and declared, "The widening stretch of the river and the bridge and buildings now in sight, would suggest we have all but arrived at Looe station."

Marjorie stood and said, "Good. The sooner we get off this train the better."

12 *Intervention:*
Kit and caboodle

1100 hrs on 27 June 1930. The parade grounds at Crownhill Barracks, Plymouth.

At 1000 hours, Brigadier O'Dochartaigh had called for all men to muster on the parade ground for full inspection at noon. Colonel Wallace had ensured that each section's sergeant was briefed and even though there was an hour to go, men were lining up and checking each other over.

Every man in D-Company had been instructed to present to parade in full dress uniform, the full kit and caboodle as Brigadier O'Dochartaigh liked to call it. As always the brigadier would be fastidious in his inspection. A full hour of pre-inspections was only to be expected.

Boots had to shine like burnished ebony and spats gleam with a near blinding whiteness except for the row of coal black buttons which must be evenly fastened to run down the side of the calf allowing no unsightly wrinkling. Every regimental kilt and sporran must hang exactly to the mid-point of the knee and the fly plaid must be neatly folded across the chest before being fastened at the shoulder with the regimental broach.

Red felt tunics must be crease free with shining buttons and a wide white belt fastened with a glistening brass buckle at the waist. The regimental tartan diced kilt hose must be turned down in pristine fashion, allowing for the hose top red flashing to be visible just above the uppermost section of the spats. The frog and scabbard would be checked to ensure it was positioned correctly and the bayonet blade tested to verify it had been oiled and was sharp enough to slice effortlessly through a sheet of blotting paper. Finally, topping the uniform off, the Glengarry would be inspected to ensure it was tilted at the correct angle and that the regimental badge was polished to reveal the full glory of its lustrous silver.

Brigadier O'Dochartaigh and Colonel Wallace watched the troops preparing from the edge of the parade ground immediately in front of the main door to the officers' mess.

"Have we sufficient transport ready?" Brigadier O'Dochartaigh asked Colonel Wallace.

"We hae five Morris light's at oor immediate disposal, sur," Wallace confirmed. "A further nine vehicles ur oan th' wey fae locations aroond th' toon, sur. Three fae th' Ryle Citadel, three fae Granby Barracks, twa fae..."

"Did I ask for an inventory, Wallace?" the brigadier interrupted. "A simple yes or no, please."

"Currently nay, sur. Bit we wull hae at mid-afternoon, sur." Wallace waited whilst his commanding officer thought this through.

"Excellent," the brigadier confirmed. "As long as we can transport the whole of D-Company for the exercise."

"As soon as th' additional vehicles turn up, we maist definitely wull, sur," the colonel confirmed. "Twelve men per motor wull allow us tae shift th' hail contingent tae th' event, sur."

"We'll keep it casual at this inspection, colonel," the brigadier confirmed. "One or two men will no doubt see this coming, but I don't want any of them going off half-cocked."

"Braw, sur," Colonel Wallace replied. "Shuid we collect bayonets th' noo, sur?" he added.

"I think we'll wait," the brigadier suggested. "No point in telegraphing our imminent manoeuvres at this early stage. Walls have ears and all that."

"Braw, sur," the colonel repeated.

"After the inspection instruct each sergeant to collect bayonets from every man in their section at sixteen hundred hours," the brigadier ordered. "There must be no chance of any knife issues in our exercise. Any man found to be in breach of that order will be subject to immediate court-martial."

"Ah wull personally clype ilk sergeant, sur," Colonel Wallace confirmed.

"Do we have sufficient Pipes and Drums, colonel?"

"Aye, sur. We hae a stowed oot complement in D-Company, sur. Mair than enough fur th' requirements o' th' exercise, sur."

"Make sure both are put through their paces immediately after the inspection, Wallace. I will personally attend to ensure that each and every one of them is competent. Given the circumstances leading to this evening's commitments, there is only one march we can use, of course."

"O' coorse, sur," Colonel Wallace agreed.

"How did Commander Hanson receive our invitation?" the brigadier asked.

"Fair defensively, sur," the colonel admitted. "Commander Hanson initially spent ferr a bawherr o' time spouting oan aboot proof afore trying tae speil th' seniority caird, sur."

"Seniority? Let me guess. Some twaddle about Devonport being an historical naval stronghold."

"Aye, sur. 'N' Plymouth, sur," the colonel confirmed.

"Will he be attending, though?" the brigadier asked, looking directly at his colonel.

"Ai politely extended yer invitation, bit he is ahhful commitit, sur."

"Unsurprising." The brigadier shook his head. "You would never see me turning tail were the situation reversed."

"Indeed nay, sur," the colonel agreed.

The two men paused to watch more of the troops march into place on the parade ground from their billets. Both were pleased to see the extent of due diligence being shown by the sergeants and soldiers on parade. A full inspection should always follow the numerous pre-inspections which they were witnessing now. One of the troops, it looked like Private Blackwood, had forgotten his bayonet, and was sent marching double time back to his billet to retrieve it.

"The men are aware that all tickets are revoked for the next twenty-four hours, colonel?" the brigadier asked.

"Aye, sur," the colonel confirmed.

"No complaints, I take it?"

"None, sur," the colonel said proudly.

"Excellent. This way, colonel." Brigadier O'Dochartaigh pointed towards the mess. "I feel the need for very strong coffee. I intend to be extremely strict when it comes to the inspection. Two shots will give me the keenest eye, I think. This will be our first Intervention on home soil, after all, and everything must be just so!" He marched forward smartly, and his colonel followed in step behind.

13 Catching the westerlies

1117 hrs on 27 June 1930. On foot from Looe Station to the Banjo Pier at Looe.

The first thing all three were struck by was the smell. They knew instantly that they were no more than minutes from the sea. Even as they passed the steam engine with its smells of rusty iron, oil and coal and the creosoted sleepers supporting the track, the air was thick with salty brine, seaweed, old tar ropes, and one over-riding unmistakable smell. The stench of fish told them instantly that this was another major fishing port, much like Plymouth. A near perpetual chorus of gulls added to the aura of the place.

"I have seen this coastline from the air and visited once, so whilst I have a reasonable recollection of the geographical position of Banjo Pier, I should be happy to bow to your superior knowledge of this quaint coastal town," Shaw said to George.

"Can you take us to the Banjo Pier, please, George?" Marjorie clarified, rolling her eyes.

George led the way along the cobbled quayside bustling with traders, hawkers, locals, tourists, and fisherman alike. All wandering to or from the narrow lanes that led into Looe away from the quay, dodging carts and horses, cycles, children, dogs, and the very occasional delivery van, still a novelty given the reliance on the railway. Marjorie stayed close to George, and Shaw followed them both, keenly observing the various street traders and their wares as well as the fishermen and their moored luggers. Several passers-by nodded or gave George a greeting with a quick word and touch to the peak of their cap.

For part of the walk, they were able to watch the various boats along the walled quayside, some moored up so their crews could off-load catches for the mid-day markets, and some boats being prepared for the next trip out to the rich Cornish fishing grounds. Even more of the fisherman called out to George, either by name or nickname, which appeared to be Georgie Boy, with George hollering a greeting back accompanied by a hearty wave.

Passing one of the larger fishing boats, one of its crewmen, a bear of a chap with a rough dark beard and matching unkempt hair, oilskins that would have made a four-man tent, and a fishing cap that looked to be several sizes too small, ran across the narrow gangway to the quayside, walkway shuddering under his enormous frame. Coming up swiftly beside the three of them he knocked George's peaked cap to the floor and said, "That's mine," angrily. Then he put his hands on his hips and watched as George bent to pick it up.

"We are not looking for any trouble, sir," Shaw said, stepping between George and the larger man while looking up into the fisherman's smiling hairy face.

The huge man placed pan-sized calloused hands on Shaw's arms at the elbows, pinning them to his side. Then with no apparent effort, he lifted Shaw two feet from the ground, turned one hundred and eighty degrees and placed him gently back down again before turning back to George.

"Charlie, you big oaf," George chided, dusting off his cap and putting it back on. "It'll be ruined before you get a chance to win it back."

The big man chuckled and turned to face Shaw again saying, "Please accept my apologies. I was only concerned for your safety, friend. George can be a little quick to... fly off the handle."

"We know," Shaw and Marjorie said together.

"Tomorrow night, boy," the big man said turning back to George again. "You give me a chance to win it back. Best of three!" He held out one huge ham hand and waited for George to shake on it.

George sighed and reluctantly moved his own open hand towards the giant's. "Really, Charlie?" he said, "Are you sure you want to embarrass yourself in front of my friends."

Charlie pulled his hand away just before George could clasp it. "Tomorrow then," Charlie confirmed, "See you at Oliver's."

"I'll be there," George promised. Slapping the big man's arm before turning away and heading along the quay again.

"Do you really have his hat?" Shaw remarked as they continued towards the pier.

"I do," said George, lifting it off and inspecting it. "It fits me much better than my own." He placed it back on his head and patted it twice.

"You are in competition?" Shaw asked.

"Every Saturday," George confirmed. "Sometimes billiards, sometimes snooker."

"And the winner keeps the cap?" Shaw asked.

"At the moment. It was his idea," George admitted. "Charlie's, I mean."

"Friendships are built on the strangest of things sometimes," Shaw observed, shaking his head, and smiling to himself.

George chuckled. "Where me and Charlie are concerned, you have no idea!"

When Shaw caught a first glimpse of Banjo Pier, he checked his watch and was pleased to see that it was still twenty minutes before mid-day. Barty would be waiting beside the beacon light in the centre of the circular stone enclosure that gave the pier, the first of its kind, such an interesting and accurately descriptive title.

"I can see why it's called a banjo pier," Marjorie noted. It really did look like someone had constructed a giant banjo from stone slabs and set it at the mouth of the East Looe River. She could see that the walled enclosure that made up the wide circular structure at the end of the pier was quite crowded, mostly with locals cast fishing, but also with a few tourists, one setting up a tripod and camera for a picture to remember their visit. In the centre of the wide circular section at the pier end was a beacon light on top of a wide post at least five yards high.

"Barty will be somewhere near the beacon," Shaw advised. "You will soon be safe and able to forget the trials of today, Marjorie." He smiled and added, "No doubt you will be as happy to see the back of me as of your brother. I did not mean to cause you distress, but on reflection I can see that I almost certainly did."

Marjorie was calmer now that she was away from the train and shook her head. "I did not mean to snap, so,

Tommy. I still cannot believe my luck in meeting you. If your friend can be as helpful as you say I shall be indebted to you for the rest of my life."

"And let us commit to it being a long and happy one, my dear," Shaw offered.

As they started to walk along the flat stone topped promenade of the pier, the sounds of shallow waves could be heard breaking gently along its wall and across the East Looe beach. The soft golden sands ran for almost two hundred yards, sandwiched perfectly between the pier and Pen Rocks. With the tide only just on the turn, the beach was at its smallest and a hive of summer activity on this fine but not overly warm day.

"Why is it so busy, George?" Shaw asked as the three began their walk along the pier.

George looked around and caught sight of bunting flags around the beach and areas of rigged up fencing on the front square set well back from the sand. "It looks like a race weekend," George noted, pointing to an area penned off from public access.

Shaw looked and his expression lit up. "That's motorcycles!" he declared.

"Yes," George confirmed. "They race here at low tide several times each summer on the flat sands. I've heard its quite the spectacle and draws the crowds in."

"After we have seen Barty I think we may stay until the low tide," Shaw suggested.

"It'll just be practice rounds on a Friday," George advised.

"I should still like to see," Shaw said wistfully.

As they approached the beacon, Marjorie was the first to spot something unexpected. She nudged Shaw and pointed, saying, "Tommy, I think that may be for you."

Shaw looked to see a young boy sat with his back against the pillar of the beacon. He looked to be perhaps twelve years old, and he was holding a cardboard sign with the words, 'Urgent message for Mr Shaw,' painted on it.

"That's a little unexpected," Shaw admitted.

The three of them walked to where the boy was sat and Shaw said, "Hello, young man. My name is Tommy Shaw, and I was expecting to meet Ferdinand Bartenique today. You do not look like him."

"Hello, mister," the boy said, standing and leaving the card on the floor. "I have a letter for you," the boy added. "But Mr Ferdinand said I was to ask you for a shilling and to see the engraving on your watch. Just to be sure."

Shaw took out his pocket watch and held it out for the boy to see the back. It was engraved with 'TEL from FAB' and the boy nodded before adding, "And my shilling, sir?"

"Of course," Shaw confirmed, taking a coin from his purse, and handing it to the boy.

"Thank you, sir." The boy touched his cap, took a sealed envelope from the inside of his course brown jacket, and passed it to Shaw before skipping away towards the town.

Shaw was frowning as he tore open the envelope and unfolded the small letter it contained. He read through it silently then turned to Marjorie and George. "Barty is not here! He has been recalled to New York and will be setting off from Plymouth on the SS Statendam this afternoon around five. He has his family with him and was unable to wait for me for fear that they might miss the liner. We must return to Plymouth immediately."

"I'm not taking the train!" Marjorie declared instantly, folding her arms again and looking worried.

Shaw looked at Marjorie and said, "I understand. I should not wish to travel back by rail, either. Madeline and Mark are threats we must endeavour to avoid." Shaw turned to George. "I am hoping that your local knowledge may suggest an alternative. Is there a bus, perhaps? Or even a private taxi service?"

George took off his hat, looked at it, and smiled. "Come with me," he said, marching swiftly back along the pier. "We need to see a man about a cap."

The Charlie's Gal was a fine 45ft Looe lugger, registered PH333 out of Plymouth and named in honour of a skipper who had captained boats for nearly twenty years. With two masts and up to five sails, the boat could easily top 15 knots in a fair breeze. Even under the more normal conditions of squally land and sea breezes that followed their daily ebb and flow over the Cornish coast at this time of year she could easily hit 12 knots under half sail.

Charlie Worral was probably the most well-known, certainly the most instantly recognisable fisherman working the coastal villages across Cornwall, and a few in neighbouring Devon. From Bude to St Ives on the north coast, and from Newlyn to Salcombe on the south, Charlie was known by all connected with the fishing fleets. Being well over six foot six tall and weighing in at near twenty-four stone, he really was a bear of a man, especially with his wild unkempt hair and beard.

George had been lucky to catch the skipper again before the Charlie's Gal had left the quay. It had taken George moments to confirm that the captain was sailing his namesake back to Sutton Pool, and only minutes to secure safe passage aboard for himself, Shaw, and Marjorie as passengers. Millbay Docks was only a short detour from the boat's destination.

George and his companions were welcomed aboard as guests for the journey, which they were assured would see them safely back on dry land in Plymouth in under two hours.

A small gang of men from other boats laid up on the quay and not otherwise engaged in any urgent duty, tracked the lugger to the end of the pier so that it could easily catch wind and be on its way more swiftly. Tracking was part tradition, part honour, part necessity and all community. By supporting each other, the crews of the boats could make their way with greater efficiency, saving time, speeding up the outward journey to the fishing grounds and getting each returning catch ashore more swiftly.

Shaw and Marjorie sat on a sturdy but not uncomfortable bench, which was actually a wide catch crate that had been upended and positioned across the beam of the boat in front of the tiny pilot house. They watched as five fishermen on the quayside hauled on the bow mooring line, which was shackled at the forepeak to a wide steel dock cleat, playing tug-of-war against the Charlie's Gal and winning easily with the assistance of the river currents now that the tide had turned.

With the mooring rope over their shoulders, each of the men was able to lend their weight to dragging the lugger to the very end of the Banjo Pier, dodging tourists, and crabbers. When the men reached the end of the pier, they let the rope drop gently into the sea and two of the lugger's crew swiftly dragged the line aboard, coiling it ready to be used to guide the boat quayside when they reached their destination.

Beside the narrow pilot house that was too small for Charlie to fit inside, George was still engaged in negotiations with the huge skipper. Passage had apparently been agreed in advance of a confirmed fare for the journey and this was now being discussed. When George joined the others to sit and watch as the boat drifted majestically out into open waters, he was wearing a rather warn and battered looking fisherman's cap which looked to be quite a poor fit. The skipper had clearly driven a hard bargain that included taking back the prize that he and George were due to contest the next day.

"I think that went very well," George confirmed with a smile. "We get free passage back to Plymouth and all for a hat, some help and a handshake." He looked over his shoulder at Charlie now proudly wearing the much nicer headgear that was normally the prize in their weekly competition. "I shall win the cap back tomorrow."

"Is that really all that's required for our passage to Millbay?" Shaw asked, sounding somewhat surprised.

"Well, the help is easy enough for me. They have a light crew on account of two members choosing to stay at Looe for the races." George leaned towards Marjorie and Shaw and whispered, "As far as the handshake goes, I've let Charlie believe he's in with a chance."

"George, we have no idea what you're talking

about," Marjorie pointed out.

"I think I might have some inkling," Shaw suggested, thinking back to the earlier encounter with the captain.

George nodded and thought for a moment. "Let me get the gaff up and I'll tell you how it all started," he offered.

Shaw and Marjorie watched as George walked to the main mast, loosening the fastening stays that held the mainsail neatly furled before pulling the topping lift to raise the boom off the gallows. George unhitched two halyards so that when he was ready he would be able to pull on both at the same time, keeping the gaff horizontal until it was in its uppermost position.

Once George was happy with the tension on both lines, he hauled them together using swift even pulls that overlapped so that the gaff rose in one continuous flowing movement, the two-to-one tackle making it relatively light work, never actually stopping until the throat halyard had pulled the luff tight. George belayed the throat halyard and continued to pull up on the peak halyard until the sail was peaked up. With the leech pulled taught and the mainsail set, he belayed the peak halyard.

The fore-sheaf of the mainsail was fixed a short way up the main mast at the tack where the boom was fastened to the mast whilst the aft-sheaf was fastened at the clew with the boom at that end currently tied off firmly just forward of the aft mast.

"Top up to windward and scandy the luff for a starboard tack!" Charlie called out to George from beside the pilot house once George had finished tying off the clew line and reef points. Charlie could see all parts of the upper deck and since he was skipper and helmsman it was easy for him to reach one huge arm into the tiny cabin area and steady the helm. After a quick glance at the sail's telltales he added, "Reeve for moderate, lad!"

George tracked across to the fastening of the aft boom loosening the mainsheet line to allow it to slowly feed through so as not to let the boom get away from him. Once happier with the telltales, George adjusted the mainsheet traveller until the boom was ideally positioned to catch the wind and remain safely under control. Anyone who allowed the boom to get the better of them on a ship captained by Charlie, never got the chance to let it happen again. Since they would be sailing to Plymouth with the windward side to starboard, the mainsail was now perfectly positioned, allowing it to make full use of the winds.

Even though the westerlies were light on this fine day, the mainsail billowed outward catching every last breath of wind and taking the Charlie's Gal on a good line that cut away from the shore following a near perfect east-south-east bearing. Shaw and Marjorie got one last good look at Looe beach as the boat picked up speed, slicing through the gentle swell and sailing well away from any dangerous outcrop of rocks that might be hidden beneath the deceptively calm blue waters near the coastline.

"It is disappointing that we shall be unable to stay and watch the races, practice though they may have been," Shaw said wistfully to Marjorie as he watched the beach grow smaller behind them.

"Well." Marjorie paused and thought for a moment. "It gives you a reason to visit again," she suggested. "The sands will still be there and perhaps you will be able to enjoy the races under less stressful circumstances."

Shaw smiled. "Thank you," he said. "That sounds like a most agreeable plan."

Their destination back at Millbay might be due east, but the Charlie's Gal would have to round the Rame peninsula to reach it. The fastest line for this leg of the journey would see the boat steadily moving away from shore, with the bow pointed towards the distant headland, visible but slightly obscured due to a gentle hazing. Whilst Rame Head was nine miles east it was also almost four miles further south than their departure point at the mouth of the Looe estuary. Keeping an even keel headed anywhere between Queener Point and Three Holes, rather than following the curve of the shoreline around Whitsand Bay, would easily reduce the length of their journey by two nautical miles.

There were two other crew on the upper deck as well as George and the Captain. They looked to be slightly older than George, experienced fishermen both, setting the foresails in much the same way as George had hauled out the mainsail. "Need more catch, skipper?" George called to Charlie once he had coiled down all ropes, double checking each one.

Charlie shook his head. "Thanks, lad. That's all. We're making at least six knots already and once that pair have the foresails up, we should make eight. If the wind drops, we'll hoist the lug, but you're done for now."

George saluted playfully and said, "Permission to lay-up, captain," as was customary when taking a break from working duties under Charlie's watchful eye. The skipper kept a tidy and a busy boat with all crew expected to pull their weight, much as George had already done in hoisting the mainsail.

"I'll call you if needed, boy," Charlie bellowed. He fastened the wheel at the helm with two ropes to keep the ship on its current trajectory, then headed for the bow to pass on some instructions to the other topside crew who had finished tying off the foresails. The nets in the aft of the boat would need checking, fixing, and layering ready for their next fishing trip.

George joined Shaw and Marjorie, taking a seat beside them on the upturned crate. He placed his now older grimier cap on his lap, leaned back against the corner of the pilot house and closed his eyes for a moment, feeling the salty breeze pass over his face which was slightly flushed and perspiring from the work of setting the mainsail.

"I can see why you observed yourself to be a jack-of-all-trades," Shaw said to George. "Though to me you appear to be something of a nautical master."

George opened his eyes and sat upright again. "Master? Not me! I just like to earn a bob or two. I work hard as an honest man is all. It keeps me fed and pays for bed."

"Madeline worked hard at seeming to be honest," Marjorie noted. "I even came to think of her as a sister. I guess you can never really know someone."

"From my entirely self-centred experience I must concur," Shaw admitted to Marjorie with a sigh. "Those few who know my true name may think they know me and in truth I envy them for that. To hold such certainty of understanding must be wonderfully liberating. I pray that one day I may be fortunate enough to know myself at least half as well as others believe they do. The sands of time change all things."

George looked over the port side gunwales across to the distant shoreline and was surprised to see Seaton and Downderry beaches already. The boat was indeed making good speed across the relatively calm waters. "My old da' used to say, you does good and good does you." He smiled at the recollection, which he had not thought on for as long as he could remember.

"Aiming for good is just playing it safe," Shaw said quietly, almost to himself.

Marjorie frowned. "As long as it's genuine, I'd take good every time."

"You think being good isn't enough?" George asked Shaw.

"I think it can be," Shaw admitted. "It's just that I have observed a great many friends work harder at the task of being seen to be good, than actually being or doing good." Shaw paused then added, "They spend so much time seeking to magnify the worth of what little they do, they fail to realise their effort achieves nothing but pointlessly inflated ephemeral opinions." He paused and closed his eyes for a moment, recalling a lifetime of personal encounters. "I often wonder how many might have achieved greatness were it not for a seemingly instinctual obsession with habitual enculturating."

"I don't know what that means, Shaw. But whatever it means I take it you mean the likes of you?" George said, emphasising that he had used the phrase before.

"My dear boy, I mean everyone!" Shaw exclaimed. "Can you imagine where our civilisation might be should each and every person live to achieve their true potential for greatness? Excelling as hero, warrior, engineer, philosopher, scientist, and the like. The

Greeks and Romans had plumbed water, in pipes, more than two thousand years ago. We are still working on achieving the same. Sometimes it feels like we are barely out of the dark ages."

"It sounds like a grand idea. I should imagine the pilchards would be pleased, but I suspect there'd be a lot of house fires," George suggested after a moments consideration.

"I beg your pardon?" Shaw asked, somewhat flummoxed by the seemingly unrelated observations. Marjorie looked a little perplexed by George's reply, too.

"Well, if the likes of me is busy achieving greatness with the likes of you, who's catching the fish?" he asked, pointing at the two men at the back of the boat who were still busy layering the nets and checking for tears as they worked. "And who'll be sweeping the chimneys? There'd be a lot of chimney fires in this world of yours filled with heroes and heroines. And don't get me started on the backbreaking toil of stacking," George added.

"Stacking?" Shaw asked.

"Stacking the carts, stacking the mail, stacking the market stalls, stacking the luggage of the high and mighty. Even stacking the rubbish." George nodded towards the shoreline. "Like back on the slipway. Or the fish baskets," he offered, looking around the boat but not finding anything to point at. He tapped the side of their seat instead.

Shaw appeared to have a lightbulb moment. "Ah. You are talking of the drudgery. The tasks no-one would want to do if everyone aspired to greatness."

"I am," George agreed.

"But I have observed you and you are, if I may say, an expert in stacking. You do not make it look like a task you find to be tedious. That deft kick of the sack truck to pick up the full load is not something most men could do. Your skill should be its own reward and valued as such," Shaw suggested.

George shook his head and said, "That's just a trick I've picked up over the years. Makes things easier and quicker. What's the worth in that?"

Marjorie looked at Shaw, clearly awaiting his thoughts.

"It's worth what you believe it to be worth," Shaw said enthusiastically to George. "I believe the only way to move forward in elevating such mundane tasks is to learn through looking back," Shaw continued animatedly. "I have recently become obsessed with what I have come to believe will be my magnum opus; an engrossing project which has already revealed one way of approaching the most boring and repetitive of tasks."

"Magnum opus?" Marjorie asked curiously.

"I am translating the original Greek text of the Odyssey of Homer," Shaw replied. "It is the most challenging work I have attempted. Barty acts as my agent."

"But isn't that just a poem?" Marjorie noted. "If it is, I'm pretty sure that it's been translated already."

Shaw raised an eyebrow. "A great many times over the centuries, my dear," he admitted with a gentle smile. "I have explored some, and most follow a poetic structure like the original, but for me the best efforts deliver its content prosaically."

"And what have you discovered? What's the secret

to the relief of boredom?" Marjorie asked.

"It's not a matter of relieving the boredom, it's about truly valuing the activity," Shaw explained. "Once a task is truly valued it is no longer tiresome or boring and therefore requires no relief. The diamond cutter's day is, on the face of it, both boring and repetitive and yet the level of skill required in combination with the value of the work ensures that it is never tedious."

"The diamond cutter produces cut diamonds, Tommy!" Marjorie pointed out, sounding slightly harsher than intended. "Does that really compare to the work that takes place on this boat? Fish or diamonds; which would you rather be offering up and the end of the day?"

"They are of equal value," Shaw suggested, enthusing again. "In fact, the greater value is in the staple food, not the embellishing frippery."

"I like your thinking, Shaw," George admitted. "I'm not sure most will have the same outlook, mind."

"Then I will find a way to educate them," Shaw declared.

"Through your book?" George asked.

"I should like to think so, yes," Shaw professed. "I have immersed myself in the original Greek transcript to produce a translation that transcends the archaic language barrier to encapsulate the entirety of its complex and multifaceted layers to discover the recondite truth."

"It's all well and good saying people need educating," George challenged, folding his arms before adding, "But if I can't understand what you're saying you can't educate me."

Shaw thought for a moment and tried again. "My

version is focussed on excavating the detail that lies below the direct translation. I mean to uncover the obscure by examining the whole text from a singularly unique point of view," Shaw explained.

"And what does your version have to say about boring old donkeywork?" George asked.

"To paraphrase one of my most recent translations, the answer lies in the recognition and reward of skill," Shaw announced, clearing his throat, and continuing loudly, *"Fifty women sit carding wool upon distaffs which flutter like the leaves of a tall poplar: and so close is the texture of their linen that even fine oil will not pass through it. Just as the seamen of Phaeacia are the skilfullest of humankind in driving a swift ship through the water, so are their women the most marvellous artists in weaving."*

"And this was within the original poem?" Marjorie asked.

"Indeed," Shaw admitted. "My version is a reflection on both the obvious and obscured meaning. All tasks, when elevated to require skill of hand or eye, must be valued as works of art or demonstrations of proficiency."

"Well, the idea that the work of the women is as valued as the work of the men is certainly refreshing," Marjorie noted.

"Indeed," Shaw agreed. "A direct translation confirms only that the fifty women excel in their task. The passage as a whole clearly intended it to be understood that the women are in fact the equal of the men."

"You should share that with your member of parliament. I think she would appreciate it," Marjorie suggested.

"I have done," Shaw confirmed. "And she did. Nancy is a very good friend who loves nothing more than to accompany me on my motorcycle."

Marjorie was momentarily lost for words before adding, "Surely it's hard enough just translating an archaic language. How on earth do you go about uncovering hidden meanings?"

Shaw smiled. "I am uniquely experienced to uncover the work's nuances from two very relevant and subjective perspectives; as one who has first been glorified as an idol, and then subsequently vilified through the unpalatable process of being very publicly dissected. Two themes that permeate the original work."

"Again, I don't know what that means but I would say you've spent a lot of time disguised as someone else," George observed. "You're pretty good at it since I still have no idea who you are. Who best to uncover what's hidden than one who spends all his time hiding!"

Shaw laughed loudly. "Wonderful, George. A third attribute I had not thought to consider." He turned to Marjorie and added, "See, Marjorie? Through our wager I get company and insight."

"Got any insights for me?" Marjorie asked, turning to George.

"About what, miss?" George said, wondering where best to start.

Marjorie just glared at him to let him know what she thought of such a dumb question.

"Oh. Well. I think we can forget about your brother and that woman. For the moment, at least," George said, trying to sound reassuring.

"That woman was my best friend! At least I thought

she was." Marjorie folded her arms and glared some more.

George looked toward the bow and the distant headland beyond. He felt the breeze drift over him again, listened to the hissing, swishing, sloshing sounds of the water and the occasional flap of sails or creak from the hull of the Charlie's Gal as it cut through the gentle swell. He felt a fine mist of sea spray and caught the unmistakable scent of the sweet warm ocean. He searched with all his senses for something helpful to say.

Momentarily inspired by an immersion in the reassuringly familiar, George tried again. "Despite a less than ideal day you have two new friends to replace your losses, which are in fact, no loss at all. Shaw can guide you to a lasting refuge and I should be honoured to keep you safe until then." He smiled feeling slightly embarrassed but was pleased to see that Marjorie smiled back. It was a warm and honest smile that shone through her hazel eyes and George had to look away, suddenly blushing shyly.

"Thank you. Both of you," Marjorie said quietly, looking from Shaw to George.

Shaw smiled and said, "George. You appear to be at your most unfettered in this moment. Now would almost certainly be the optimal time for you to extricate your contribution against our wager."

George looked blank for a moment and Marjorie just huffed and said, "Shaw, you may very well be the most egregiously erudite man I have ever met."

George laughed, but only because Marjorie's tone was much like he remembered his mother's to be whenever he had done something that was slightly naughty. He wasn't sure what Shaw had said, but he had no idea what an egregiously erudite man might be like, either.

"Again, with the compliments." Shaw smiled, turned to George, and added, "You seem to be most comfortable here. Now might the best time for you to tell a tale of your choosing. That was our agreement, after all."

George looked around the boat for a moment and said, more confidently than he might have expected "There is a true story I can share. A tale of events that led to me being invited to work regular aboard this very boat."

"True stories tend to be the best, young George," Shaw admitted. "But do not be afraid to embellish where the tale can take it. And never understate any aspect of relevance, since to do so will only serve to undermine the more grandiose aspects of the whole. Your audience may be inclined to bring their own prejudgment, anyway, so do not give them reason to doubt you."

George looked at Marjorie blankly. "Don't be afraid to exaggerate, never belittle yourself and be confident regardless of how those around you may react," she translated.

"Well, I'm not a storyteller...," George began. Then cringed slightly, realising he was doing one of the things he had just been advised not to.

"The first I worked the Eddystone relief was a day I shall never forget," George began, leaning forward to rest his elbows on his knees. He had removed his now older cap and began twisting it nervously in his hands.

Shaw and Marjorie sat quietly and listened, the sounds around them providing a perfect backdrop to

ON TIDAL SAND

George's tale of a very different journey at sea.

14 The tale of the Golden Hand

Looking back, I think I was little more than a child with grand ideas of being all grown up when I first worked under Captain Charlie Worral. It was cool for May as I recall, and I think it would have been five, maybe six years past. Doesn't seem that long ago, mind.

Before I start proper, you've probably heard of the Golden Hind. Sir Francis Drake made it hard to forget that one. Taking it round the world like that must have been quite the adventure. Being first captain to ever do so makes it so as even the likes of me get to know your name, and the boat you sailed into the history books, even though it was centuries past.

Drake was a Plymouth lad, you know, like me. Well, I think he might have been born up on Dartmoor somewhere, but Plymouth was key to his fame and fortune. He had to sail from somewhere.

He didn't have an island back then, though. It was St Nicholas Island, but he still had a lot and my old dad used to say Drake could scoop treasure straight out of an empty pond. Dad could remember when Drake's Leat brought fresh water streaming into Plymouth, a man-made river that snaked into the city for hundreds of years. You get to build things like that when you're a Member of Parliament and Mayor of Plymouth, I guess.

Twenty miles from the moor, built the whole way into the city with huge granite blocks to keep the water clean and clear, ready to feed straight into Drake's very own reservoir. A giant dam built up at Burrator left the leat dried out near thirty years ago when dad was a boy, or so he said.

Queen Elizabeth paid for the leat to steal water from a moorland stream for her navy crews working out of Plymouth's Barbican. Someone probably made a pretty penny from the works digging out a watercourse all that way. Perhaps Drake saw the opportunity for riches in that, paying men coppers to line the leat with stone slabs whilst lining his own pockets with gold. If he didn't add to his riches that way he did when it was finished, on account of the dozen or so mills he owned along its route, all tapping that new supply to turn their wheels and grind the corn.

You ain't ever heard of the boat called the Golden Hand, mind. Least ways not the one that used to run trips out to the lighthouse and back in these waters. Swapping men, delivering food, fuel, and stuff to keep everything clean, especially the glass so as to make sure the light shines bright and true. A lot of folks depend on Douglass Tower to warn them of the reef that sits mid-channel on the way into the various docks and quays of Plymouth and the like.

We shan't see the tower or the rocks up close today on account of them being near eight miles out from the tip of Rame Head. You can see the stump of the old light and the big new one in the distance from here though. Looks like a needle on the horizon even through the haze. But that's about as good a view as we shall get today of the working light.

Old Smeaton's Tower, or the top half at least, you might have seen already up beside the main Hoe promenade. Weren't nothing wrong with it except the rocks it was built on started crumbling away, so the people of Plymouth voted to bring it ashore like some trophy or memento when the new one was built. It seems to fit in, even if it is just for decoration.

There could have been a line of four towers up on the Hoe if someone had wanted a collection and it weren't for the tragedy that seemed to mark the reef as cursed. A sailor, Winstanley somethin'-or-other, had his crew build the first light before the start of the eighteenth century. Not three years passed when it was badly damaged by a storm, so Winstanley brought his men back and fortified it with huge stays. He was so sure of their work he took his crew out in the fiercest of storms to prove its measure and show that the light could shine even through the darkest of nights. The following morning the reef had been scoured clean. No ship, no men, not so much as a splinter of wood to show where the light had been.

Rudyard's tower replaced that one and it lasted near fifty years until the top half was destroyed by fire. The legend of Henry Hall was born the night it burned. Henry was the oldest of its two keepers and records said he was near a hundred, though my dad said he probably just looked that old and enjoyed playing the codger.

His age ain't the legend, mind. When he was trying to put out the fire, he went down to the sea to fill buckets with water and when he glanced up to the burning wood of the tower above, a flood of molten lead spilled down from the roof of the light, making him scream. He managed to dodge it all except for one big dollop which went straight down his throat. Legend has it Henry just gulped it down and ran up the stairs with his buckets of water. Plymouth boy, see.

When Henry and his fellow lighthouse-man was plucked from the rocks beside the smouldering remains of the light, he was already feeling ill, but no-one believed his story. Even his partner from the light just scoffed. Henry died a couple weeks later, and a surgeon examined his body to see what killed him and found a piece of lead the size of his fist in Henry's stomach!

Anyway, my first trip out to Eddystone Reef on the Golden Hand would have been just another day at sea, blending in much like any other if it weren't for my introduction to a trial of strength with a certain captain I knew only by reputation. I'd been warned by others of the crew that it was coming, and for some strange reason I was looking forward to it. I think it was the idea I might finally find someone who could best me, or at least come close.

The bosun, Danny Moss, warned me even before I was on board. He'd worked the trip to the Eddystone Light for almost two years and said he would never forget his first. Captain Charlie Worral has a way of making a lasting impression when it comes to the end of your first time under his command. Danny knew me well enough to know I would never shirk from a challenge, but he felt the need to caution me just the same.

I was started off tending the bow hawser when we left harbour that first trip, something I was familiar with. I'd never been aboard a steamer before, so it felt a little strange at first. It was quite exciting looking back. It was noisier than any fishing boat I'd crewed before, and the large stack was billowing steam as we left the harbour. I could feel an unfamiliar vibration through the deck, the pound of the steam engine and the thrust of the shafts turning the screw at the back of the boat. We were still rigged with sails, so I guessed the boat was good for all conditions.

As I finished coiling the huge damp rope, the skipper came up to the forepeak and welcomed me aboard with a reassuring smile, which I had been warned by Danny was just a ruse, an act to put me at ease, the better to catch me for the unexpected test which Charlie would present at the end of the day's voyage. He was certainly as big as I had been expecting from the tales already shared with me. I was not quite seventeen but already turning stocky. Charlie was nearer forty, easily three times my weight and next to him it was obvious I was still more boy than man. Still, he didn't intimidate me, so looking back I was either very stupid, very certain, or perhaps a little of both.

From that first encounter, I knew it was his experience that made him respected more than his huge frame. He made me feel as much one of the crew on that trip as those had served with him a dozen years. Some folks have a way with them like that, and Charlie had the gift in spades. He told me he'd known my dad and was quick to complement his skills on the few trips they'd made together. Said dad would have made a fine bosun one day if it weren't for the horrors of the war, might even have made captain. He told me he was sorry for my loss, even though it was more than five years ago.

He knew it was my first trip to the lighthouse but still thought to ask me that he had that right. Wanted to know if I'd worked a breeches buoy before or had any experiences stoking. He laughed when I said I was good at carrying sacks of coal, which I was. He laughed but I knew he wasn't laughing at me which I remember made me smile. He complemented my familiarity and speed with coiling the forward line between the pillars of the mooring bitt, said it reassured him I was quick enough to show willing whilst still being careful enough to set the rope safely. Said he liked all things done proper and had no time for slapdash.

Even before he'd asked me to check all the ropes were as tidy as that which I'd already coiled down, I was finding it hard to believe the tales I'd heard about him were true. Looking back, I think it's the manner of telling that makes the difference. I could tell this tale and make you think Captain Charlie Worral was an ogre of the seas, a man ruling by fear alone, but that wouldn't be right. That'd just be me trying to make you feel the way others tried to make me feel before my first trip working for him. They wanted me to be scared or at least to seem scared, and I think that had just become part and parcel of the folklore surrounding him. He was big enough to start with and this just meant the myth of the man was magnified.

I'd finished checking the other mooring lines before we'd rounded Drake's Island, so Danny came and told me to help out in the stokehold, said the boat was short of a trimmer and as the new lad it would be me. He took me down past the noisy engine to the boiler room and said I was to help the fireman, mostly with moving coal from the main bunker to the stoking locker but then with anything else I was told to do by old Nelson. If I'd known then what it was like to be a trimmer, I might have jumped overboard and swam for shore. But I never was a quitter so probably I would have done what I did that day, gritted my teeth, and knuckled down to it.

Nelson wasn't his real name, but it suited him, and he was proud of what he could do. He looked to be little more than dirt and skin thrown over a skeleton, but he was actually wiry muscle and sinew, built for the heat of the steam engine furnace. He was proud he'd been a fireman for near fifteen years and could get any steam powered engine up and running in minutes. Told me he didn't care for that new diesel engine most new boats and refits were getting now. Said there was nothing so good as steam, except steam and sails, since then you had the best of all worlds.

I'd never seen a man wearing more dust that clothes before, least that was what it seemed. When Nelson moved, he was at the centre of a cloud, and a dark cloud at that. Coal dust made him look a bit blurred, more shadow than man, especially in the poor light of the boiler room. I didn't know then that I'd be pretty much the same in short order.

Shovelling coal took a lot longer than I expected. Not just shovelling, neither, but trimming the larger lumps by hitting them with the flat of the shovel or a lump hammer if they were stubborn. I had to unblock the feed chute from the main coal bunker which seemed intent on blocking every few minutes, much to my annoyance and Nelson's amusement.

It was tough going that first trip, but even the stifling heat of the boiler was nothing I couldn't handle. I think the worst was the coal dust which had not just a very particular smell but also a taste. My few experiences with trimming coals gave me a lot of respect for those who work day in and day out down the pits. Made me pleased to be living in a fishing town rather than a mining one. Sea can be cruel, but it ain't dusty on any day, let alone every day. Two hours was enough for me, and I was pleased to be released back to the fresh air of the top deck when Nelson told me he had enough coal stocked and ready to see this and the next trip out and back.

On deck, I spent a fair time dusting off in the cool air, then found Danny mending nets in the aft section, keen for my next job. I'd missed all the action at the lighthouse, and we were already halfway back to the harbour. I'd hoped to see the work that goes into getting things on and off the light, especially with the breeches buoy. The steamer's need for coal put paid to that on my first trip.

Danny had another job for me, but as it was something I'd not done before, he showed me the ropes of the lifeline; literally. The rocket line for the breeches buoy was a particularly light rope made of Italian hemp. It had been coiled on deck near the main mast and Danny said I could pack into its storage chest called a Dennett's Faking Box. Danny showed me the way to feed the line into the chest, winding it between tapering pegs in a pattern from peg to peg diagonally, so that it couldn't foul or tangle when next fired across to its target. He said once the line was safely faked it would be ready for use again.

Danny said lives might depend on faking the line right, so he watched me wind the rope between the pegs, following his first feed until he was happy, then he left me to it. It was just a matter of zig-zagging the line between the pegs, making sure that each repeat followed the exact pattern of the one before. It looked odd at the time, and I remember asking Danny before I took over why the pegs didn't get in the way and snag the line. He said there was a trick to making sure the line flew true every time, but he didn't let on what that was. I was disappointed to miss out on seeing it in use that first trip, but I was certain my time would come.

When I was finished, Danny asked me if I wanted to see the secret to how the line worked, and I made the mistake of saying yes. He flipped the box over, gave it a few sharp knocks with his boot, then lifted the crate by its rope handles secured at the narrow ends. Sure enough, the weave of Italian hemp rope slipped neatly from the pegs, leaving the diagonal weave of the rocket line in its woven pattern on deck. He complimented me on a job well done and said the line would definitely have done its job. I was pleased to know I had faked it correctly until Danny grinned and asked me to put the rope back in the box. I started by trying to turn the box upside down again but quickly realised that even if I could press the pegs back onto the right loop ends, I wouldn't be able to right the box again without the rope just slipping back out.

I shook my head and knuckled down to weaving the lifeline into the crate a second time, starting from the beginning this time with Danny just checking my first weave before patting me on the shoulder, chuckling, and heading back to his own chores with the nets.

When I finished packing the line that second time, I looked up to see that we had already passed between Drake's Island and Mount Batten and were coming up on Fishers Nose. Once we rounded that final outcrop we would be into the narrow channel and slowing down for entry into Sutton Harbour. The few craft I saw as we approached were already giving us a wide berth. It didn't matter that we were no bigger than the sail powered luggers, sail gives way to steam.

The old Elphinstone Barracks on our port side and Queen Anne's Battery to starboard looked to be little more than ruins, both in dire need of some new life. Commercial Wharf was busy enough and our skipper kept us on a perfect line between the East and West piers so as we could enter Sutton Harbour and lay up at the quay. The next trip for this boat would likely be for trawling, perhaps Eddystone to Dodman Point if local catch was good, or down to Michael's Mount and Wolf Rock if not.

The quay was already bustling, and the Golden Hand was tethered to another boat called the Handsome Transom which was already moored quayside. The captain was first to the port side to see his crew safely ashore and most importantly to put me in my place, as I had been warned would be the reward at the end of my first trip.

Captain Charlie Worral shoved an upturned crate against the port gunwale with one kick of his enormous boot to provide a step his crew could use to jump aboard the other boat before climbing a mooring ladder to shore. There were six crew on board from that trip apart from me and the captain, and all were gathered on the top deck, clearly waiting for me to leave the boat first. I sighed and then took a few steps towards the crate at which point the skipper took a small leather pouch from his jacket pocket, taking a few coins and handing them to me. I can't recall the exact amount, but

I remember I was pleased and said so before tucking them in my own pocket. Then the captain held out his enormous right hand and smiled, waiting for me to offer my own so that I might give a handshake of thanks, or so he made it appear.

I sighed, held out my own right hand and locked it with his. In turn he looked down on me with a cocky smile and began to squeeze. I can recall his grip was formidable, vice like, trying to crush the bones in my palm together so as to cause sufficient pain to make me drop to my knees. That's what I had been told by other crew members was going to happen to me, anyway. He would wait for me to say, 'mercy', as was tradition in this childish test of strength that many men still felt compelled to engage in, and then he would stop, victorious in yet another battle.

What he didn't know, couldn't know, was that my own grip was one that had never been beaten in any of my own childhood playing of this game. When I was eleven, I could trounce any older boy that dared to challenge me and when I was fourteen, I could do the same to any man. I squeezed back, and it must have seemed to Charlie like having one vice caught in the grip of another, and the most memorable game of mercy I've ever played began.

Charlie's palm was wide but not so wide I couldn't curve my own fingers around it to exert my own grip in our testing handshake. I almost made a mistake allowing Charlie to start his crushing grip a few seconds ahead of my own response. Almost. I think Charlie would have bested me if I hadn't ratcheted up my own grip to fortify my resilience, straighten the bones in my palm and begin to inflict a measure of pain back into my challenger's hand.

To anyone watching our silent battle was completely invisible. Only the crew knew what was playing out, but I kept my eyes fixed on Charlie's so couldn't say how they were reacting. The look of surprise on Charlie's face told me that my earlier confidence in my own ability was not misplaced.

I could feel why the others had been so quick to warn me since he had the strongest grasp I had ever endured. Charlie levered his right elbow out slightly, working to bolster what was already a pretty punishing grip. I did the same, feeling the muscle and sinew in my whole arm tense in support of my wrist, hand, fingers, and the grip I was determined to increase further in response to his challenge.

We stood, locked in our silent skirmish, probably looking to the rest of the crew like some bizarrely frozen lifelike statues. For all the height and weight that gave Charlie the literal upper hand to bear down upon me, I was a match, presumably through my natural strength powered by my limitless youthful energy and self-belief.

For Charlie this was a ritual challenge, one which he had used on every new crewman to test them, to test him, and confirm himself to be not only captain but also the stronger man. For me this was a chance to apply myself with gusto to the ultimate test, to take on a challenge that all who had faced before me said I was doomed to fail. Even those few who knew of my own largely hidden strength did not believe that I might be a match for the legendary captain. Look at us both. How could I be?

Time passed with each of us trying to gain an advantage over the other. We remained locked in a painful battle of wills, one which we both endured refusing to yield or even acknowledge any suggestion of weakness. The sweat of exertion began to trickle down Charlie's brow and I could feel the same on mine. The earlier smugness had emptied from his smile, turning instead to a gritted grin of dogged determination. His left arm rose slowly like a wing out to one side, as if he was trying to pour strength from one into the other. In contrast, my left arm was pulled tightly against my body since I had often found that to be most effective in powering the clench of my right hand.

I heard one of the crew, it might have been Danny, call for us to declare a draw. I really don't know how long we had been bound in our tussle at that point. I hadn't seen any of them move but now noticed all six of the crew were crowded around, probably eager to be heading home. I could see from Charlie's expression that a draw would never be acceptable as I was sure he could see the same in me. Our silent duel would continue until one of us gave way and we both remained certain that it should eventually be the other. Charlie had his reputation at stake, and I had my own personal demons driving me on. We were both resolved to give no quarter.

It was Danny and Nelson eventually forced our hands, quite literally. Both brought a large wooden bucket filled with ice and water from the boats fish hold, and before we knew what was happening, Charlie and I were doused in the freezing liquid which hit us both square in the face. The unexpected deluge made us inhale sharply, and by reflex we pulled our hands free from the contest, gasping at the sudden chill and wiping icy water and fish scales from our faces and hair as we turned to see who had drenched us.

Danny apologised and said he had no choice but to break us up since we'd been locked in our silent contest for a quarter hour, with no sign of it ending anytime soon. He declared his interruption made our contest null and void; no draw, no winners, no losers, just a postponement to allow the crew to head home.

The captain wasn't happy but could see the sense in it, and he paid the rest of the crew from his leather coin purse, thanking each one and allowing them on their way. As the crew left the boat, each one looked at me differently than they had before. In some I could see reluctant respect, in others downright disbelief, and one was joylessly jealous.

When all crew except Danny were on their way, Charlie Worral turned to me, rubbing his right hand with his left, trying to ease some of the tensions and pains we had inflicted on each other. He suggested we declare a truce and return to our contest at some future point of his choosing, and I accepted, since I was as keen to be on my way as the others now that our contest had been broken up so dramatically. Danny congratulated us both on what he called our foolish pig-headedness, then made his way off the boat, too.

Charlie slapped me across the shoulder before striding off toward the pilot house. He came back immediately with two ragged but clean sheets of towelling, handing one to me so that I could dry myself off. I expected the skipper to be angry, but he wasn't. I felt a little cheated, but mostly I felt happier than I'd ever been. This was a man who had crushed all he had tested.

Charlie was as honourable in our stalemate as he

would have been in victory, which given our chat on my boarding did not surprise me. He said he needed strong and dependable men for next week's fishing rota aboard the Charlie's Gal and asked if I would like to join his crew. I said yes, and we shook on the agreement after a moment's hesitation and a shared wary smile...

...left-handed, of course.

15 The captain's connivance

1327 hrs on 27 June 1930. On board the Cornish fishing lugger Charlie's Gal, less than one nautical mile west of Rame Head, sailing on a bearing east-south-east for Millbay Docks in the city of Plymouth. Visibility is good. The sea state is slight. Winds are veering but currently steady from the south-west at 12 knots.

"Wotta lotta twaddle!" a gruff loud voice cut in scathingly, as George finished his recollections.

Shaw and Marjorie turned to see one of the crew, one of the two that had been fixing the nets in the aft section of the boat, half sitting, half leaning against the port side gunwale behind them. The man had clearly become more engrossed in George's tale than in his own chores. He looked to be at least ten years George's senior and easily as big as Charlie, though his bulk looked to be more fat than muscle.

The man looked across to the captain who had also been listening whilst steering the boat, one arm still reaching into the pilot house to steady the helm. "What? Oh, yes. Absolute tosh, Johnno, and I should know," the skipper agreed seriously.

Johnno's chubby face had an expression that was as scathing as his voice sounded. His chins were covered in thick greying stubble and his matching hair was thinning and slicked over his wide round head. He wore a white knitted sweater and had rolled up the sleeves to show his thick-set forearms. His bib and brace looked to be handmade, sewn from heavy duty brown canvas, and from the obvious staining needed a good clean.

"Forget the truth, boy," Shaw said, defending George. "The story always comes first and that was magnificent. Your earlier lack of confidence was completely misplaced. Your mother was right, you tell a good tale. It was well spoken, perfectly paced, recalled with just the right balance of detail and information, and leaving us wanting more. The lighthouse history was particularly splendid. Bravo."

"There is a fine line between exaggerating to build a good story and self-flattery, though," Marjorie interrupted, looking at the captain. "I am wondering if you might have crossed it slightly, George."

"It was certainly not how I remembered it," the skipper agreed, with an unreadable smile and a nod at Marjorie.

George looked shocked. "But every word was true!" he declared, looking first at Marjorie, then Shaw before finally turning to the skipper who just continued to smile and said nothing.

"Pah!" the fisherman called Johnno said. "Cap'n Crush'm 'ere is one thing, but you'm n' more 'n a b'y churnin' out fairy stories."

Charlie nodded again and George reddened further.

"You should put him in his place," the captain suggested, looking at Johnno. "Your wariness in constantly refusing me is one thing, brother. Perhaps you can challenge this deluded boy. I shall call it quits as far as our own test is concerned," he said seriously.

George just stared open mouthed and looked from Charlie to Johnno and back, a sudden realisation hitting him. He had seen the man he now knew to be called Johnno a few times before, but only in passing, so didn't really know him at all. What he knew now was that this man had refused the captain's challenge, and from his time working with Charlie it was one thing to give in with a swift cry of mercy, but quite another to refuse the hand of challenge altogether.

"Sounds good t' me," Johnno declared, stomping loudly across the deck to stand directly in front of George. He leaned forward, held out his open right hand and said, "I refuse 'im 'cause he's me brother-in-law," he flicked a thumb towards the captain. "And I know what he c'n do, see. Care t' put your 'and where your mouf is?"

George sighed and looked across to the captain who now appeared to be struggling to keep a straight face. He turned back to Marjorie and said, "It really was all true, you know."

Marjorie shrugged, clearly choosing to take more heed of the skipper's response to the story than to George's assurances. Shaw was unusually silent but watching everyone keenly.

"Poppycock!" Johnno exclaimed, clearly delighting in George's continued embarrassment, and demanding his attention. "I seen more meat in a maggoty biscuit."

The skipper had been joined by the other fisherman that had been fixing nets, and both laughed at this less than flattering observation of young George. It was true he was still smaller than either Johnno or Charlie, but in some regards size and strength do not always go together.

"I know which hand I favour," Charlie announced with a thumbs up to Johnno. "If I was a betting man, I'd put money on it."

George stood slowly, giving his old and grubby hat to Marjorie to hold as he did so. "Are you sure, sir," George asked, still looking slightly flushed and flustered by the unexpected ridicule from this man in response to his recollections of the day he had faced the skipper's challenge.

"Jus' gi' me your 'and b'y," Johnno demanded.

George sighed again and slowly reached forward. Johnno grabbed at George's right hand impatiently saying, "Stop bein' such a wim...EEEE.......OOOOOWWWWW!!!"

Johnno dropped to his knees, screaming suddenly and very loudly, and to those watching it really did look as if George did nothing at all. The skipper almost doubled over in a fit of laughter, Marjorie let out a yelp at the shock of the large man dropping instantly and heavily to his knees in front of her, and Shaw just watched, dumfounded but clearly impressed.

"You have to say mercy, brother," Charlie declared loudly, trying to make himself heard over his brother-in-law's yelps of pain.

"You can say it for him if you like," George said nonchalantly to the skipper as he continued his relentless crushing of the fisherman's hand. "He doesn't seem to know how the game works."

"I'm sure he'll pick it up," Charlie replied, still chuckling.

"Me... AARRGGGHHHH!" Johnno screamed, trying to snatch his hand away but finding it caught in a grip that was relentless, merciless, indomitable.

George couldn't resist a further ramping up of pressure to teach the man a lesson for the ribbing, teasing and downright bullying he had had to endure. This man would think twice before doing the same to another.

"Mer... AARRRGGGHHHH!"

"Come on brother, you can do it! Just get that word out and it will all be over," Charlie said through a hail of guffaws.

"MERCY!" Johnno managed in one loud staccato burst.

George released his grip immediately and Johnno slumped forward in a heap on the deck, cradling his right hand and whimpering quietly like a small child.

Marjorie sat open mouthed, and Shaw was beaming, clearly delighted to have witnessed the spectacle first-hand, so to speak.

"Sorry, sir," George said, sounding genuinely apologetic as he looked down at Johnno who was now sniffling and rubbing his right hand with his left. "I stopped short of a full grip so as not to break anything." George turned to Marjorie and smiled before taking his hat back from her.

"Oh, lad, that was marvellous!" the skipper said loudly. "I've been trying for years to get him to meet my challenge. Here, you take this and give me that back," he said, holding the newer slightly larger cap back out towards George with his free hand. "I really can't let you pay further for the trip after that magnificent display. The help and the handshake are more than enough."

George smiled and took the smart cap from Charlie, handing the older grubbier one back to the captain.

"Bloody bastar'!" Johnno snapped at his brother-in-law as he finally managed to stand, still cradling his crushed hand. He hobbled past the captain towards the aft deck and the nets that still needed tending. "You plan' that!" he said, dipping his hand into a bucket of cold water near the back of the boat to try to soak some relief into his aching joints.

Charlie shrugged, looking wide eyed and innocent.

"I would put it down to opportunism," Shaw suggested to the wounded man. "As an independent witness, of course."

Charlie tried hard not to smile.

"Why did you call George a liar?" Marjorie asked, turning to the skipper. "If George's story was true enough, we didn't need a demonstration."

"I don't recall saying he was a liar," Charlie said defensively.

"Ah! So, you were playing with words," Shaw observed.

The captain grinned impishly.

"We all heard you say George's story not as you recalled?" Marjorie pressed, keen to unpack the way in which the captain had steered his brother-in-law into competition with George.

"It wasn't quite right, is all," Charlie admitted with a chuckle. "As I recall, George and I were locked in battle for nearer thirty minutes than fifteen!"

Shaw grinned and said, "Cleverly done."

Marjorie just rolled her eyes but couldn't help smiling at George's victory.

"Bastar'!" Johnno whinged again from the back of the boat.

"Maybe I should help him with the nets," George offered to Charlie.

"You'll do no such thing, lad," Charlie ordered sternly. "My boat, my crew. He needed bringing down off his high horse, anyway. He'll be right back on it soon enough."

"If I 'ad 'n 'igh 'orse you'd be under 'im, right enough!" Johnno called out to the skipper.

"See?" Charlie rolled his eyes and shook his head.

"How come he's been able to refuse your challenge anyway?" George asked. "I thought it was a condition of being on your crew."

"It is!" Charlie confirmed loudly. "Normally. But that wily old codger managed to find the one and only loophole."

"And marry her," Shaw finished for him.

"Indeed!" Charlie confirmed, impressed with Shaw's understanding. "He can turn me down every time and I still have to have him back on account of blood is thicker, and all that."

"And today you found a way to force his hand," Marjorie noted, smiling broadly at the gloating captain. "Albeit into George's."

"If not me it has to be George. Sometimes an opportunity falls into your lap," Charlie chuckled, and George smiled at the compliment. "I had no idea Johnno had stopped working until George finished his story. Johnno gave me the idea and the opportunity by being his usual self; quick to judge, quicker to bully." He paused and smiled before adding, "I might have been able to predict that part."

"I 'eard that! Bastar'!" Johnno shouted out from the back of the boat. He appeared to have recovered since he was busy checking the nets for splits and tears again, using a wooden shuttle wound with repair twine to fix any he found.

"There, there, Johnno," Charlie called back. "It's all over now."

There was some muttered grumbling from the back of the boat followed by the sound of someone sniggering and then the two men fixing the nets began to squabble loudly but continued working.

"And..., everything is back to normal," Charlie announced. "George. We'll be rounding Rame and Penlee Point in a few minutes. I might need you to help with the sails once we're into Cawsand Bay."

"Just say the word skipper," George confirmed.

"Remember the door's always open for you, boy," Charlie offered.

"One day, Charlie," George replied. Then he watched as the skipper began to steer the boat first east, then slowly turning north into the wide channel between Rame on the Cornish coast to the west, and Heybrook Bay on the Devon coast to the east. The boat began to hold more wind in its full sails as it turned, making it tilt slightly to starboard as it rounded the headland. George was braced and ready to make any adjustments to the sails which the captain might order, but it was already beginning to look as if none would be needed.

Once the skipper finished setting the boat on its new course, the Breakwater and Drake's Island were almost straight ahead. The boat was maintaining good speed in the slightly reduced breeze that continued southwesterly and the captain would be steering a course that would take them in west of the breakwater and east of the island.

"I can see Mount Batten," Shaw declared happily,

pointing at a rocky promontory on the Devon side of the estuary. "This really was an excellent idea of yours, George. I fly so rarely, and the speed makes it impossible to take in the beauty of such fleeting views."

"Mount Batten?" Marjorie said quizzically.

"The air base at which I am currently stationed, Marjorie," Shaw replied. "A remarkable refuge."

Marjorie stared for a moment toward the steep cliffs Shaw seemed to be pointing at. "How on earth do planes land there?" she asked. "Is there an airstrip on the hillside above somewhere?"

Shaw chuckled. "No, my dear, the planes land almost exactly where I am pointing. Seaplanes! The base currently has three."

"And you fly them?" Marjorie said, sounding impressed.

Shaw laughed. "Of course! Not often though, and only because I am indulged since I am not a qualified pilot. I mostly work on the motorboats that provide support for those who do, especially for those who might be forced to land in rough waters. The boats are essential."

"It's remarkable that you should choose to move on as you have," Marjorie stated. "Working with seaplanes and motorboats seems odd given your achievements in the..." She glanced at George, indicating to Shaw that she was trying hard not to give anything away. "...in warmer climes."

"This is not my first nor only placement outside of... warmer climes," Shaw said playfully. "I tried tanks, but they are frightfully hot and decidedly smelly, and I did not agree with the army. Or perhaps the army did not agree with me. Here, I have been fortunate to be needed for my ability to speak several languages, my topographical astuteness, and my memory recall. In truth I suspect I am tolerated mostly because of my administrative skills. Flights tend to be infrequent, a little tedious, sometimes challenging and mostly top secret, but they remain enjoyable, nonetheless."

"You make it sound like you're still a spy," George said with a wide grin. "You're not. Are you?"

"Not just now," Shaw replied seriously, managing to keep a stern, straight face until all three could hold their true feelings in no longer, filling the deck with laughter as the boat sailed on its last stretch toward Millbay.

16 *Intervention:*
The protracted stand

1330 hrs on 27 June 1930. The military planning room at Crownhill Barracks.

As always, Brigadier O'Dochartaigh was the last to join and sit at the Long Table. This was a meeting for his unit's commissioned officers only and the following were in attendance: Colonel Wallace, Lieutenant Colonel Mackay, Major Ackerman, Captain McKinley, Lieutenants Michaelson and Addie, and Second Lieutenants Callister and Hendrickson. All stood to attention as the brigadier entered the room and took his place at the head of the table.

"At ease, gentlemen," the brigadier said brusquely. "Please sit," he added, taking a seat himself.

"A' requested ranks ur the noo 'n' correct, sur," Colonel Wallace confirmed once everyone was seated.

"Yes, yes. I can count, Wallace, and I know all by name but you," he said, pointing at one of the now seated officers with his swagger stick. The young officer had short cut ginger hair, a pale freckled complexion, a pencil thin moustache, and was the largest man at the table being so tall that even seated he appeared to tower above his fellow officers. "Name?"

"Second Lieutenant Callister, sir," the man boomed. To the brigadier he looked to be the youngest officer at the table, probably around the age of twenty.

"Stand up when you introduce yourself, man!" the brigadier barked. It was all rather unnecessary, but you had to keep new blood on their toes.

The young officer jumped up, stood to attention, and repeated, "Second Lieutenant Callister, sir!"

"I said at ease, lad, didn't I?" the brigadier continued to harangue the new man.

The young officer stood at ease, "Second Lieutenant Callister, sir," he tried a third time, with slightly less gusto.

"Better. Good to have you as one if the team, lad," the brigadier continued. Turning to face the remainder of the men at the table who all nodded in agreement.

The young officer began to sit again.

"Second Lieutenant Callister, I need you to pay a visit to the stores," the brigadier interrupted, stopping the young man in his tracks. "Please ask Keeper for the Reference Volume Protracted Stand. We shall need it for my presentation."

Second Lieutenant Callister began to stand to attention again, thought better of it, and simply said, "I shall return with it directly, sir," before turning from the table and heading towards the door.

"Good luck with that," the brigadier whispered under his breath.

The second lieutenant paused, turned briefly, and said, "Begging your pardon, will there be anything else, sir?"

"I said, good work. Just the stand, laddie," the brigadier confirmed.

Second Lieutenant Callister turned around smartly, left the meeting room, and headed down a dimly lit corridor, walking at a brisk pace towards two old wooden doors at the end. The corridor was empty, and his boots echoed noisily as he stepped purposefully into his errand, keen to make a good impression but knowing already that it was unlikely.

It was a short walk across the barracks compound to the main stores building situated behind a row of eight Nissen huts currently used as accommodation by a full complement of junior ratings. At the end of July, almost everyone stationed at the barracks would be journeying to the British settlement of Tientsin City, a major port in China, currently anticipated to be a deployment to support the Second Battalion The Royal Scots in overseeing and supporting peacekeeping in the region. There had been some minor territorial disputes recently, mostly around the edges of the Japanese settlement, and a bolstered military presence would no doubt provide a swift restoration of more ordered civility.

Three privates on route to the mess hall gave the second lieutenant a sharp salute as he passed, and he returned the greeting. Of all the battalion's commissioned officers, Callister was nearest in age to most new regulars, and this seemed to afford him additional respect. Prior to his first posting he had been concerned that he might find command a challenging prospect, but the younger soldiers looked up to him and taking charge had been easy. Being the lowest ranked commissioned officer was still not without its challenges, but they tended to come from ranks above and the higher the rank it seemed the greater the challenge might apply.

Right now, he was playing the game of getting accepted. The brigadier had sent him on a fool's errand; it did not take much reflection to realise this. All he had to do now was figure out how best to complete the test in a way which minimised his own humiliation whilst simultaneously affording the higher ranks a jolly good laugh at his expense.

Callister entered the main store and marched directly to the serving hatch which looked into the main repository of goods and consumables all set out in row upon row of sturdily constructed wooden shelf units. The store was gloomy looking with poor natural light provided by a series of small skylights during the day, and a few small gas lanterns that could be carried and hung on conveniently placed hooks during the hours of darkness.

There was no-one visible, but Callister recognised the voice of Lance Corporal Cooper, the battalion quartermaster, supervising the storemen in setting and checking inventories of items to be packaged for the trip to the orient. They were currently discussing stocks of soap already in storage and the additional quantities to be ordered in advance of the battalion's deployment.

"Shop, Keeper!" the second lieutenant called sharply to draw attention to his presence. There was a bell conveniently placed on the serving hatch of the storeroom, but that would most likely be ignored until the stock check with the lance corporal was complete or reached a natural break, and his task was urgent.

There was a moment's silence and then the sound of multiple footsteps making their way towards the open serving hatch. Lance Corporal Cooper appeared first with Quartermaster Sergeant Mitchell, holder of the honourable title of Keeper, a few paces behind. Both men presented a smart salute which Callister returned.

"Howfur kin ah hulp ye, sur?" Keeper was first to speak. Hailing originally from Islay with some schooling in Barrhead his accent was as broad as his frame. In contrast the lance corporal was slender, and to Callister the pair looked akin to Laurel and Hardy in finest Scottish military fancy dress.

"I have a request from the brigadier," Callister began, in an accent so tamed by comparison it might have passed for Queens English.

The two men turned to each other briefly, exchanging a knowing look before the lance corporal said, "'Tis a wee bit streenge, sir."

"Aye. 'N' whit's it yi'll be needin', sur?" Keeper asked with a chuckle in his voice.

"I am here for the Sing...," Callister began before being immediately interrupted.

"...Single Volume Protracted Stand!" the lance corporal finished for him.

"That is correct," Callister confirmed.

Keeper sighed and said, "Ye wid think he cuid come up wi' something mair tryin' oot."

"Aye," the lance corporal agreed. "Is it handy?" he asked, looking at Keeper.

"'Tis proppin' up a shoogly buird wey oot th' back thare," Keeper pointed, then disappeared into the recesses of the storeroom adding. "I'll away 'n' fetch 'm."

"So, howfur's plannin' for th' 'rests goin'?" Lance Corporal Cooper asked while Keeper was busy.

"Arrests?" Second Lieutenant Callister wasn't sure how to respond.

"Aye, sir. After the drillin' the men are fair fetchin' it," the lance corporal confirmed. "As a man they stand ready, sir. The colour-sergeant's beatin' from a gang of bally bobbers needs addressin'."

"The men know about Campbell and what happened to him?" Callister asked.

"Aye, 'tis th' blether of the loaby, sir. If it wis nay for all tickets bein' pulled, there'd have been a right royal rammy a' th' toon t'night."

"I'd 'ave bished th' shone oot 'o oony jimmy wi' a cap," Keeper offered, as he returned carrying a large old book which he landed loudly directly in front of the second lieutenant. Dust billowed outwards and upwards around it, driven by the tiny explosion of air created by the sudden thump of the heavy tome hitting the hatch.

"Aye," the lance corporal agreed. "Only a lassie stood in to gi' 'im hulp. Tay a man nay others dun nothin'."

"An' the wynd was fair buzzin' wi' ithers peepin', ah heard," Keeper added with a knowing nod. "Ah wid nay skelp a wifie bit ah wid rammy oony mon."

Callister looked at both men, nodded and realised he needed to report this back immediately. "What is that?" he asked, pointing at the old book and the clouds of dust settling around it. It looked like it was leatherbound, but the once red cover was now mostly faded to a dull pink and almost scaly due to a web of cracks and crackles over the binding. There were also some deeper square divots in the cover.

"That wid be th' single volume, sur," Keeper confirmed.

"But it's a book," Callister pointed out.

"Aye, right enough, sur," Keeper replied.

"Page twa hundred eighty foor," the lance corporal nodded towards the book.

Callister picked it up, wiped some of the more persistent dust from the spine and said, "Ah." He opened the book to the suggested page, scanned it dutifully and chuckled before adding, "Protracted! Bugger!"

"Yer single volume," the lance corporal said, pointing at the book this time.

"Aye, an' ye hay hud yer staund," Keeper said seriously.

Callister closed and handed the dictionary back to Keeper, thanked them both and headed back to the meeting room. He could kick himself for having fallen for one of the oldest practical jokes in the literal book, albeit hidden in an unexpected volume on this occasion: *protracted (adjective) - drawn out or lengthened in time or duration; long.* Ha!

Callister may not have had a particularly long stand in the stores, but it had turned out to be an exceedingly fruitful one. The detail he had gleaned about the mood of the men presented an overriding urgency. He had to report back to the brigadier and other officers. They would want to know before there could be any escalation of bad feeling into dangerously retaliatory action against the bally bobbers.

Stepping out in double time, Callister marched straight back to the meeting room to share what he had discovered.

17 The Isambard

1415 hrs on 27 June 1930. Disembarking from the Cornish fishing lugger Charlie's Gal to the quayside of Millbay Docks in the city of Plymouth.

The Charlie's Gal was laid up swiftly at the quayside of the main basin of a heaving Millbay Docks. A couple of longshoremen that had been working on moving barrels from near the quayside edge to a huge open storage area were quick to help. Two men tied the boat off fore and aft, wrapping the hawsers around quayside bollards, whilst the chief among them made sure to check what business the Charlie's Gal had. When the Captain explained it was a brief stop-off for an unexpected taxi service, they seemed satisfied and returned to their tasks, still keeping a watchful eye just in case. Piracy was rare these days but not unheard of, so it paid to remain vigilant.

Captain Worral was advised his boat would be allowed to moor only briefly since the entire quayside was reserved for a steam ship delivering coal to the Millbay fuelling station. It was expected to arrive later that afternoon so Charlie's Gal would need to be away sharpish.

"I do believe we have travelled in a near perfect

equilateral triangle," Shaw announced matter-of-factly to George and Marjorie as they climbed a ladder to the quayside. "If you join the dots on a map, at least."

"You are probably the only man in the world who might think it normal to make such an observation," Marjorie suggested, shaking her head in near disbelief.

The Captain followed them ashore, and George thanked him again for his fortuitously timed assistance. "You really are a life saver. I think you should keep this after all," George offered, removing the grand cap, and trying to hand it to the captain.

"No, no! You've paid me ten times over," the captain insisted, looking briefly towards the stern of his boat.

"Did you know when you struck our bargain?" George asked, also glancing briefly towards the captain's brother-in-law, and raising one eyebrow. "I had expected a challenge from you!"

"I had a few poor thoughts on how I might real him in, but it seems he carries his own hooks and they're far bigger than any I could offer up. Together with the weight of all the chips on his shoulders, I'm surprised he has the strength to stand up." He thumbed towards the back of the boat where Johnno was keeping his head down working on the nets, still silently fuming.

"I c'n 'ear ya', ya' bastar'," Johnno called across without looking up, before muttering and spluttering incoherently to himself.

"I must repeat my good friend's ardent gratitude," Shaw confirmed, reaching to shake the captain's hand, and changing his mind at the last moment; having witnessed the possible outcomes of such a simple action, it seemed prudent. He gave the captain a wry smile before patting him gently three times on the elbow.

"It was a pleasure helping, my friend," the captain replied, slapping Shaw on the shoulder. "In truth this has been little more than a quick diversion rewarded beyond expectation."

"I shall certainly never forget you, or the trip," Marjorie said, taking the Captains hand and shaking it with no qualms. The captains hand felt like it was coated in tree bark in place of skin, all calloused and lined, rough and hardened by the relentlessness of a life lived mostly at sea. "Or your tolerant and gracious brother-in-law," she added tongue-in-cheek, whilst waving across to the man still busying himself with the nets.

"Pah!" Johnno snorted without looking up.

"That's a little cruel," the captain said loudly and seriously to make sure Johnno could hear him; building bridges seemed the order of the day. More quietly he added, "No more than he deserves, though." He gave a quick wink that only Marjorie could see.

"Look after your good lady," the captain said, turning to George. "She's quite a catch," he added with a more obvious wink and a nod.

"What?" George spluttered. "No. I mean, yes. I mean... No!" George reddened noticeably, and Marjorie had to turn away to stifle a giggle rising at George's blushes.

"This way, George," Shaw said to offer the young man a route out of his discomfiture as he pointed towards a row of buildings set some way back from the quayside. "And thank you again, good sir," he added with a hearty wave at Captain Charlie Worral before heading away with Marjorie beside him and George following, still a little flushed.

"I hope we are not heading for the station again," Marjorie said to Shaw as they marched towards the largest of the buildings beside the busy quay. Some concern had returned to her voice, in part because she had to pick a path carefully along the cobbled quayside to avoid multiple trip hazards of ropes, rail tracks, coal spills, patches of oil and grease stains. "Mark will almost certainly make his way back to Plymouth. Most likely he'll be heading to the guest house I was staying at. I don't think I could bear to chance running into him again."

"The station would be a necessity for us to find most people, but Ferdinand is a creature of habits," Shaw replied reassuringly. "Not all of them good ones."

"Please don't tell me he's a drunkard," Marjorie said, pleased to hear they would not be returning to the railway but wondering if they were instead headed for the nearest public house. "I was just beginning to feel safe, and I don't think my nerves could take it!"

"Good heavens, no!" Shaw exclaimed. "Ferdinand is teetotal, like me. He does, however, have one vice which I tolerate but could never share. Fine cigars!"

"He'll be headed for the Isambard," George said knowingly.

"The Isambard?" Marjorie said.

"A gentlemen's club," George replied. "The gentlemen's club. Well, the only one around here anyway."

"In Plymouth I would go so far as to say the Isambard is his second home," Shaw confirmed. "Ferdinand will not depart for the Statendam until five at the earliest and the liners are more often than not a little on the late side. He will first make sure his family are happily ensconced in a quietly comfortable waiting area, then make his way directly to the Isambard. He could be there already."

"Wonderful," Marjorie breathed a sigh of relief. The thought of being able to stay within the quayside buildings was immediately comforting.

"Would you be so kind as to lead the way, George?" Shaw asked as they entered the busy passenger terminal section of the Millbay complex. With the SS Statendam arriving offshore later that afternoon, the huge public hallway was already packed with people. Some were clearly booked as passengers awaiting the arrival of the incoming ocean liner, others were here to meet friends and loved ones who would disembark. There were also hawkers and traders offering everything from daily papers and cigarettes to shoeshines and postcards.

"I've never been inside the club, but I know where it is," George confirmed winding his way through the crowded concourse towards a side stairwell with Shaw and Marjorie close behind.

The three of them made their way up four flights of stairs to the second floor of the terminal building which was still decorated in its original Victorian garb dating back to when it first opened, making it look both grand and tired at the same time.

The first and second floors were constructed in a mezzanine style with wide balconies overlooking the hordes of travellers and traders below. A high iron balustrade allowed safe viewing to the public concourse, the better to spot loved ones in a crowd.

The gentlemen's club was named after the man responsible for the biggest developments at Millbay, Isambard Kingdom Brunel. On most days over a thousand people would pass through the quayside terminal building. Almost all of those arriving and departing were very rich, very famous or both. By far the majority were American, taking the ultimate booze cruise to a destination with no prohibition and ample supplies that could be purchased in bulk and taken home for private consumption. Plymouth was favoured for disembarking after crossing the Atlantic since a fast train service to and from London via the adjoining Millbay Station saved almost a day over remaining on any liner that might be headed to berth in either Southampton or Tilbury.

The second floor was separated into two sections, an open public viewing gallery and the very private Isambard Club. The viewing gallery was set out with seating and tables overlooking the docks through huge arched windows. A small café working from an anteroom of the Isambard Club served teas, coffees, and cold drinks through a wide ornately decorated hatch. Passengers bound for, or from, one of the liners could present their boarding pass or ticket for unlimited beverages, only having to pay for any comestibles they might choose to purchase.

The Isambard club was strictly members only and George wondered what Shaw's plan for gaining access might be. None of his friends had ever visited. The only man he knew that had ever frequented the club was Mr Sursden, owner of a fine tailors in George Street and purveyor of fine cloth from a stall in the market. George often worked the stall, carrying bolts of cloth from carts at the main entrance to the huge shelf stacks of the stall itself. Mr Sursden would often share tales of late-night drinks and cigars with his most distinguished clients.

"Can I help you, sirs? Madam?" a wide set doorman asked politely looking at each in turn as they reached the entrance. He looked to be just a few years older than George, but much bigger. He wore smart black trousers and shoes, a clean white shirt with stiff white collars was embellished by a shiny black bow tie. He looked comfortable in his smart attire, clearly taking pride in his role.

The man stood mid-way between two heavy swing doors; both painted a very dark matt black. Wide brass bar handles gleamed against the dark of the doors and small glass windows set at eye level showed nothing of the interior. Marjorie thought she could just make out a dimly lit corridor leading to an identical pair of doors at the other end, obscuring the mysteries of the gentlemen's club.

Shaw stuffed his cap into a large pocket then removed his long air-force overcoat for the first time that day, revealing the finest three-piece suit George had ever seen. All this time George had assumed Shaw must be wearing his uniform beneath the long coat. Instead, he was wearing a suit with the finest tailoring including a double-breasted waistcoat. The material looked to be so fine and light it might have been silk rather than wool, it was a pale grey with fine white pinstripes. A pure white shirt with wing collars added to the transformation from airman to fine gentleman and a deep grey bowtie that had been hidden under the coat rounded everything off nicely.

"Would you be so kind as to hold this for me please, George?" Shaw asked hesitantly, holding out his overcoat.

"Not at all, sir," George replied, trying to sound

deferential in case this might be important to Shaw's plan for gaining entry. He took the coat by the collar, folded it smartly lengthways and then flipped it over one arm so that it draped neatly.

The doorman waited patiently, less impressed than George since most of the guests of the private club would also be finely attired. Shaw reached into an inner pocket of his suit and pulled out what looked to George to be a small blue and gold pamphlet which he handed to the doorman. The doorman opened it, looked at Shaw, stood open mouthed for a few moments and managed to look confused and conflicted about what he should do next.

"I take it that will be sufficient to allow admittance?" Shaw declared expectantly to try to resolve the obvious indecision that was currently travelling back and forth between the man's face and his mind.

The doorman handed the small blue and gold pamphlet back to Shaw with a nod and then pulled one of the doors open to allow Shaw to enter, saying, "Sir, it is an honour to meet you!"

"This way, please," Shaw said, looking over his shoulder at George and Marjorie.

The doorman's inner turmoil returned as he saw Shaw's companions begin to follow and he said hesitantly, "Sir, this is a gentlemen's club! Strictly..."

Marjorie cut him short, leaning in towards the doorman's left ear. She cupped her hand between her mouth and the side of his head and whispered something too quietly for either George or Shaw to hear.

"Really?" the doorman said, his eyes widening as Marjorie pulled her hand away.

Marjorie looked at the now quite startled looking man and just nodded seriously.

The doorman pulled the door wider to indicate that he was happy they all enter and said, "If you need anything, anything at all, call for me. Just shout for Brian. That's me, by the way."

"Thank you, Brian," Marjorie said and meant it. She entered first followed by George and then Shaw.

"No one is to know I am here," Shaw whispered to the doorman as he passed and entered the corridor. "Especially not him!" Shaw pointed at George's back.

The doorman frowned and a look of deeper puzzlement returned.

"It's a long story," Shaw sighed. "At least, it feels like one. Please, just do not say my name or you will ruin a wager."

"I wouldn't dream of it, sir," Brian declared. "It really is an honour to meet you, though," he added with a smile. "And you, sir, madam!" he called after George and Marjorie.

Shaw smiled back, saluted smartly, and followed George into the corridor after which the doorman pushed the door shut behind them.

"That was your passport you showed him, wasn't it," Marjorie stated quietly as soon as the doors to the corridor were closed behind them. "In your real name."

"Indeed," Shaw confirmed. "And a small newspaper cutting I carry with it. Even so, I did not expect admission for all of us to be so easy," he added, clearly interested to hear what Marjorie had said to the doorman.

"Yes. How did you get us in?" George pestered immediately.

Marjorie looked from George to Shaw and said, "Blackmail!"

"I beg your pardon?" Shaw said, completely taken aback whilst George just looked at Marjorie blankly.

"The big new talkie last year staring John Longden. You have the look of him, George so if anyone asks, that is who you are," Marjorie smiled, clearly quite pleased with herself.

"What?" George said, sounding as if someone had stood on his foot.

"And I am Marjorie Hitchcock," she declared. "We are scouting locations for a new talking picture my cousin is working on following his success with Blackmail. I told Brian there will be a scene for an authentic doorman and that he was currently at the top of our list."

Shaw gave a short laugh and George just shook his head in disbelief.

"If you tell someone you are going to put them in the movies, they will pretty much do anything you want them to," Marjorie finished confidently.

"I wonder if it was wise to resort to the use of pseudonyms?" Shaw said flatly.

"Well, there's the pot calling the kettle black!" Marjorie retorted. "And besides, surely someone of your standing will be in similar company. You being you makes it instantly believable."

"Touché, my dear. But whatever gave you the idea?" Shaw asked.

"I'm ashamed to say I fell for a similar ruse some years ago," Marjorie replied. "Madeline saved me from making a real fool of my...." Marjorie paused and even in the dim light of the corridor Shaw and George could see the colour drain from her cheeks.

"Oh! My! God!" Marjorie exclaimed each word loudly.

"It is ok to be angry, my dear," Shaw said calmly, realising immediately the deduction Marjorie had made and placing one hand on Marjorie's shoulder to try to comfort her.

Marjorie turned and said, "But I'm angry at me! The ruse I fell for wasn't about being in any movie at all, was it! It was Madeline rescuing me, getting close enough to become what I would grow to think of as my best friend!"

Shaw said nothing because there was nothing he could say. Marjorie was almost certainly right, and Madeline had never been a real friend, especially in light of this revelation.

George looked at Marjorie, at how desperately miserable she appeared and said, "I think I speak for both of us when I say that after today, we are and always will be your truest friends."

Marjorie sighed, turned to face George, took a step to place herself directly in front of him, put one hand on either side of his face and kissed him.

"Is everything all right, sirs? Madam?" the doorman called to the three of them as he pulled the door open slightly. "I heard some shouting."

"Just checking the lighting for a possible close up," Marjorie managed to say quickly, pulling away for George, who was glowing scarlet once more. "It seems fine," she declared, turning away, and heading for the doors at the other end of the corridor.

Shaw smiled and followed, leading George by the elbow so as not to leave him behind in the state of near stupefaction which Marjorie's sudden show of affection had left him.

The three entered the Isambard together, finding themselves in the most sumptuously decorated bar room George and Marjorie had ever seen. The walls were ornately trimmed with wood panelling and the ceilings were decorated in fine plasterwork including framed covings layered in gold leaf. The floor was laid wall to wall with luxuriously soft deep pile carpet in a regal looking pale red. There were thick mahogany tables with matching plush leather padded chairs, each table was set with an elegant tiffany electric lamp, a crystal ashtray, and a solid silver guillotine style cigar cutter.

At the far end of the room a multi-tiered mantlepiece supported a magnificent, marbled clock, sandwiched between two art deco vases each sporting a mixed bouquet of fresh flowers. Below this, a small fire was lit in the hearth providing more in the way of ambience than heat. Around the room, panelled doors matched the surrounding woodwork making the routes to the other rooms of the club quite hard to pick out.

Two gentlemen were seated at separate tables either side of a tall, narrow bay window hung with heavy gold and red drapes that blocked out most natural light. Both were looking over a broadsheet newspaper, one of them was smoking a large cigar and the other was sporting a pipe. Neither of them looked up from their reading to see who might have entered since such nosiness was not gentlemanly. The room was otherwise unoccupied except for two smartly dressed barmen who watched completely unphased by a woman in the gentlemen's club as the three approached the bar.

"Miss Hitchcock. Mr Longden. Sir," the nearest of the barman welcomed them, looking, and nodding at each of them in turn. "I am delighted to welcome you to the Isambard, which I hope will meet your needs today and for the future. My name is Hudson, and I shall be your host. What may I get you to drink?"

"Impressive," Shaw said. "Your caller nomenclature is remarkable," Shaw noted, pointing at a rack of speaking tubes, six in total all topped with an elegant looking silver whistle, each in the shape of a different animal.

"Indeed, sir. We have only the best at the Isambard," Hudson stated flatly.

"I have seen any number of unusual designs but yours is singularly impressive," Shaw complimented. "I would guess the main door to be the owl, or possibly the wolf. Each has a recognisable pitch, no doubt."

"Ordinarily," Hudson said. He unhooked the rubber pipe topped with the silver wolf whistle to confirm that this was indeed the one connecting with the doorman, and added, "These are currently silent since the reeds have been removed. Each has a small silver stopper attached to a fine chain which is blown free by the caller making a barely perceptible chime as it falls. This ensures guests are not disturbed but remains sufficient to draw our immediate attention." He smiled, gesturing to his colleague, then neatly hooked the speaking tube back in place again.

Shaw could see that below the rack holding the six pipe ends, the rubber tubes fed through one of six wider holes in the wood panelling, each would be running to different locations around the club enabling instant communication.

"Well, I must thank Brian for his discretion," Shaw smiled gratefully.

"Oh, I know who you are, sir," Hudson declared. "The doorman is required to give me details of all who enter the club. It is the reason we have a corridor. I am able to welcome all guests by name," he paused and smiled knowingly. "Unless they request otherwise."

"In that case I must thank you for your discretion," Shaw declared.

"I am here to serve, sir," Hudson confirmed.

"I wonder if you could confirm whether a friend of mine is here? Ferdinand Bartenique?" Shaw asked.

"No, sir," Hudson advised. "Monsieur Bartenique has not yet arrived, if such is his intention for today."

"Splendid," Shaw declared confidently. "We have plans to make... for our film... our movie... project," he said, looking at Marjorie and raising his eyebrows playfully. "Would you be so kind as to facilitate a quiet room in which we might take tea and coffee please, Mr Hudson?"

"Of course. And it's just Hudson, sir," Hudson replied. He lifted the bar flap then pulled open the hinged front section. "This way, sirs, madam," he said as he led them across to a panelled door to the left of the large fireplace.

The door led into a long, narrow corridor, much longer than the one from the double doors at the lounge entrance. The three of them could see it ran all the way to the end of the building complex and a tall single window, so far off that the corridor needed to be lit with electric lights mounted in wall sconces at this end. The lights illuminated baroque patterned red flock wallpaper interspersed on both sides with sections of ornate wood panelling, some of which framed open or closed doors into the club's other rooms.

The first door they passed on their right was closed but the second on their left was open and looked in upon a billiard room with a single well-lit table. The two men playing at the table did not appear to notice them as they passed quietly by.

Hudson stopped at a section of the corridor with panelling on either side. It did not appear to include a doorway but when Hudson gently pushed against one of the wooden panels on his left, a door opened into a small room with one wide, arched window. There were no curtains making the room incredibly bright in comparison to the corridor. A single table like those in the lounge was set with four matching padded chairs.

"Our tearoom," Hudson declared as he led them in. A lead-crystal ashtray on the table held a cigar butt and a pile of ash. Beside that was a deck of well-worn playing cards face up showing the six of diamonds. Hudson tutted and picked both up.

"I do not suppose you will be smoking whilst you take tea," Hudson declared.

"Neither shall we be playing poker," Shaw confirmed. "But please allow Ferdinand to join us, and to bring a clean one of those to the room when he arrives, please, Hudson," Shaw said, gesturing towards the dirty ashtray.

"Allow me to pay for the room and the tea please, Hudson?" Marjorie declared, reaching into her handbag.

Hudson took one step back towards the door holding his empty hand in front of him and declared, "Miss Hitchcock, the room and our hospitality will be entirely complimentary. I must insist."

"Well now. In that case, how 'bout some fine biscuits, partner?" George asked, trying to put on an accent like those he had heard in the westerns. "Or some other tucker, sandwiches, p'rhaps? It's been a mighty long day."

Shaw and Marjorie just glared at him, and he gave an almost imperceptible shrug.

"Of course, Mr Longden," Hudson confirmed happily. "I shall ensure tea is served with a provision of both."

"Please don't forget the coffee," Shaw replied.

"Tea, coffee, biscuits, sandwiches," Hudson confirmed pleasantly, looking at each of his guests in turn. And to confirm he was not in the habit of forgetting any request he added, "And when Monsieur Bartenique arrives, I shall send him in. With a clean ashtray." He smiled genuinely, nodded, and closed the door behind him as he walked out into the corridor.

"What on earth possessed you to talk like that?" Marjorie asked in a half whisper, clearly a little vexed as she turned to George.

"I saw The Virginian last year," George replied in his normal voice. "I thought since I was a famous movie star, I should probably sound like one." He smiled disarmingly.

"John Longden is an Englishman, not a Yankee cowboy," Shaw advised, pulling a seat back for Marjorie to sit at the table.

"Oh!" George said.

"Indeed," Shaw smiled. "Thankfully being an actor probably allows you to speak in any way you wish. You can always claim to be practicing a forthcoming role."

"Yes," Marjorie agreed taking the offered seat and thanking Shaw with a nod and a smile. "If he asks..."

"I don't think he will, my dear," Shaw interrupted.

"...but if he asks," Marjorie continued. "You are working on your accent for a film you will be making with Gary Cooper in the fall."

"The fall?" George wondered out loud.

"It's what the American's call Autumn," Marjorie replied. "It will sound more authentic."

George smiled, shrugged properly this time, and just said, "Ok, partner," in his rather poor American accent.

Marjorie could not help but smile back.

"I suggest we continue our wager, George," Shaw said, taking the seat facing away from the window. "Until Ferdinand arrives, at least."

There was a polite knock at the door to their room and George, who was still standing, stepped across and opened it. Hudson carried in a large silver tray set with two pots, presumably one of tea and the other of coffee, a milk jug, sugar bowl and spoon, cups and saucers, a large plate filled with three neat rows of sandwiches cut into triangles and a smaller one piled with spectacular looking biscuits, some lined with swirls of what looked like white or dark chocolate.

"Compliments of the Isambard, sirs, madam," Hudson said, carefully placing the tray diagonally across the low, wide table. Shaw thanked him, Marjorie smiled and nodded, George said yeeha, and then all three watched him leave.

George placed Shaw's long-coat over the back of Shaw's chair then took a seat himself before also taking a sandwich, only half listening to Shaw who was pouring the three of them a hot drink and introducing another story.

He decided he liked being John Longden. Being someone else felt incredibly liberating. It seemed to come with a freedom from both expectations and limitations. As someone else he felt he could be or do absolutely anything. Perhaps this was why Shaw appeared more than happy to be Shaw. Maybe this new and unique experience would help George to better understand who Shaw might really be.

George took another sandwich and a cup and saucer that Shaw proffered to him then leaned back into his seat, returning his concentration to Shaw's next tale.

18 The man who saw five centuries

I do not know what journey my life might have taken were it not for the unexpected but welcomed sponsorship of my academy. The work we completed in Carchemish as an archaeological team was received at Oxford with a mixture of admiration and astonishment. Our rigorous application of processes built on systematic analysis, critical interpretation, historical context, methodical evidence-based conclusions, and empathy with and for the nomadic tribes that called the now barren lands home, set us on a path to change the world.

For almost six weeks at the beginning of 1914, I had the pleasure of undertaking a monumental project. It was a task which, though I had no notion at the time, would shape a nation, or at the very least, shake one to its core. It would no doubt seem both torturous and arduous to most, but to my friend Charles Woolley and I, it was nothing short of heavenly.

It was just before Christmas 1913 that Woolley and I were approached and offered a unique opportunity. We were to set off on a reconnaissance mission from Gaza, following as near straight line as we could across the desert roads, if such they could be called, to Ain

Kadeis. Had we more time we would have travelled together to survey the lands beyond, but our deadline was fixed. To ensure completion of our mission we separated, Woolley travelling north to Beersheba and I following a route first south to Akaba before heading north-east to Maan.

I think in those days my mind was even more a sponge than it is today. If I close my eyes, I can feel the texture of every last gain of sand that I touched, feel the overwhelming heat of each day and the deep and unexpected chill of each night. I relished a total immersion in fresh but all too familiar landscapes, especially those presenting the most inhospitable and challenging of conditions.

We called most places we encountered the wilderness; it was far more complex than a mere sandy desert, but it seemed name enough given the haste required of our mission. Six weeks over such distance would allow us to complete only brief observations of both the wonderous desert and its archaeological treasures. Our skills in cartography were cooked far too literally in the searing heat of that wide and sandy magnificent landscape. We were not the first to travel those lands and we would not be the last. Their significance was and is profound, and it was no small thing to wonder if we were treading paths first shaped under King Solomon.

We each had our theodolite, camera, picture plates, notebooks and writing companion with us, tied with care to our most trusted companions in our rushed journey, our pack camels. We knew from works undertaken by those who had investigated these lands before us that there would be an abundance of water in the known oases, but we were all too aware from our experiences in Carchemish that to rely on such without personal knowledge of their exact location would be folly. Our food rations would be meagre, but we were if anything over-cautious with the quantity of water skins that we felt compelled to carry.

Our survey work was to be shaped by clear objectives set for us by the academics funding our travels. First and foremost, we were to map the original route across the deserts of both ancient and more modern trade caravans travelling from Palestine to Egypt. Should we identify any site of possible archaeological, and more specifically biblical, significance, we were to pay particular attention in noting both the location and condition of such discoveries.

Our limited time would not allow us to undertake any detailed investigations so our instructions on what to note and how were very clear. In a land populated by a nomadic people and subject to such a fluctuation of landscapes, the identification of sites referenced in the bible was never a realistic task given our timescale and even before we set off, we knew this element of our mission to be an entirely bogus objective.

Until Woolley and I separated on our journey, we were supported by one very accommodating guide who seemed to value our company, taking as much interest in our culture, and understanding, as Woolley and I did in his. Erfan Bey became a trusted friend and supporter of our work. As the Governor of Beersheba or, Kaimmakam, as was his customary title, he held a formidable knowledge of the Bedu, his people.

I have never before travelled in a land so welcoming

and openly friendly to strangers like Woolley and myself and yet so hateful of their common neighbours. The Bedouin were incredibly insular to the point that they held their own in the highest regard whilst seeing every other tribe as beneath even the dirt on their feet.

This short tale is not my own. I share the detail of its context purely for our challenge. There is much that can be gleaned in this tale of long forgotten history. It was shared by Erfan during the first days we set out from Gaza.

Later, I recall, his tale burned in my mind through the early days of the war, and though it raged against the machine in the months immediately after, it did not convey sufficient promise to successfully deliver a nation's foundation. Politics may claim to be rooted in the needs of the people, but in my own pitiful experience it is only ever about wealth, power, resources and money. The people ruled under any political structure may at best be considered as an afterthought.

In its own unique way, Erfan's tale was to prove to be as inspirational as it was fanciful. A seed to guide me, perhaps. A tale of a unified Arabia.

In the years before the Muslim conquest succeeded in the seventh century, the Sassanid Empire ruled the lands stretching from the eastern Mediterranean to the Punjab in the west, and from southern Arabia to the Black Sea in the north for many hundreds of years. The Empire of Iranians, as it was also known, held sway through blood bonds between brother tribes, most notably the children, or Banu, of Judham, Lakhm, and Amilah.

There was a larger faction also bonded at that time known as the Quda'a. The Quda'a was the first true sign of hope in a kingdom that struggled to hold itself together due to the fractured nature of its people. The Quda'a was not one tribe, but many hundreds of smaller tribes, united in a true partnership of equals, the first gentle ripples of possibility in what had hitherto been a nation riding a storm-driven sea of instinctual hatred and distrust of any man, woman, or child from another tribe.

The Quda'a did not form quickly. It was a slow building of networks, a slow erosion of hardened barriers to change, and specifically a seeding of a greater acceptance of others, a subtle growing of alliances built on trust and honour. Slow and steady was the secret of its success. A unification forged over five centuries and all at the bidding of one man: Zuhayr of the Muʿammarūn.

Zuhayr dared to speak not as an equal, but as one willing to serve his neighbours and their children and their children's children. Placing every tribe he encountered above his own, he was swift to open his food stocks to all in times of hardship, to pour his waters for all in times of drought, to offer shelter from the fiercest sandstorms. The wisdom of his generosity was rewarded first with fame, then fortune and most importantly with fidelity. The more he gave to others, the more others were willing to give to him. First in gratitude, then in tribute, and finally in unquestioned allegiance.

Within two centuries the Quda'a had grown a hundred-fold under the guardianship and guidance of Zuhayr. Over the next three centuries it grew a thousand-fold as more small tribes ceded their independence and joined this conglomerate of empowering brotherhood. It grew not as a cult might, but as a true confederation of peoples. The history of hatred began to be forgotten.

This fable, for such it must be seen, was firmly believed by Erfan as the undisputed truth. Zuhayr, Erfan assured us, died shortly after his four hundred and fifty-second birthday. He saw the world change across five centuries and was mourned at his burial by his own grandfather Hubal, who outlived his grandson by almost two hundred years. Proof indeed, Erfan assured us if ever proof was needed, that miracles can emerge from even the harshest desert.

"And what of the tribes now?" I asked him when his tale was finished. I watched him carefully as he led us across a stretch of landscape that was indeed a wilderness. Nothing to see in any direction but sand, baked hard and crusted, unyielding like it's people, perhaps. "What chance of unification do you see?"

Erfan pondered my question briefly before responding with, "I dare not to dream, but show me one with the wisdom of Zuhayr and four hundred years of life to dedicate to such an achievement, and I will be first in line to bow to such a man."

I thought on this reply for longer than Erfan had considered my question and then simply said, "What one man achieves in four hundred years, four hundred men may achieve in only one."

Erfan laughed and said, "English! You think too big."

I laughed in turn and said, "Bedu! You dream too small."

When first I was called upon by the war office to use my skills for the army as a cartographer, I found myself directed to map out little sections of Arabia, pieces of the landscape that might be useful for some or other strategic manoeuvre. In short order I had enough parts of a jigsaw to see the magnificence of the whole, to consider the grandeur and potential to forge a unified Arab nation. I believe it was Erfan's tale that drove my own dreams, my own determination to stand alongside my Arab brothers, to work as their emissary, to strive to see those little pieces come together again as one united and glorious whole. An Arab nation ruled magnificently by its own people, rising like a phoenix from the hot dust and sand to..."

19 Barty the bull

1555 hrs on 27 June 1930. A small anteroom of the Isambard Club on Floor 2 of the Millbay Passenger Complex in the city of Plymouth.

"You're not still dining out on that old chestnut, are you?" a gruff and booming voice interrupted, bringing Shaw's recollections to an abrupt and unexpected end.

"Barty!" Shaw declared standing to shake his friend by the hand enthusiastically. "As predictable as ever. Please, sit, and I will fetch additional refreshments. Coffee?"

"Sure," Ferdinand Bartenique replied in an accent that was genuinely American. He took a seat at the table placing a large square ashtray at the nearest corner before adding, "Anyone mind?" He held up a large fat cigar, rolling it between his thumb and middle finger.

Marjorie and George both shook their heads timidly.

Marjorie thought that Ferdinand looked to be at least twice the size of George and Shaw put together. His blue striped suite was cut exquisitely but also deliberately snug so that his body looked somewhat like an inflated beachball with a head. He wore a deep grey custom Homburg with a pale blue trim and in combination with his thin grey moustache made him look like a gangster straight out of the movies.

"I understand from Hudson that you are Marjorie Hitchcock," Ferdinand declared loudly, still playing with his cigar.

"Well, I...," Marjorie began.

"It's a real pleasure to meet with you ma'am," Ferdinand interrupted before turning to George, frowning, and adding, "And who the hell are you?"

George looked at Marjorie for reassurance before replying, "I'm Ge... John. John Longden?" Without thinking about it he really did make it sound like a question and Marjorie kicked him in the shin. At least he hadn't tried putting on an American accent.

Ferdinand arched both his eyebrows. "Oh, really?" he said, making it immediately apparent that he knew this to be false. "Pleased to meet you. John."

"Shaw tells me that you may be able to help me," Marjorie began, looking behind to see if Shaw had returned to the room.

"With what, exactly?" Ferdinand replied sternly before striking a match and drawing carefully onto his cigar, turning it between puffs to get an even burn going.

"Well, I'm not sure where to begin, really," Marjorie replied, a little flummoxed by Ferdinand's manner. He was nothing like she might have expected.

"Well, I can help you find the real John Longden, for a start," he said, glaring at George. "I don't know who the hell this pretty-boy is, but he sure as sherbet ain't no goddam John Longden."

Marjorie blushed and so did George.

"Ah," George managed. "I can explain."

"Not to me, pal," Ferdinand replied through a puff

of smoke. "It's Miss Hitchcock you need to apologise to."

Marjorie looked from George to Ferdinand, realising that he genuinely believed her to be Marjorie Hitchcock. "Sir, it's complicated," Marjorie began.

"No, Miss Hitchcock, it's perfectly simple. I can see that you're a nice-looking gal, and guys like him make me sick. Making you think he's famous just so's he can schmooze you." He indicated towards George with a twitch of his cigar and George reddened further.

Marjorie couldn't help but giggle at the absurdity of what Ferdinand was saying. She was also beginning to doubt that this man could be of any help after all.

"Did I say somethin' funny?" Ferdinand asked bluntly.

"Well, almost everything, really," Marjorie replied honestly.

Ferdinand looked blankly at her with his mouth wide open.

"Now, that is a sight I do not see often," Shaw declared as he closed the door of the room behind him and returned to the table with a large, steaming carafe of coffee and an additional cup and saucer for Ferdinand.

All three turned to look at Shaw who smiled quietly as he took his seat around the table.

"Lost for words, dear boy?" Shaw said to Ferdinand as he poured another coffee, leaving it black as he knew his friend would like it. "What did I miss?"

"Well, he knows I'm not John Longden," George admitted after a moment's hesitation from all three.

"But he still thinks I'm Marjorie Hitchcock," Marjorie added.

"Wait a goddam minute," Ferdinand puffed. "Is everyone here using a false name?" He looked specifically at Marjorie who just smiled and shrugged.

"Apart from you, dear chap. But for good reason," Shaw replied.

Ferdinand raised his eyebrows again, smiled, cleared his throat and said, "Of course. Apart from me."

"Ferdinand, allow me to introduce my friends, George and Marjorie," Shaw said. "And George, Marjorie, allow me to introduce my soul mate, Ferdinand Bartenique. I'm sure he will allow you to call him Barty."

"Do you mean to embarrass me on purpose?" Ferdinand barked at Shaw before turning to George and Marjorie. "Allow me to apologise for my earlier outburst. I should have known things would not be straightforward when it comes to this vainglorious rapscallion."

"You have always been somewhat of a bull in a china shop, Barty," Shaw noted. "Fortunately for me." He paused briefly to hand his friend the coffee he had poured. "I am hoping you will agree to support Marjorie in the way you supported me. Specifically, regarding my identity and the hiding thereof."

Ferdinand placed his cigar on the edge of his ashtray and leaned forward to take his cup and saucer from Shaw. With his free hand he removed his hat and placed it on the floor beside him, revealing a shock of tight, curly black hair that was somehow oiled and shiny. Now he really did look like a gangster. Frowning he turned to Marjorie and said, "I almost certainly can, but I have to be honest, miss, you have to be willing to travel. And I mean right now."

Now it was Marjorie's turn to frown. "Do you mean what I think you mean?" she said, glancing at Shaw and then looking directly at George.

"I do. You'll take the Statendam with us to New York. Do you have your passport?" he asked, immediately switching to considering practicalities.

"Well, yes, but...us?" Marjorie wondered, suddenly feeling like everything was happening too fast again.

"My family and me," Ferdinand confirmed. "You'll love Shirly, and the kids won't be no bother."

"I see," Marjorie said, quietly disappointed that it was not the 'us' she was hoping for.

"That settles it then," Ferdinand confirmed confidently before adding, "Who's paying? Is this one on you buddy?" He looked at Shaw.

"I pay my own way!" Marjorie said sharply, finding her voice again. "And I don't yet know that I will be accompanying you!"

"It might be safest if you did," George said, turning to her quickly. "It's the last thing your brother is likely to expect."

Marjorie frowned.

"Hey, I'm easy either way," Ferdinand noted, before taking a noisy sip of his coffee. "I can help you, but you have to want my help and you have to be able to come with me so's I can give it. If I could stay here I would, believe me."

Marjorie looked at George again and George just smiled in a way that made Marjorie's heart ache like she had never felt before. She wanted to stay, needed to stay, longed to stay. But somewhere deeper down she knew she had to go. For both their sakes. George had humiliated her brother in a way that placed him in very real danger, and she could only remove that by going away. Today.

"How long will it take?" Marjorie asked, turning back to Ferdinand. "Before I can return, I mean?"

"Most likely less than two months," Ferdinand replied. "No more than three. Prohibition has opened more doors than it's closed."

"You haven't asked me why?" Marjorie stated.

"Why what?" Ferdinand replied, taking up his cigar for another puff.

Marjorie folded her arms and just glared at him.

"Hey, your business is your business," Ferdinand added, throwing his arms wide. "I trust my best friend here. So why would I ask?"

Marjorie sighed. She could see the sense in his reply, but she wanted to speak, wanted to tell her story again, to see if it might help her understand what choices she had and which she should take.

"Given the events of today I can understand your hesitancy," Shaw reflected, seeming to recognise the internal quandary she had reached. "As you stated earlier, it seems too good to be true that we should meet as we did. It is beyond serendipitous. It feels as if Fate herself has stepped in personally, steering you gently to this very moment. And now her role is complete, and you stand at a fork in the road. The choice now is yours alone."

"I am faced with a dilemma. Do I turn left, or do I turn right?" Marjorie admitted.

"You should write this down, buddy," Ferdinand noted quietly, nudging Shaw gently in the arm. "If you were to turn your fascination to fiction, you could do worse than start with this kind of material."

"My entire life has felt like a work of fiction, Barty," Shaw replied. "I could not dare to fill my waking hours with any more of it."

"Oh!" Ferdinand jumped slightly and reached into a jacket pocket, withdrawing a thick brown envelope, and handing it to shaw. "Payment for your work so far. In cash as always."

"Thank you," Shaw said, placing the envelope in his own jacket pocket. "I will have the final pages of my translation to you by the end of July, possibly sooner."

"Tell me about Shaw," Marjorie demanded, looking at Ferdinand.

For the second time Ferdinand looked blank, glancing from Shaw to Marjorie.

"Not everything," Marjorie clarified. "I need...something...to help me decide. What did you do to help Shaw become Shaw?"

Shaw nodded at Ferdinand.

"I take it you know who he is, then?" Ferdinand began, looking at Marjorie and George.

"I don't!" George was quick to admit. "I just know he used to be famous. Oh, and there was a bounty on his head. And he likes digging for treasure, sometimes in France but mostly in the desert."

Ferdinand looked at Shaw who shrugged and said, "I have a wager with young George. I have challenged him to uncover my identity before the end of the day."

"The name, that's it," Marjorie added. "Tell me how you go about changing a name."

Ferdinand scratched at his left temple, searching for the best way to respond.

"It has to fit," he began. "Shaw was not my first suggestion. Nor his first new name."

Marjorie raised one eyebrow quizzically.

"My first assumed name was John Ross Hume," Shaw admitted. "It did not last."

"Only because you failed to stick to it!" Ferdinand noted. "It was a perfect fit."

"It was too unknown," Shaw complained. "Too nondescript."

"John Ross was a great man, a great leader," Ferdinand interjected.

"In America," Shaw noted. "And his leadership is remembered as much for its failures as its successes. Like the Trail of Tears."

"And Hume was a magnificent Scottish philosopher," Ferdinand continued, ignoring Shaw's reservations. "Hence, John Ross Hume was a perfect fit for one such as you." He looked at Shaw.

"I prefer T E Shaw to J R Hume," Shaw said simply.

"Of course, you do," Ferdinand admitted. "The Shaw's treat you like one of the family. So, it fits you more snugly."

George and Marjorie looked at each other. Marjorie frowned and George shrugged.

"George Bernard Shaw and his wife Charlotte are very dear friends," Shaw explained.

"Well, if you want to keep using that name, I suggest you be a bit more careful," Ferdinand advised. "I knew you were here before I arrived!"

"Really?" Shaw said, genuinely surprised. "I did not think I had been recognised in any way today."

"That's not necessary when you actually go about telling people who you are, is it?" Ferdinand complained.

"Not people," Shaw corrected. "One person."

"It only takes one person," Ferdinand insisted. "And besides, you made the biggest mistake of all."

"How so?" Shaw asked, genuinely interested.

"You told that person not to tell anyone else!" Ferdinand said, clearly annoyed at Shaw's actions.

"It seemed the right thing to do in the moment," Shaw replied. "The simplest way to gain access to your club. I thought you might already be here."

"Our made-up names are my doing," Marjorie confirmed, sounding apologetic. "I saw a way to follow Shaw's lead and win us the access we required."

"Your made-up name is flawless," Ferdinand complimented. "Marjorie Hitchcock is a perfect fit for the identity I shall be able to create for you. I believed it to be your name instantly."

"Really? Why?" Marjorie asked.

Ferdinand pointed at George and said, "For the same reason I knew immediately that this young man is not John Longden. Even though Hudson had told me he was."

George tried unsuccessfully not to blush again and said, "I was quite enjoying being John Longden."

"Exactly," Ferdinand confirmed. "It was just a game to you. You can't play at being someone else. It's no good just wanting it, you have to believe it. If you don't, I won't."

Marjorie thought for a moment and realised that she had indeed embraced the idea of being Marjorie Hitchcock. She had worn the name like a mask, allowing it to provide some relief from the thought that her bother might find her.

"Your real name doesn't matter right now, Marjorie" Ferdinand said. "What matters is that you've created an alternative that fits. I can work with that."

Marjorie smiled and though she was still uncertain said, "I should like your help, please, Mr Bartenique. I formally request it and hope that you will assist me."

"You want it, you got it, ma'am," Barty said.

"Thank you, Barty," Shaw said. Turning to Marjorie he added, "Good luck, my dear."

Marjorie stood, pulled Shaw from his chair, and hugged him. "I guess I was in the right place at the right time," she said before turning to face George.

George stood gingerly and Marjorie hugged him, too, harder than Shaw. George put his arms around her and hugged her back, bittersweet feelings preventing them saying anything further.

Ferdinand checked his pocket watch, stubbed out his cigar and said, "We'd better be heading off, Marjorie. Let's get you a ticket and I'll introduce you to the family. We can't afford to miss the tender out to the Statendam. At least, I can't."

"The very best of luck with everything, my dear," Shaw said as they left the club's tearoom together. "I should like to keep in touch, if possible," he added as the four of them walked down the long corridor that would take them back to the club's bar.

"I shall send correspondence to RAF Mount Batten for the attention of 338171, Thomas Shaw," Marjorie promised. She winked at Shaw before adding, "I have a pretty good memory, myself." She turned to George and stopped him for a moment.

"No point in writing to me, miss," George admitted. "My lodgings are rarely the same month to month."

"In that case I shall be back, George." She paused, frowned, and added quietly, "I do not even know your full name!"

"George Edwin Devereux, miss," George replied, also keeping his voice down just in case Hudson was near enough to overhear them.

"Well, George Edwin Devereux," Marjorie smiled and slipped her arm under his. "I shall have to return to see you personally. Keep in touch with Shaw and he will tell you when I'm due back."

George blushed yet again, but for the first time today it felt good. When they reached the end of the corridor, George was proud to walk Marjorie through the bar arm-in-arm.

They each thanked Hudson as they passed, and he gave them all a cheery farewell before thanking them for their patronage.

As they left the club, Shaw spoke briefly with Brian the doorman to let him know he wasn't happy that he had failed to keep his secret. Brian apologised sheepishly and said he hoped it wouldn't go against him when it came to his being able to appear in the movie. Initially he claimed only to have told Hudson, but Shaw just looked at him as if he knew very well that was not the whole truth. Brian soon admitted to telling his wife when she had brought him some late food, saying she had always been a big fan and in her excitement would most likely have told one or two friends. It wasn't every day that you got to meet a genuine hero.

Shaw said that there was no harm done on this occasion but suggested Brian work on his discretion skills.

Shaw and George walked with Marjorie and Ferdinand to where Ferdinand's wife and children were waiting in the viewing lounge beside the Isambard.

After some brief greetings and introductions, George and Shaw said their final farewells to all of them and headed towards the stairwell and the exit.

"I can take you back when you're ready, Shaw," George confirmed as they headed for the stairs. "I should like to stay in contact, mind, and not just because I know Marjorie will be back some day."

"Why, thank you George. How about we round the day off with one further wager," Shaw suggested. "Let's end things on a more relaxing note with a game of snooker. It has been on my mind since your exchange with the Captain and seeing those chaps playing in the Isambard has reminded me how much I enjoy it. Best of five. What do you say?"

"You're on!" George said eagerly. "Oliver's will be quiet this time of the afternoon and it's just round the corner from the Octagon."

"Wonderful," Shaw confirmed. "And if you win, I will tell you my name and you will take double the pay, as agreed."

"I'm not sure about that," George admitted. "It feels like today's adventures have been enough."

They exited the concourse of the Millbay complex, and George led them down Martin Street to the Octagon. From there it was two minutes to the best snooker club in the city.

Oliver's was just a licenced bar but much of its success was down to the large games section at the rear of the deep low building, with nine snooker tables and more than thirty round tables set with anything up to eight chairs for punters to play cards, draughts, dominoes, table skittles and shove ha'penny. It filled a much-needed gap left by the other watering holes on

Union Street; there was more to do than simply getting drunk.

It was the most colourful building on the street with outside walls painted a brilliant blue whilst the window frames were painted a pale lilac. George led them in through a brilliant yellow entryway, one of two wide arched doorways that were permanently propped open, the better to entice passers-by inside. There was no name on display outside the bar, but inside, the owners had invested in something they knew would become the talk of the town and catch the eye of passing punters. A sixteen-foot neon sign spelled out 'Oliver's' across most of the wide bar mirror in a garish sea-green colour.

Even though it was barely after five, Oliver's was unusually crowded. The bar was stacked with sailors, all seemingly eager to get their Friday night off to the best of starts.

"George!" a thin, reedy man behind the bar called out as he spotted a regular. "It's Friday ye' know. You'm always in on a Sat'day," the man called across with a chuckle.

"Malcolm, I honestly have no idea what day it is," George replied quickly. "Any chance of my usual table?"

"Sure," Malcolm replied cordially. He grabbed a clipboard from behind the bar and flicked through several sheets until he got to the page he was looking for. "It's free till eight," he called.

"Cheers," George said. "Slate me in till seven, that should be time enough."

"Done," Malcolm agreed. "Anythin' t' drink lads?"

"Do you have black coffee?" Shaw asked.

"We have anythin' you want," Malcolm replied

chirpily.

"Black coffee, no milk, no sugar. Please?" Shaw said before looking at George to see if he wanted anything.

"Just the usual," George said casually. "On my tab."

"I'll bring it over drektly," Malcolm promised, "But you may have to wait a while since I'm on my own 'till six and this place has never been so full this early!" And then he was away, happily taking orders from the unusually crowded bar.

"Best of five it is," George agreed with Shaw's earlier suggestion, as he led the way to a table that was furthest back on the left. It was a cool relatively quiet corner being as far from the bustling bar area as it was possible to get. Both removed their coats and threw them over the back of a sturdy wooden chair set beside a small round table pushed against the wall.

"Will there be a cue I can use?" Shaw asked, looking over the table and at the sparce walls that seemed to be made of bricks painted a shiny dark brown. All the colour on the inside seemed to have been reserved for the neon sign.

"There's several in the stack corner but some can be a bit wonky, so you'd be best to use mine. We want a fair match, after all," George insisted as he wandered over to a section of the games room in the opposite corner that seemed to have a wide row of pipes hanging from hooks on the wall just below the high ceiling. George found the pipe he was looking for then rooted around his jacket pockets for a key. At the bottom end of the pipe was a small padlock and when George unlocked it, he was able to open a small, hinged plate. Shaw watched as George's cue dropped from the pipe, which was of course a cue case, and George caught it easily.

There was a small square of blue chalk on the edge of their table which George picked up when he returned with the cue, using it deftly to chalk the tip ready for use. Shaw helped George to rack the snooker balls in place on the table and then flipped a coin to see who would be making the first break. George won the toss and made a magnificent break shot, smacking the cue ball into the side of the triangle of reds, and setting balls scattering around the table. Then he handed his cue to Shaw and the match was underway.

"If we are not playing for my name, what stakes do you feel would be appropriate?" Shaw asked, setting up a shot and pocketing a red easily before lining the white up ready to fire onto the black.

"You look competitive enough to me," George declared. "So how about, if you win, my assistance today is free of any charge, and you keep your name to yourself. We can revisit your original challenge on another day of your choosing."

"And if I lose?" Shaw asked as he easily knocked the black into a corner pocket, rebounding off the top cushion and leaving a number of options for another red.

George retrieved the black from the corner pocket and neatly set the ball back on its spot. "Great start, Shaw," he said genuinely impressed. "How about if I win you hold onto my payment until Marjorie visits? I should like to be able to pay my way when I see her again." For some reason, all thoughts of Molly were largely forgotten.

"What about our original wager?" Shaw asked as he lined up another red, this time into a middle pocket.

"Let's have this match stand on its own. Best not to muddy the waters," George suggested. "I've tried and failed to work out who you are. It's been fun, though. Good shot again, Shaw," George noted as the red fell neatly into the middle pocket and the white stopped perfectly for either the pink into a top pocket or the blue into a middle one.

"There are more tales I could share," Shaw admitted, neatly potting the blue. This time the white stayed tucked against the side cushion so the next red would not be so easy.

"No! Really?" George said cheekily. "You do surprise me!"

Shaw picked out a red of choice, lined up the white and struck it confidently with the cue. The red ricocheted between the jaws of a corner pocket but didn't fall. Shaw handed the cue to George.

"That is a nicely weighted cue," Shaw observed.

"Thank you," George replied, re-chalking the cue tip before responding to Shaw's opening break with a comparable performance potting red, black, red, black, red. He missed a difficult pink and chalked the tip again before handing the cue to Shaw.

Malcolm brought their drinks without disturbing the two men's concentration, placing a black coffee and a pint glass of lemonade filled with ice on a quarter-table that was tucked into the shadowed corner before returning silently to the bar.

Shaw and George were content to play in relative silence now, reserving their few exchanges to short compliments for either a difficult shot well executed or a break higher than a score of twenty.

It had been a most unusual and eventful day filled

with unexpected twists and turns, and both were pleased with the way things had turned out. They could relax into the game now, satisfied that they had been able to guide Marjorie to someone who could help her in just the way she needed. Both were quite contented, happy to think of as little as possible and just concentrate on their game of skill and tactical safety play.

It felt wonderful that such a challenging day was ending in the relative peace and tranquillity of such an unhurried gentleman's sport upon the green baize. Sometimes things just worked out right.

Outside, more sailors than Union Street had ever seen in one day continued to pour into the bars and ale houses.

20 *Intervention:*
The Campbells are coming

1730 hrs on 27 June 1930. A convoy of military trucks travelling from Crownhill Barracks to Union Street in the city of Plymouth.

Second Lieutenant Callister sat proudly between Colonel Wallace, who was driving lead in a convoy of fourteen vehicles, and Brigadier O'Dochartaigh, commander of this most unusual of military exercises. They were in the newest of the military trucks available, most of which had been effectively seconded at short notice specifically for this operation. Each magnificent behemoth had been thoroughly scrubbed and cleaned by the platoon's squaddies earlier that afternoon, each now looked to be in pristine condition, as if just driven off the production line. Metalwork was gleaming, paintwork buffed to a reflective shine, tarps scrubbed, and tyres scraped, degreased, and polished with copious amounts of shoeshine.

Callister's reporting of the dark and angry mood across the camp had been well received by the brigadier, though the commanding officer had not seemed the least bit surprised. Brigadier O'Dochartaigh had congratulated his second lieutenant on his candour in bringing the information directly back from his testing errand at the stores. Callister was then instructed to ensure he made his way to the lead vehicle at exercise muster that afternoon and had expected to be the duty officer in the back of the wagon.

"What are you doing, Callister!" the brigadier had barked as the second lieutenant moved to join the contingent of regulars that had already climbed into the back of the truck.

"Sir?" Callister had asked, bracing himself for another possible test situation.

"Front!" the brigadier had ordered, pointing at the cab of the truck with his swagger stick.

And so here he was, in the lead vehicle, on the way to secure equity in recompense for the unjust brutality against the company's colour sergeant. Truth be told he was still uncertain how the exercise was going to play out. In missing the whole of the briefing through his fool's errand, the exact details had yet to be shared with him.

The convoy took only twenty minutes to travel from the barracks to ha'penny bridge at Stonehouse and was brought to a brief halt by a traffic jam caused by a cart with a wonky wheel. A policeman was quick to direct a line of carts and a few cars and bicycles to one side so that the army trucks could continue their journey with minimal delay. Military vehicles of all kinds were always given right-of-way, so each rolled noisily across the bridge as they closed in on their destination, bearing right after the old Toll House to join Edgcumbe Road which, within a quarter mile would become Union Street.

The convoy slowed again as soon as the Western Hotel and Palace Theatre came in sight, each vehicle crawling along to slow all traffic behind and be sure of stopping at just the right place, first passing a crossroads with Battery Street, then continuing on until the eighth truck in line, a gleaming Scammell Pioneer driven by Lieutenant Addie, stopped directly in front of the theatre entrance. The next two trucks in line behind Addie's pulled across two side junctions, one blocking Phoenix Street that ran south beside the theatre, the other sealing off Manor Street beside Union Corner to the north. The four vehicles at the back now turned side on, blocking all traffic from gaining any route around them, closing off all access to Union Street from the west.

The front seven rolled on slowly until Colonel Wallace stopped just past the Octagon intersection. The wagon behind him pulled off to the left, blocking Octagon Street and the next one pulled off to the right blocking Martin Street. The final four trucks pulled past the brigadier's lead vehicle, and each turned side on across Union Street, closing off access from the east. The principal booze district of the city centre was now effectively sealed off.

"This is your first Intervention under my command, Callister. Correct?" the brigadier asked the second lieutenant as he pulled open the door of the Morris cab and dropped lightly onto the road.

Callister followed saying smartly, "Yes, sir! And very much looking forward to it, sir!"

Colonel Wallace chuckled as he exited the cab on the driver's side before marching around to join them.

"And what do you expect we should achieve, I wonder?" Brigadier O'Dochartaigh asked, looking searchingly at the young officer. "I am genuinely interested, and you may answer freely. Tell me what you really think."

"Given the mood of the men, sir, I believe those responsible for Colour-Sergeant Campbell's injuries must be identified, apprehended and judiciously punished, sir," Callister offered up, proudly sincere, and clearly believing his suggested proposal to be the correct course of action.

"Excellent!" the brigadier agreed, a broad grin spread from ear to ear but there was a steely look in his eyes. "Tell me how we might achieve that, and this whole exercise today is yours to command." He held his swagger stick out at arms-length for Callister to take, absolutely serious.

Callister looked at his commanding officer dumbfounded.

"Gay aheed, laddie," Wallace prompted. "Tell us howfur."

"Well, I... we...," Callister faltered, suddenly finding it difficult to pinpoint the steps that might contribute towards delivering against the practicalities of his proposed outcomes.

"Your suggestion is laudable, lad," the brigadier commended genuinely, returning his stick under his arm. "But completely impracticable."

"Yes, sir!" Callister replied, slightly embarrassed but also relieved since he was uncertain of anything further to say.

"Such stuff and nonsense must be left to this lot," Brigadier O'Dochartaigh noted, pointing with his swagger stick towards a small group of policemen gathering beside the truck blocking Martin Street. "I suspect they may try to do exactly as you have suggested when our colour-sergeant has recovered enough to be able to speak with them."

Callister watched the small contingent of police officers as they began ambling slowly towards them. They each looked as if they were out for a Sunday stroll, no stepping in time, no urgency or immediacy, no obvious purpose beyond appearing to be representatives of the law.

"No, Callister. We are not here for justice. I had the same discussion with the chief constable this afternoon. There he is now," the brigadier noted, pointing at the lead officer. "He has brought his men ready to protect the public."

"Permission to speak, sir?" Callister asked, eager to probe the brigadier whilst the chief constable was still some way out of earshot.

Brigadier O'Dochartaigh nodded.

"Why are we here if not for justice, sir?" Callister asked frowning deeply. "It's what the men were calling for."

"We are here to wage peace, Callister!" the brigadier affirmed loudly with a genuine smile, tapping the younger man lightly on one shoulder with his swagger stick before turning to his second in command. "Wallace?"

"Sur!" the colonel barked sharply.

"Get the men out of the trucks and in formation whilst I brief the chief constable."

Wallace marched smartly away from the lead truck until he could see the back of all seven and shouted, "Squad! Dis! Mount!" At which point, the troops of D-Company filed out of the back of the vehicles parked at the Octagon. A similar faint call could be heard from the blockade at the other end of the street; Lieutenant Addie had already been briefed on relaying the colonel's commands.

"Fall! In!" Wallace bellowed, followed by an echo repeating from the other end of the street.

The brigadier and second lieutenant watched as half of D-Company lined up into their practiced drill formation facing their comrades who were also lining up to form a blockade. Four evenly spaced rows of Scottish guardsmen set up in swift formation, a parade straddling the full width of Union Street; twenty Drums at the rear, twenty Pipes in front of them, each carefully inflating their bagpipes, and finally two rows of hardened highlanders to the front, all stood to attention, eyes front and centre.

Beside the entrance to the Palace Theatre, the other half of D-Company also formed up into four rows of regulars, minus the pipes and drums. There was a smattering of applause from the crowds gathering around the troops at either end, clearly impressed by the precision of the unexpected military drilling. Eighty men now stood on parade at each end of the isolated section of Union Street.

"Callister? You stay with me, and we shall see that you learn a thing or three," the brigadier commanded as he marched first to the lead truck, opening a storage flap below the side door and removing a tin megaphone painted a mottled green. It was dented slightly below the handle and the brigadier tutted before clipping it to his belt at his right side and then heading off towards the approaching police officers. Callister stayed in step behind him.

"Danny, delighted to see you, old man," the

brigadier greeted the chief constable convivially.

"I wish I could say it was a pleasure, sir," the chief constable replied, sounding unapologetically disapproving. "But I do understand," he added brusquely.

"How many are you?" the brigadier enquired.

"Sixteen in total, sir," Chief Constable Daniels confirmed, indicating the officers that were behind him awaiting his instructions.

"There's quite a few civvies to clear down there," the brigadier indicated towards the stretch of road between the two military blockades. They could see some rather befuddled looking shoppers caught on the streets between the lines of soldiers, all wondering what all the fuss was about. "And we're beginning to pick up a crowd here, too," he added, indicating a number of people milling around uncertainly.

"I'll send half my men to clear the street and keep everyone behind your vehicles at the theatre, sir," the chief constable confirmed. "And the remainder will cordon off all access beyond your lead vehicle at this end."

"Excellent, Danny," the brigadier replied, tucking his swagger stick below his arm.

The chief constable called his men around him and set each to their tasks, eight immediately set off to shepherd any bystanders out of the street and he led the remainder in creating a cordon thirty meters back from the lead truck, moving all members of the public behind his line.

The brigadier marched to stand with Wallace directly in front of his men, and Callister followed obediently.

"Summon the team, Wallace," Brigadier

O'Dochartaigh instructed.

"Officers! Pre! Sent!" the colonel shouted, at which point the brigadier's senior staff joined Wallace and Callister to stand in line before their brigadier.

"Pay attention, lads," the brigadier began, addressing his officers whilst taking a small fold of paper from a top pocket and flipping it open carefully. He glanced towards his lines of troops at the other end of the street and could see that the eight policemen had all but completed their task of clearing pedestrians away. He waited a few moments whilst the last few bystanders were carefully shepherded through his lines of troops then moved further back until they were well behind the trucks parked up at that end.

"Each of you will now instruct all men within the following establishments to move out onto the street. Punters only. Women and staff are to be instructed to remain inside and to lock doors. No Exceptions. Is that understood?" the brigadier said.

"Sir! Yes, Sir!" the seven officers responded in unison.

"Wallace? The bar of the Western," the brigadier read from the top of his list and pointed with his swagger stick, seemingly towards the theatre building.

"Sur!" Wallace confirmed, with a stiff salute before marching at double time in the direction of the Palace Theatre, which did indeed incorporate the Western Hotel. Its grandiose nautical façade built from red and terracotta brick included windows shaped like portholes, four striped brick chimney's mimicking a liner's smokestacks, and a replica lighthouse dominated its roofline. Two semi-circular tiled panels almost five yards wide covered the exterior wall on the first floor, celebrating Plymouth's greatest moment in maritime history with the Spanish Armada setting sale from Ferrol in the first, and their resounding defeat against the might of the British Navy in the second.

"Mackay? The Posada."

"Sur!" the lieutenant colonel replied, following immediately behind Wallace but on a line that would take him to the opposite side of the street to a far less grand frontage, though picked out easily enough by one huge billboard dominating a high side wall proclaiming Posada Wine Bar.

"Ackerman? The House of Lords."

"Sir!" Major Ackerman acknowledged before heading off towards an inn separated from the Western by a boarding house and cabinet supplies store. The inn had a single grand entrance and wide arched window and appeared to have been constructed from deep green marble blocks embellished with faux gold ropework and ornate sconces.

"McKinley? Farley's bar." The brigadier continued through his list.

"Sur!" Captain McKinley grinned eagerly before marching away towards a building that was three stories of plain red brick, easily picked out through the huge sign below the windows of the third floor declaring WALTER'S FARLEY HOTEL.

"Michaelson? The Castle."

"Sir! Yes, Sir!" Lieutenant Michaelson said smartly, saluting briskly before heading off to a frontage on the same side as the theatre but at the mid-point between the two blockades. A two-story public house, its single feature of interest highlighted by the grey painted walls was the mock battlement topping the second floor with rather lacklustre looking crenellations, further spoiled by a far from medieval looking slate roof.

"Hendrickson? The Star Inn."

"Sur!" the second lieutenant hollered enthusiastically, heading off to a tavern opposite the Castle, which was the plainest building on the street with two stories just whitewashed except for the glossy black woodwork surrounding the windows and doors.

"Callister?" the brigadier glanced at the buildings on either side of the street, trying to spot the last remaining venue on his list. "Yours must be that one over there," he pointed his stick at the most garish looking building on the street. It looked as if someone had decorated it using paint pots that could only have been leftovers, rejects or returns.

"Sir! Yes, Sir!" Callister smiled as he saluted before marching towards the last bar on the brigadier's list.

The brigadier waited and watched, as each of the seven watering holes began to empty their customers onto the street between the two blockades formed by his soldiers. By far the majority of the men were sailors as expected, and more than might be usual at this time on a Friday evening. The brigadier smiled knowingly.

Wallace had been instructed to brief the navy commander and invite him to participate specifically to secure this outcome. Whilst the naval commander-in-chief had refused an invitation to attend in person, the request itself had achieved the desired effect. Commander-in-Chief Hansen had taken umbrage and issued an immediate blanket shore leave across his naval fleet, seeking to show that his own men were a match for the brigadier's platoon.

The two most notoriously bawdy taverns seemed to

hold more sailors than physically possible, dozens upon dozens spilled onto the street. The bar of the two hotels were evidently the least crowded at this time, most likely too mild for the tastes of the crews finding themselves on a short and unexpected release from duty.

The brigadier's officers followed each venue's customers onto the street, closing the doors firmly behind them and standing smartly to attention in front of each doorway that would now be locked by the staff within. Callister was last out.

Brigadier O'Dochartaigh estimated way over three hundred men had exited the establishments all murmuring and milling around between the two contingents of his platoon in a state of obvious confusion. Almost all were in naval uniform, as expected. The brigadier smiled proudly, satisfied that when it came to the manipulation of other military colleagues, he was still able to consider himself a master.

The brigadier unclipped the megaphone from his belt and put the speaking end to his mouth. "Welcome," he said, his voice carrying easily through the use of the loud hailer. It's small dent clearly had no impact on its efficacy as the whole bewildered crowd turned to face him, eager for some details on the interruption of their drinking and forced eviction. This was not turning out to be the kind of evening any of them might have expected.

"I am Brigadier O'Dochartaigh, Commanding Officer of this evening's exercises," he began, silencing the last remaining mutters. "You have the honour of being instructed to take part in an essential inter-service competition that will secure reparation for a heinous crime." He took a few slow paces towards the crowd, in part to maintain composure, but also to emphasise the next part of his announcement.

"Your commander-in-chief has given his blessing to our endeavours, granting many of you shore leave at short notice so that you might participate." Some in the throng glanced at colleagues, wondering what this was all leading to.

"In the early hours of yesterday morning, a dozen or so men from one of these very establishments," he indicated the buildings on either side of the street with a sweep of his swagger stick, "set upon my colour-sergeant, beating him in the most savage and ungentlemanly fashion. All of them sailors...," he paused, in part to calm himself, in part to allow what he was saying to sink in, but mostly so that he could steer his cold and angry gaze across the rabble before him, making eye contact with as many as he could, "...and as a single mob they set upon my officer like a feral pack!"

"Much as yesterday morning I am pleased to see that we are outnumbered," the brigadier continued. "But today we do not stand alone. Civilians and cowards among you may elect to avoid participation at any time by simply sitting. My company, unlike your craven cronies, will not strike at any man not standing, neither will they fight in anything other than a one-to-one engagement."

A few older looking civilian gentlemen sat immediately amongst the crowd, some younger ones, too, leaving just the sailors and a one or two civilians still standing. The brigadier could see a number of the younger navy lads looked as though they wanted to sit, but peer pressure and bravado engendered by their superior numbers appeared to be preventing them. That would change.

"When you have had enough, simply stay down. Last men standing shall be declared victors!" the brigadier confirmed, addressing the mob and his men evenly.

"You represent the might of the modern navy, whilst we are a simple Scottish regiment of His Majesty's Army, the second battalion Argyll and Sutherland Highlanders," he said humbly.

"This exercise clears a debt! Is that understood, men?" Brigadier O'Dochartaigh called out to the crowd but also very specifically to his own regiment. This was closure.

A single unified cry resounded from his troops at both ends of the street, "Yes! Sir!"

"Let the skirmish commence!" he cried, pointing at the crowd with his swagger stick.

At his final word, Drums immediately struck a first rat-a-tat-tat roll and Pipes kicked in loudly with the most fitting regimental march. The lines of highlanders stepped together in perfect unison from both sides of the street, bearing down upon the massed sailors to the glorious strains of The Campbells Are Coming.

As his men completed their march past him towards the nervous looking crowd, the brigadier turned to find Callister at his shoulder, returned unexpectedly. "You should be in the thick of it, lad!" the brigadier snapped immediately.

"Forgive me, sir. Two men refused to leave Oliver's, sir!" Callister declared loudly, to be sure of being heard over the wailing pipes and reverberating snares, squealing, and thumping out the regimental march.

"What?" Brigadier O'Dochartaigh barked incredulously, throwing the megaphone to the floor, adding some new dents.

"One of them said he was a Colonel in the army and refused to be bullied by a junior officer, sir," Callister reported. "The other wanted to leave but was prevented, sir."

"Is that so, Callister?" the brigadier snapped, angrily. "Let's you and I knock some sense into the brigands!" And he marched with Callister in tow behind, both dodging the clamour of fist fights filling the street around them, Callister joining in occasionally when a sailor not otherwise engaged strayed too close to the brigadier.

At this early stage in proceedings, Brigadier O'Dochartaigh was not surprised to see that every man under his command was still standing. Whilst a significant number of blue and white uniformed sailors littered the floor, clearly intent on staying there, not a single man down could be seen in a red jacket. Pipes and Drums were still playing full volume, not yet needed to support those engaged in the restitution he had brought his men to deliver. Outnumbered by two-to-one and his men were still superior, entirely as he expected given their training, experience, and very personal motivation for this essential engagement. His battalion was not called the Thin Red Line for nothing.

"Right, Callister!" Brigadier O'Dochartaigh declared as he stepped through a narrow doorway painted a sickly yellow. "Where are these cowardly dastards."

21 Snookered

1815 hrs on 27 June 1930. The games area of Oliver's Bar on Union Street in the city of Plymouth.

"That's not something that you see very often," Shaw said to George flippantly as he led them back to the snooker table.

"I've never seen the like! Shouldn't we just go outside and sit down?" George suggested, sounding genuinely concerned.

They had both heard the brigadier's announcements, having followed Second Lieutenant Callister to the doorway and watched him walk back to report on Shaw's refusal. The irate soldier had towered over Shaw by a clear foot when attempting to order him out onto the street, but in their verbal exchange it was Shaw who had come out on top, much to the young officer's obvious annoyance.

"Certainly not!" Shaw responded immediately, sounding most put out by George's suggestion. "I am neither civilian nor coward, but I am most definitely not inclined to accept a punch in the face from an angry Scot!"

"You're dressed like a civilian," George pointed out. "Your cap and coat are at the table so no-one would know you're in the services."

Shaw stopped and turned to George slowly and deliberately. "My dear George, I should know," Shaw declared. "Besides, as I pointed out to the second lieutenant, I have no intentions of allowing myself to be bullied into anything. Never again. As I detailed in our earlier exchanges I do not suffer bullies gladly. Come, let us continue our match. It will help me to think." And he strode back towards their table.

George shook his head and followed, wondering again if Shaw might get him into trouble after all.

"It's two-one to you," George said as the pair began to rack the balls up again, George placing the reds into the wooden triangle whilst Shaw spotted each of the colours. "Your break," he said once all the balls were in place, rolling the cue ball to balk ready to be placed in the D.

"We are," Shaw declared, as he leaned forward and smashed the white into the top cushion so that it rebounded into the back of the pack, scattering reds around the table, "if you will forgive my deliberately outlandish alliterations: outnumbered, outmanoeuvred, outclassed, outmatched, out-positioned, out of time and out of luck." He turned defiantly to George handing him the cue and adding, "That does not mean that we are out of options. I may be somewhat outdated but when it comes to tactical thinking my mind remains outstanding. I believe we can outwit this superior adversarial force if you will but ally your strength to my strategy. Do we have a deal?"

George just nodded, unsure in every conceivable way about what was going to happen next, but certain that he trusted Shaw. The reputation of the Argyll and

Sutherland Highlanders was formidable and widely known across the city. Whatever idea or plan Shaw might come up with, George would go along with it. He found himself hoping, almost praying, that it was going to be a good one.

"As soon as the brigadier chap comes in, as I am certain he will," Shaw said quietly after George had potted a red. "Sit quietly in a chair at the table in the corner."

"Right," George agreed, knocking a black into the corner pocket and settling into a great position for building a strong break.

"Let me do all the talking," Shaw suggested as George checked out the way the reds had split to see which one to play next.

"Not a problem," George agreed again, knocking a red, that was blocking the black, into the top right pocket and settling perfectly onto the pink.

"You, there!" a loud voice called from the entrance as a stocky Scotsman in fully decorated military uniform entered the bar followed by the returning Second Lieutenant Callister.

Shaw looked at George and nodded. George did as he had been instructed and walked immediately to sit at the table in the corner, fading into the shadows. Shaw walked towards the bar to meet the brigadier as far from their snooker table as possible. His plan depended on unknowns, uncertainties, and over-opinionated self-confidence. If he could get the balance right, give just the right impressions, he was certain he could lead the brigadier to just the outcome he desired.

"Brigadier O'Dochartaigh," Shaw said brightly as he came up in front of the commanding officer. "How wonderful of you to join us, can I order you a drink?"

The brigadier stopped dead, feeling immediately that he was dealing with a very slim customer and resolving to think carefully before responding to anything this smooth talker might say. The man looked older than himself by at least ten years, and he was short and slight in comparison to the brigadier's stocky build and immediate height advantage. Callister was six inches taller than the brigadier, so when he joined them both he looked like a giant compared with this little man.

"Now listen, sir," Brigadier O'Dochartaigh said sternly, ignoring the offer. "Who are you?"

"Tommy Shaw, sir. I am here with my friend George trying to relax at the end of a day you simply would not believe," Shaw said, pointing towards the snooker tables. "I am winning and do not wish my concentration to be broken."

"That is no excuse, man. I order you to leave this establishment immediately!"

"And ruin a perfectly good suit?" Shaw said, indicating his fine clothes.

"I am your superior officer, and you will do as I command!" the brigadier barked leaning down to be level with Shaw's face.

"You wouldn't happen to have a lozenge or mint of some sort, would you?" Shaw said quietly.

"I beg your pardon?" the brigadier snorted.

"Never mind," Shaw continued diminutively.

"Colonel Shaw. I order you to leave this establishment. Now!" the brigadier declared, pointing at the exit, through which the sounds of fighting could be heard to be continuing with much gusto.

"I'm not a colonel, sir, not anymore. As I explained

to your man, I was a colonel. Your second lieutenant did not understand the significance of the tense and left the premises before I had a chance to clarify," Shaw continued with a wily smile.

The brigadier calmed himself, realising that as an ex-serviceman he was no more subject to any military compulsion than a civilian, except in an emergency, which this exercise could not be classified. He could see at least one barman cleaning glasses and watching them, and the other person that had refused to leave was also here, over by the snooker tables, somewhere.

"I fear we may have gotten off on the wrong foot, sir," Brigadier O'Dochartaigh declared, calming himself significantly. "I am indeed Brigadier O'Dochartaigh, and this is Second Lieutenant Callister."

"Pleased to meet you," Shaw said timidly. "That was a very good speech. Outside."

"You heard me get the exercise underway?" the brigadier asked, with a curt nod towards the exit onto the noisy street.

"I did, sir," Shaw admitted.

"Then you know that it would be a simple matter for you to step outside and just sit down," the brigadier confirmed. "As a civilian that is really all that is being asked of you. It is a matter of principle that I secure a victory over all those present at these premises this evening."

"We could sit there, sir," Shaw declared, pointing at some empty stools at the bar. "That seems reasonable, don't you think?"

This chap was really beginning to annoy him now, but he had to keep his cool. "No," the brigadier replied stiffly. "That does not seem reasonable."

"I do not wish to sit on the floor outside, and you will not accept my sitting inside. That is a predicament," Shaw declared quizzically. "If only there was some way of getting around it?"

Brigadier O'Dochartaigh picked up that Shaw was hinting that he might have a suggestion. Just the sort of thing that he would do. He thought carefully before responding, deciding to take the bait, whilst also being ready to steer any resulting momentum in his own favour. One way or another, this man would regret refusing his instruction.

"What do you suggest?" the brigadier asked pointedly. "I should like to re-join my men in short order so please, whatever you might think to offer by way of resolution I am willing to consider."

Shaw looked pensive for several moments and then said, "What about a simple competition?" He paused for a moment as if thinking it through and as the brigadier opened his mouth to say something added quickly. "A test of strength, perhaps. In here."

The brigadier looked at Callister standing head and shoulders above Shaw. He might just as well be looking at David and Goliath. "What did you have in mind?" the brigadier asked, intrigued.

"There is a wonderful local challenge I have seen today," Shaw said, deliberately pushing one slender hand through his white hair. "A game called, mercy. Perhaps you have heard of it?"

Brigadier O'Dochartaigh looked at Callister who nodded and smiled confidently. "I am mess hall champion, sir," Callister stated, at which the annoying little man suddenly looked a little unsure of himself, as if perhaps regretting the suggestion.

"Well, we only have a local champion of sorts...," Shaw began, sounding a little concerned.

Seeing a weakness and thinking to outsmart the annoying little man the brigadier cut in quickly. "If my second lieutenant and I win in this game of your choosing, you will join us immediately on the street," he barked, making it sound like an order, which in truth he was intending it to be.

Shaw frowned and a look of concern flashed across his face. The brigadier could see he was clearly not expecting such a suggestion, most likely hoping that the test of strength alone would be sufficient and excuse them from joining the fray.

After a moment's hesitation, Shaw said uncertainly, "And if one of you does not win?"

The brigadier said calmly, "You can remain to finish your game."

"We *may* remain to finish our game," Shaw corrected.

"What?" Brigadier O'Dochartaigh snapped, annoyed at such an overly pedantic correction. "Yes, you may remain to finish your game, if one of you...,"

"Wonderful," Shaw agreed, cutting in immediately as the brigadier had done to him a moment ago. "That is settled, then."

The brigadier watched as the annoying little man went to fetch his companion. Both he and Callister snorted at the sight of the youth returning with Shaw from the shadowed corner of the games area. He looked to be about sixteen! The brigadier looked at Callister and both smiled broadly, these two were in for a right royal drubbing.

"Allow me to go first, sir?" Second Lieutenant

Callister requested eagerly.

"Of course," the brigadier agreed.

Callister took a step towards the approaching pair and held out his right hand.

George took a small step forward to meet his adversary, the current champion of the Regiment of Argyll and Sutherland Highlanders, six-foot-six of muscle and sinew honed by military training and service. They seemed a similar age, so any advantage of youth George might have hoped to bring to the test was lost.

For the first time in his life George accepted he was about to lose, felt it with a level of certainty he had never known. Here was a man he knew instinctively to be his better, a colossus he could not hope to match, let alone conquer. Friends, family, even Cap'n Crush'm, as Johnno had called him; they were a local testing that he had been able to either eclipse or withstand. But this giant was the best of a whole regiment of trained and hardened soldiers. This titan was in a different league.

George sighed and tried to prepare himself mentally for the biggest test of his life. He didn't want to let Shaw down but in his heart of hearts he believed it to be inevitable, and entirely Shaw's fault. He really felt that Shaw should have come up with a better plan, something that might have given them a chance, given *him* a chance, however small. If this was the best Shaw could do, he wasn't sure the man was as smart as he'd hoped him to be.

George took another small step forward and began to raise his arm slowly, steeling himself for the inevitable outcome, preparing for the unremitting pain that he was about to try to bear whilst simultaneously but ineffectually also attempting to inflict. An unexpected defiance suddenly rose within him, and he understood Shaw's unwillingness to just walk outside and sit down. No matter the damage, hurt or injury he was about to endure, he found himself immediately resolved to giving this contest his all. For Shaw, for sure; but mostly for himself.

As hand was about to clasp hand, George was first shocked, then confused when his arm was briskly barged away. Shaw stepped lightly in front of him and grabbed the huge soldier's right hand with his own.

"One for the Phoenix!" Shaw said seriously to George with a subtle glance towards the brigadier which only George could see. "Or perhaps, just to share with Marjorie."

George wanted to simultaneously laugh and cry but managed to hold all signs of emotion in check. He felt conflicted, cheated, elated, infuriated, relieved, offended and gratified all at once. But mostly, following a quick glance at the brigadier, he immediately felt more confident.

Shaw looked up briefly into the face of Second Lieutenant Callister, allowing his own to mirror the smug expression he saw there, then he turned away, locked eyes with the brigadier, smiled and said, "Do not worry, sir. You will not have to face our champion, since this young officer of yours is sadly not capable of delivering a victory, as he believes."

"I'm bloody-well sure I can, old man!" Callister said, managing to sound, for all his size, both defensive and petulant at the same time.

"But you see, dear boy, you have to win this childish game. I, on the other very literal hand..." He paused deliberately and glanced down at their grasp. "I only have to not lose."

"I've crushed men twice your size and half your age," Callister declared confidently, gripping slightly harder to give the old man a taste of things to come. "I can promise you one thing. This is really going to hurt."

Shaw smiled warmly, showing no indication whatsoever that Callister's increased grip was causing either discomfort or pain. "Well! It's quite funny you should say that, eh, George? Sadly, for you, a stalemate is assured. I know which hand I favour," he said, turning deliberately to George this time with the broadest grin George had seen all day. "And if I was a betting man, I should put honey on it."

The brigadier and Callister looked at each other, frowning.

George saw their puzzled expressions and could hold things in no longer, doubling over he filled the empty pub with joyful hearty laughter, a full belly laugh that came close to drowning out the sound of pipes, drums and the gargantuan skirmish still filling the street outside. George even had to wipe away tears of laughter that began cascading down his face.

Shaw was a puzzle all right; he stood stock still smiling serenely, not looking the least bit uncomfortable, let alone in any kind of pain. As Callister's face turned from pink to purple with an effort that was clearly causing nothing more than personal frustration, George realised that he would never doubt this enigmatic man again. Whoever he may be.

EPILOGUE

0455 hrs on 30th June 1930. The Barbican Wharf slipway, Plymouth.

George Edwin Devereux had one early job to do before meeting up with James and Donald at the Pannier Market to tout for work on the stalls. There was always someone who wanted something moving or fixing or needing help with loading or deliveries. All three young men were known to be honest, trustworthy, and reliable, and extra work came their way easily. Just one routine delivery to make and he could head into town to find his friends, or that was the plan, anyway.

George loaded a small rowing boat with six bags, each filled with various groceries including, fruit and veg, cooked and raw meats, butter, lard, milk, flour, sugar and other supplies for the caretaker, his wife and family. George lifted each bag easily from the sack truck he had used to wheel them from the store shed at the top of the slipway. He was careful to share the weight between the bow and the stern, placing each sack into position before pushing the boat out into the quiet waters of Plymouth Sound.

Almost silently, George began to row the cargo across to Drake's Island in the stillness of the early dawn that made everything appear flat. Buildings and trees visible only as featureless silhouettes against a dark and moody sky, overcast this morning and threatening to spoil the start of the week with thundery summer showers. There was a low breeze making waters slightly choppy, but it was nothing he couldn't handle.

In little more than forty minutes, George crossed the quiet channel to the island. Once there, he carved his name into the sand, then, when the caretaker arrived, offloaded the supplies and wheel-barrowed them to the island's kitchen, shared a welcome breakfast, and took their order for fuel oil, coal, and the like, and then set off back towards shore again.

His weekend had been thoroughly uneventful, at least in comparison to the way the previous Friday had played out. Sure, he'd caught up with James at the panier market on Saturday morning and they'd made a dozen or so deliveries of groceries to some old folk and rich families who kept regular weekly orders rather than spending time at the market themselves. He'd retained the grand cap in his weekly competition with Charlie. He'd even bumped into Molly on Marlborough Street, or rather she had bumped into him, literally, since in truth he didn't notice her until she deliberately nudged him. She looked a little put out when all he said was 'good day' before carrying on walking.

The world was different. No, he was different. Yes, that was it. He was different and the world would never be the same again.

He was less than halfway back when he heard a familiar sound, and quickly scanned the skies, looking for a flying boat since after last week's encounter he immediately recognised it.

He could see nothing anywhere near and continued

rowing ashore, glancing around every now and then to try to pick out the source of the distant rumbling hum. When he did spot the aircraft, it wasn't flying, at least not yet. It was heading out from the air base at RAF Mount Batten, skimming across the water towards the channel George was passing through.

"Not again," George said quietly to himself, speeding up to avoid any possibility of a collision with the swiftly approaching seaplane. From never having seen one close up, suddenly he was having his second encounter in a matter of days.

George picked up his rowing pace, in part to make sure he was able to steer clear of any possible danger, but also to try to make it back before the skies opened. He could tell it was going to rain. It was just a matter of when.

The Blackburn Iris continued to whiz his way, a white and foamy spray whipped up behind it by the speed it's broad hull cut through the water but also from the backdraft of the three propellers driving it. Someone was really in a hurry this morning and it was barely seven o'clock.

George continued to row towards shore making certain he was well away from the narrow waterway that the seaplanes favoured as their take-off strip. He became quite concerned, however, when the plane failed to turn where he might have expected but continued to bear down on him. This really was too much.

George was just considering diving overboard as the huge props came so close, he was almost deafened and then, at almost the last possible moment the plane turned suddenly to the left, one huge underwing float passing beyond his rowboat to leave George rocking under the wing as the wake of the plane pummelled the small boat. All three motors powered down immediately to a slow chug, leaving the aircraft on a bearing that would take it back to the more usual channel for take-off.

The head that appeared at the spotters cockpit was clearly Shaw's and he immediately began to beckon George to the side of the boat again, before disappearing for a moment so that he could throw a rope ladder over the side ready for him to climb out. "I'm not your personal taxi!" George called up as he approached the side of the plane, only half in jest.

Shaw appeared again and shouted something that, over the noise of the props, George thought sounded like, getting. Getting what? He rowed a little closer, waiting at the base of the ladder, looking up and steadying the small boat ready for Shaw to join him.

After a few moments Shaw's head appeared looking straight down the side of the plane at George. "I said, get in!" Shaw shouted.

George heard it clearly this time and was now very confused. The thought of being treated as a taxi service forgotten, he obviously had to refuse the request. "I can't," he called back up. "I have work to do. I have to get this boat back, for a start."

"George, this is hard for me to say," Shaw admitted, looking concerned. "Mark has Marjorie, and it is all my fault. We have to stop him!"

"What!" George shouted, a mix of concern and terror rising inside him in a way he had never known.

"Get in!" Shaw shouted again. "We have to go! Right now! We have a boat to catch!"

George grabbed the ladder and began to climb, all thought of work or the rowboat or his friends or the market swept aside. Marjorie was in danger. A pressure of panic and anger rose like an inferno from his heart, filling his chest, arms, neck, and finally the whole of his body.

George climbed the rope ladder and tumbled through the hatch into the belly of the Blackburn Iris in a daze. He sat in shock where he landed, his back to the hull, trying to make sense of what he was feeling. Shaw was standing near a thin doorway into the forward section of the seaplane, white as a sheet. On a row of fold down seats beside Shaw, looking very much the worse for wear, a bandaged and bruised looking Barty was mumbling. George's heart sank momentarily as he realised that somehow they had failed after all.

"I think you might have broken him," Barty managed groggily. "See? Nothing good comes from telling people you're Lawrence of Arabia, does it Lawrence? Sorry! I mean, Shaw!"

Shaw was speaking, or perhaps it was Barty, but George couldn't hear, couldn't make out any of the actual words. His mind was racing as implications began to sink in. Marjorie, his head and heart wailed, drowning out everything else.

A rage began to build, and the rage became a howl and the howl kept building, enveloping not just George, but everything around him. He was filled with an unquenchable fury the likes of which he had never known. In that instant he could feel nothing, smell nothing, taste nothing, hear nothing; but when it came to the world around him, everything was tinged in the same vermillion hue. The world might never look the same again.

George would do everything he could now to turn the tide of loss that had so unexpectedly risen against him, stealing a future he was certain should be his destiny. The thought of losing Marjorie forever was more than he could bear, more than he was willing to accept. He glanced at Shaw and then at Barty, standing slowly, hands clenched into fists.

"Where are we going, Shaw?" George said sounding uncharacteristically harsh and resolute. He was still seeing red as he promised, "I'm going to save Marjorie. Then I'm going to make sure Mark remembers my name for the rest of his life!" One way or another Mark would regret what he had done.

How long Mark might live to regret it...? Well, that might just depend on how deeply George would be forced to carve his name to be sure of it never being forgotten, never washed away no matter the tide or passing of time. When next they met, Mark would be facing a very different George and he really wasn't going to like this one. He wasn't going to like this one at all!

ABOUT THE AUTHOR

Paul G. Devereux is an ex-MOD weapons-radio specialist turned novelist. Roles between have included primary teacher, education officer, marine engineer and, following the completion of his creative writing master's degree in 2023, very mature student. He lives with his wife and muse in a quaint Cornish town with their best friend Charlie Sproodle. Paul is an accidental and extremely grateful author currently working on his forth novel. On Tidal Sand is his first published work.

Printed in Dunstable, United Kingdom